INTO THE MYSTIC

KATHRYN CALLAHAN

DEDICATION

To my Two.
To my Four.
To my Thirty-five.

CONTENTS

ACKNOWLEDGMENTS

Thank you to the readers that cheered for the next chapter before I could even write it. Without you I would have and could have questioned the value of my story, and never returned to it. Thank you to my writing partners for making me feel at home in the writing world and giving me access to your beautiful minds. Thank you to the one and only, the greatest: Coach, who's words inspired me: "Keep chipping away at that idea in your head. One day it will demand release, and when it does, watch out."

INTO THE MYSTIC

KATHRYN CALLAHAN

ONE

GOLDEN YEARS

I needed wine. And my label maker.

I knew what was coming when my principal peeked in through the tiny sliver of a window set in the classroom door, grinning like an idiot who just showed up to a party he wasn't invited to. Holbrook never popped in for social calls, which meant a parent had called. Again.

I checked the clock. Thirty-five minutes until I would need to pick up my class from PE. With my insides already in uncomfortable protest, I smoothed and tugged at my cardigan. *Here goes nothing.*

Thirty-eight minutes later, I signed and dated my formal reprimand: *Corynn McKay, April 6, 2017.* I left Mr. Holbrook in my room and sprinted, now late, to pick up my students. Letting my caramel hair fall out of its makeshift bun, I concealed my red, flushed face. I wasn't crying — I hadn't cried in almost twenty years since my grandmother died. But after my exchange with Holbrook, fierce eruptions of boiling blood simmered up to the surface of my skin.

Too strict? Parent calls? Four kids hate coming to school? The "my way or the highway" attitude has to stop? I teach kindergarten — it *is* my way or the highway. If I didn't set up high expectations for them in their first year, the whole rest of their schooling would go to shit.

Wine. Label maker. But when I got home with my heart set on therapeutic-drunk-closet-reorganizing, another unwanted visitor waited on my doorstep, wringing her hands. My mother perched next to an aged cardboard box with, *Rynn*, marked across it. For the second time that day, my stomach lurched.

I didn't recognize the box bearing my name, but I knew what it was. While cleaning out the garage earlier that week, Mom mentioned finding the vanity my sister, Nora, had inherited when our grandmother passed away. This box, I knew, held *my* inheritance. Little trinkets hidden away all these years because nine-year-old Rynn was too distraught to accept them back then.

Nearly twenty years later, I still felt unprepared for this. I stared at Mom from the car, unsure if I could get out. Maybe I could just make chitchat with her, and then push the box aside to deal with later. Or never.

Why today? Why did Mom have to show up today?

Loosen up. Loosen up. It can't be my way or the highway...not all the time, I guess.

"Looks like I beat you home," Mom greeted me cautiously as I walked up the sidewalk. Sweating palms betrayed my conviction to be "loose," and I thrust them into the pockets of my slacks for fear they'd give me away.

"Hi, Mom," I responded, half-hearted. My keys shook as I unlocked the door.

"So," she hinted as she followed me in, "this is yours. I found it in the garage..." She set it down on the coffee table, waiting for my reaction. Her hands hovered at her sides as if preparing to grab me if I fainted.

"Yeah, ok," I responded without looking at the box. "So...what have you guys been up to?" I walked into the open kitchen, hoping to draw her attention away from the imposing package.

She understood my not-so-subtle intentions, and answered from the living room. "Oh, you know, still trying to clean out the garage," she looked at the floor as if realizing her feet were stuck to it, "Your dad wants space for hobbies, although I don't know what he's planning on taking up," she forced a laugh. "I should probably go, though, I have six crates of donations still in the car." She hopped free from the floor and reached for the door. "Just...wanted to bring this by..." she looked back, her eyes troubled. I don't know what words could have helped, and neither did she. She blew a kiss and said, "Love you," and ducked out the door.

So maybe I would just continue with my wine and labeling. Slap a "DO NOT DISTURB" tag on the cardboard box, and then I could shelve it for another twenty years.

Loosen up. Loosen up.

This box represented every reason I needed to loosen up. Maybe if I opened it, some of the carefree spirit my grandmother embodied would seep out and touch my life once again.

I slammed my hand on the countertop, strode over to the couch, and sat down. The rhythm of my heart hastened so forcefully that my body rocked to its beat, and my formerly sweaty hands were now the source of ice spreading throughout my entire body. I closed my eyes and reached for its rough sides, sliding it onto my lap.

The box was so old I wondered if my memory had changed any of the details of what it actually contained. A quilt would be on top, hexagonal floral swatches of what used to be my great grandma's clothing, alternating with a cheerful gold. With a chill, I remembered the reason I closed the quilt up in the box in the first place: it still held my grandmother's scent.

The air became too thick, like sucking in a milkshake through a coffee stirrer. My oxygen-deprived brain choreographed dancing fireflies in my vision. I closed my eyes, but still saw them. I opened up my mouth to swallow in deep gulps. Surely after all these years, it wouldn't....could it?

But I wanted it to. I wanted it to smell like her and her house and everything that I loved from back then. I wanted the scent to rise up to me, calling me from the familiar fog I had clung to during the time of her death. As if searching for something I had lost and expected to find in that box, I threw open the lid and tossed it aside, grabbing the quilt that remained right where the nine-year-old me left it years ago.

I barely processed the beauty or the softness of the fabric as I gathered up all of it and brought it to my face, burying my nose in it, breathing it in. Tears welled in my eyes as I realized it did in fact still have remnants of her scent. It smelled of a combination of woodsy and something like honey — sweet, without being too floral.

Memories surfaced of watching TV specials cuddled up under that blanket with Nora and Grandma, drinking creamy hot chocolate and eating warm gooey baked-from-scratch cookies. My mind jumped to Nora's lanky legs and tow-headed blonde hair circling Grandma around the quilt. Grandma always cheated, darting through the middle, tackling one of us in fits of laughter. Then to sitting on the quilt in the backyard or down by the creek, snacking on crackers and cheese. And last, lying back on the quilt, gazing up at the stars, laughing and talking about whatever might be going on in the life of a little girl.

I thought I'd be devastated. I thought the fog would creep forth and consume me just as it had when she died. But that didn't happen. In fact, rather than being shattered again like I expected, instead I felt...warm. Cozy. Like Grandma's hugs. The air in the room returned to breathable, filling my lungs with what felt like helium, lifting my mood and my outlook. I knew I could now place her things in view to appreciate them and let their presence trigger memories of the best moments of my childhood; maybe the best moments of my whole life.

I set the quilt down on the couch beside me, making mental notes of where I might want to display it, before turning my attention back to the box. Under the quilt was a music box that had never worked, and random tchotchkes — Grandma called them "treasures" — from her antique shop, wrapped in protective tissue paper.

I took out the music box, taking in its scent as well. I couldn't pinpoint the type of wood, but it had a similar smell as the quilt. Immediately, it took me back to the days we spent in Grandma's antique shop.

As I lifted the music box out, I noticed a small notebook slip down to the bottom of the box. It must have been standing on its edge, wedged between the music box and the cardboard side, but I didn't remember this being something Grandma had passed down to me in her inheritance.

It was thick, but small in size, like a Bible with fewer pages. Time and use had worn the leather binding thin and soft around the edges, and a strap of the same leather wrapped around it, tying it closed. A new memory flashed like an electrical current, and it wasn't one I wanted to relive.

The river pasture. The tree, curiously growing around the rock. Nine-year-old Tucker and me. Seven-year-old Nora. Inquisitive inspections revealing a notebook wedged between the rock and the tree. Pulling the tree, heaving the rock. Nora wrenching the notebook free. Tree bark indentations on one side. Grooves from the rock on the other. Running to show Grandma. Mom on the front steps, waiting with red, wet eyes. The notebook slipping from my hands. Fog consuming me.

The day my grandmother had her stroke — the day I lost her, was the day we found this journal.

Because it materialized here in the box, I assumed I must have recovered it from where it slipped from my hands, but during those days I didn't form memories of seeing or thinking or hearing anything. For years afterward, I would hear talk of events during this time and need to be reminded of what had happened, like the break-in at Grandma's shop that occurred that very same day. I lost weeks, maybe even months. I could only imagine that after she died, I subconsciously put the notebook in the same box, literally and metaphorically speaking, as the rest of my grandmother's treasures that I'd hoped I'd never see again.

I turned it over in my hands. We had discovered it wedged

between a rock and a tree, and even after all these years, faint indentations remained on both sides. I thought about calling Tucker to see if he remembered finding it that day, but it felt too personal to share at the time. We had never even opened it up. An aching lump caught in my throat. What would Grandma have said about this unique find if we had gotten the chance to show her?

She would have advised me not to cut the straps, but I wasn't interested in preserving this now — I wanted *into* it. I bolted to get my kitchen shears, and without holding back or allowing time to talk myself out of it, I severed the leather near the tight knot.

The cover gave a slight crackle as it separated from the pages for the first time in God knows how long. My first glimpse inside the notebook showed that it had no title or name of the former owner, at least not on the first page. It did, however, have a very neat and tidy cursive, in the format of a journal entry. I turned a few more pages and could see the same general outline: dates followed by short paragraphs.

June 1, 1793

I found a newspaper that says the year is 1986. That is all I can understand, as this is apparently a Spanish speaking country. A heavily populated area, like I have seen on occasion before. Busy. Looking at the faces of people that walk by, no one is familiar. No houses here, more of a market area.

Sitting back, I tried to process this strange journal entry. It described somewhere like Mexico City, but the dates were perplexing.

If the writer didn't understand Spanish, he or she must have read the newspaper wrong, taking the number 1986 to be a date, when it surely pertained to a volume number or article. The writer seemed to be taking notes on his or her surroundings, but why wouldn't he or she know where they were?

I turned to the next page and found it to be similar to the first one:

June 8, 1793

> *Extremely rural area, I don't see people or dwellings or even a sign of life. Cold, but my clothes were well planned as usual. I'm in a very heavy coat made out of a material I'm not familiar with, and my pants are of the same. The boots have some type of animal fur lining the inside. It is not snowing, but there are patches of it on the ground. No information on this trip, so I'll merely wait to be returned to the warmth soon. Only one turn this time...won't be long.*

Only one turn this time? Weird. And what kind of jackass goes somewhere snowy, then acts surprised that they're dressed for snow?

My exhale sputtered through my pursed lips like a whoopee cushion. This "treasure" we found turned out to be nothing but a lunatic writing on the luck of proper snowsuits and the hustle and bustle of foreign cities. I flipped through more pages of the journal to see if this is what I could expect from the whole thing.

Halfway through, though, I found something more interesting in the notebook. Literally *inside* it. The writer had cut out a section of the pages, like in *Diamonds are Forever*, when the old lady hid the diamonds in a Bible. Nestled safely between the crazy adventures of this lost traveler, lay an old key.

It felt heavy and big; too big for a door key, even for a door in the 1700's. I imagined everything from around that time to be lavish and beautiful like the things in Grandma's shop, but this was different, more like an ornament. An attractive clover decorated one end, and on the other, three prongs stuck straight out the bottom rather than to the side like typical door keys.

I lay out on the couch, dangling the strange key above my head and wondering why it would need to be hidden in the notebook. For the next few hours my attention bounced back and forth between the journal and the key, blissfully released of the crappy day and plans of fixing it by labeling my music collection. Page after page, I read of more adventures, until an orange glow appeared in the mirror over my mantle, announcing the sunset in the backyard.

MY BODY WIGGLED awake before the rest of me, subconsciously dancing to the tune of Elton John's "Saturday Night's Alright for Fighting," as my bedroom alarm clock radio sang through the house. Thanks to falling asleep on the couch, I rose with stiff limbs, still clutching the key to my chest. The journal begged to be explored, but unfortunately would have to wait. If I'd had an office job my boss would have found me locked in a supply closet with the notebook and a flashlight. Thankfully, I would spend the day distractedly in motion, ringmaster of a circus of five-year olds.

I didn't expect to be so taken with this notebook. Especially after I snuck one more peek at it before leaving for school, and another mystery revealed itself. The writer penned the first entry in 1793. 1922 documented the last. Yeah, of course it did.

Yet...yet I couldn't help leaving school early — without even cleaning the whole room with Clorox wipes or laying out the next day's lessons — and sitting down with it again as soon as I got home. It's not like I wanted it to be true, or that I believed in some magical explanation, but it drew me in with an unexplainable curiosity I'd never felt before. Grandma would have had a fabulous tale for it, no doubt: a man trapped in endless time, searching for his one true love, and I would have gone to sleep dreaming about it, like I had with all her whimsical stories.

A chuckle escaped me. I'd spent nearly twenty years ignoring eccentric notions like this. Trying to live every day without acknowledging the images of her life reflected in my own, because it hurt too much. In the nine years I had with her, Grandma inadvertently shaped who I was — then and now. Some things I couldn't refuse, like her habit of shortening my given name, Corynn, to just Rynn, or the way she always had a song in her head. A song that usually erupted unexpectedly, yet purposefully, joined by a chorus line of Nora, Tucker and I. She imparted the song habit on me, too, although by choice, I learned long ago to keep my music in my own head. Habits and nicknames are no longer painful reminders, but I had admittedly become a very boring adult, suppressing bubbles of quirky spontaneity as if they were offensive burps.

But this journal and key were anything but boring, and it felt good to embrace Grandma's sense of adventure once again. I found the journal right where I left it, on the couch, closed up with the key nestled in the cutout of its pages. The rest of the items from the night before were still laid out on the coffee table, ready for me to continue browsing, but my attention focused solely on the journal and key. Thinking maybe the key held something more that I hadn't noticed last night, I took it out to examine again, twirling it between my fingers. It was attractive, smooth and polished, despite having spent a considerable amount of time outside in the elements. The unique spot between the rock and the tree had preserved it well. Sadly, though, the key did not appear to hold anything more than the three prongs and the decorative clover. No engraving or stamp on it. No clues.

I grabbed my phone, deciding the time had come to tell someone about my rediscovery. Up until last weekend, I would have called Tucker first; my automatic best friend reaction. I second-guessed myself in light of the new relationship news, though. They threw me for a loop for sure, but after a lifetime spent as the three musketeers, it wasn't the bomb of he and Nora's budding romance that knocked me on my heels. It was the apparent fear they had over whether or not I would approve.

My sister's face evidenced this when Tucker wrapped up his band's set on the stage of Dirty Legs bar with the unexpected announcement of his undying love for Nora. Instead of relief or happiness, her face turned a sickly white. What did she think I was going to do, say they weren't allowed to date? Tucker, far less bothered, joined us in our usual booth, casually leaning back without a care in the world. I swear I caught him shooting the occasional cautious look in my direction, though.

Of course I was happy for them. Of course I would approve. Unexpected? Yes. A major change in our friendship? For sure. Irritated that they left me so in the dark? Sadly, that stung the worst. And now, in the back of my mind I felt like I'd been knocked on my heels regarding where I fit with this new dynamic. Tucker was my best friend — but would Nora be jealous if I called him? Maybe if they'd just included me from the beginning... But I should have seen it. I knew them better than anyone and this happened right under my nose. Too secure in our friendship's history, I naively assumed its future would be unchanging.

After the announcement, the night turned into a drunken celebration of sorts, perhaps in effort to acclimate me to their love affair by deadening my senses. I never even got a chance to ask how long they'd been dating, or who admitted feelings first. Nora didn't appear ready to divulge all the romantic details before I fully committed to my blessing of the relationship.

Loosen up. Loosen up. I took my chances and dialed Tucker's number. Voicemail. I checked the clock: 4:45. Although he usually answered his phone even during business hours, he could have been out of range or meeting with clients for his father's construction company, so I tried Nora. She didn't answer either, but texted me back within minutes, saying she was in a meeting and would call when she finished.

The wheels were turning in my head about what they would

think or say about the strange adventures of the lost journal writer. The more I thought of it, the crazier it sounded, and I started to talk myself out of even telling them. We all found it together, though. They would want to know.

To pass the time until I got a return phone call, I cranked my David Bowie collection, opened up the windows, and brought a beer and the journal out to my back patio. Unpredictable Texas weather sent a still-chilly April breeze penetrating through my school hoodie with a bite, so I went back in for Grandma's quilt and grabbed the music box as well.

"Golden Years" resonated in my modest backyard, where new native Texan buds and greenery were brimming; a beautiful contrast to the last few months of typical dreary brown winter effects. Just as I sat down on the outdoor sofa, my phone rang. I deliberated for a moment, not sure who I wanted it to be. Nora's grinning face lit the screen of my quivering phone. My stomach fluttered. *Loosen up. Loosen up!*

"Hey," I said, "sorry if I interrupted your meeting earlier."

"No, it's fine, I had it on vibrate. Whatcha doin'?"

"Just sittin' on the patio. Guess what?"

"Chicken butt," she answered, the usual response.

"Yep, but something else. Mom came over yesterday." I paused for a breath and said the words I never expected to deliver so casually. "She brought over my inheritance from Grandma."

"Oh. Are — are you okay?" My eyes rolled, even though her reaction was valid. Why didn't they ever just slap me?

"I didn't think I would be, I really didn't. But yeah, I am. And to top it off," my voice picked up speed, "I found something else in the box."

"What do you mean, wasn't it just little figurines or something?"

I plunged. "The day Grandma had her stroke — do you remember what we had been doing that day?"

Silence echoed on her end as she revisited the day in her memory, until she came up short, "Uh...I don't remember. Probably running around like always?"

"Think, Nora — when we found out about her stroke, we were running back from the woods to show Grandma something." Nothing still. "Down by the river...between a huge rock and — "

" — And the tree!" she interrupted, "That book! Holy crap, we were going to show her, but mom stopped us on the front steps and... and that's it. I never thought about it after she told us about Grandma. What happened to it?"

"I don't know, I guess I put it in the box of Grandma's things eventually, because it surprised me in there when I got it all out yesterday."

"Whoa. Have you told Tucker?"

My stomach panged. At least she still acknowledged the habits of our old trio. "I called, but he didn't answer. But listen, I opened it and..." I didn't know how to describe it adequately. I didn't want to sound too enraptured by it, but I didn't want to sell it short, either. "It's weird. I don't know what to make of it..."

I told her about the tree bark imprints on the leather, the key in the cutout of the pages, the entries detailing places and times, and how the writer, who I identified as a man, seemed as if he didn't know where (or when) he visited. Nora listened intently the whole time, while I recounted a few of his entries, and finished up with the little tidbit that the journal entry dates started in 1793 and ended in 1922.

When I wrapped up my summation, she responded with, "Maybe there are two writers, you know, like one carried on the journal when the first guy died?

"I know, I thought that, too. But everything is the same — the handwriting, the format of his entries, the way he speaks...it's the same guy."

"Okay, so he's nuts." She seemed happy with that resolution.

"Yeah, I guess." I blushed, thankful she couldn't see it through the phone. Even though I had come to the same conclusion, somewhere inside me glimmered a rare Grandma-like optimism that I had actually come across something more interesting than a crazy man's journal.

"What about the key? What was that doing in there?"

"No idea," I sighed. What did it matter, if the guy was just a lunatic?

"Hmm...well I gotta run, but I want to come look at it, okay?" I heard her shuffling around like she had reached her car and searched in her purse for her keys.

"Yeah, okay. I'll talk to you later. Love you."

"Love you, too. Bye."

After hanging up, every inch of me flushed. I didn't know why, but I started to regret telling her about it. It wasn't possible, any of it, therefore I needed to just shelve it now, before I started convincing myself that it could be real. It should just be an interesting "conversation piece" on my coffee table, like my other treasures from Grandma's shop.

I turned my attention to the music box, but found it just as I remembered it. Beautiful carved wood, empty inside, and no music. I thought about the days after Grandma had passed away, when my dad would placate me by looking at it, trying to figure out how it worked. He said it looked like it needed a tool to turn the music mechanism, but because it was so old; there could be little hope of finding its original match.

I bent down to see the side better where the tool would be inserted. I hadn't cared enough to look closely back then, but now I thought maybe dad or Tucker could fashion a new tool of some sort.

It looked like the spinner would need three notches of equal sizes on the end of it. It needed to be long, too, and have a handle on the other end so you could turn it. I sat back and put my feet up on the patio table, wondering if a wire coat hanger could be bent and reshaped to fit the outer notches.

I cringed, ashamed that I had avoided these items for so many years in fear that I couldn't take the memories that would surface with them. Not only was I now truly enjoying bringing Grandma's things out into the open and taking pride in them, but the journal provided an absolutely palpable bonus factor.

I flipped the pages of the journal again, fighting the urge to dive headfirst into the perplexing entries once more. My whole life had been spent finding order and logic and patterns. Control. Something about the writer had me ignoring my tendency to reason logically, though. Maybe he wasn't crazy. Maybe there could be more to his story. An insatiable nosiness came over me; I had to figure this guy out.

As I turned page after page, skimming again the words describing coast to coast and around the globe, I reached the space where the key had been kept all these years. With my finger, I traced the outline of it, wondering why he kept something like a simple key in such an ingenious place. Hide it? Keep it safe? From what?

When I reached the bottom of it, my fingers rested on the three prongs. Three prongs of equal size. Roughly the same size as the notches in the music box. And the key was long. About as long as the opening on the music box. And the clover sure would make a nice handle to turn.

I sat straight up with a shot. "No." My head involuntarily shook. "No way." It would be completely illogical to think this random key from a crazy man's journal would fit the music box. If someone else had been trying to believe bullshit like this, I would have told them they were being an idiot.

But no one was there to tell me I was being an idiot, so I charged forward like one.

I sat the music box upright again on my lap, and took the key out of the journal. I could no longer hear David Bowie from inside the house; drums beating in my head with every heartbeat drowned him out. I eased the pronged end of the key into the opening, sliding it until it stopped. With a slow clockwise turn, the prongs slipped right into the notches. A perfect fit.

Unbelievable. I swigged my beer, held the bottle to the sky, and said out loud, "Here's to you, Grandma! I'm sorry it took me twenty years to do this!" I breathed deep, steadied myself, and turned the key to the music box for the first time.

I spun the key several times, and the chimes of the tune began to vibrate the box, but I never heard the song. Like a black hole had opened up around me, an invisible force pushed my body into a slump. Every part of me caved under pressure from all angles; unyielding weight forced my eyes closed, yet somehow they begged to explode wide open at the same time. All the breath rushed from my lungs, which threatened to collapse.

I couldn't even think, and just when I started to lose consciousness, the sensation lifted. My lungs screamed for air. I swallowed it in in enormous gulps. I had lost my sense of sight, but once upright and aware, a flash of understanding hit me. Although I had no idea where I was, my backyard no longer surrounded me. And in my hand, I held the key.

TWO

THE FARM

Footsteps trudged through the flooded mess outside William Bennett's Nantucket cabin, rousing him from his fireside slumber. Muscles tensed. Breath caught in his chest. The faint sound became louder. Closer. Had one of the animals spooked with the storm? Mr. Jacobs must have been fetching him for help.

Expecting to see his boss on the other side, he threw open the door. Instead, Charlotte Jacobs stood, completely drenched and shaking, water dripping from her ebony curls onto her dress' bustle. Even soaked through from the rain, she was beautiful.

Part of him longed to pull her inside to continue yesterday's passionate embrace. The other thought it better to close the door in her face.

He stepped aside, and Charlotte entered through the open doorway, carrying a curious wooden box. His gaze followed her as she chose the chair by the glowing fire, where just moments before, he had slept so deeply. The rhythm of raindrops rapped at the windows, as if the farm beyond fought for his attention, or perhaps gave warning.

"I hope it's all right that I stopped by, William," Charlotte spoke, her hands shaking as they fingered the lace of her dress.

He cleared his throat, unable to commit to an answer. An awkward intensity had built between he and Charlotte the past few months, but whereas she quickly acted on her feelings, William knew better. Her father's enraged face was all he could see in his mind's eye.

One hand rubbed his furrowed brow, as memories from the previous day intruded on his thoughts: the hungry look in her eye, the way her fingers caressed his chest. Her lips, like velvet. Just as he always imagined they would be. But it was a mistake.

William's head shook as if he could expel the memory from his head. It was not his place to traipse around with the boss' daughter. William respected Mr. Jacobs far too much to give in to Charlotte's propositions.

Their most recent encounter had left William in a nauseating predicament. If he were to act on his instincts, he would betray his boss — the man who took him in at age twelve when his own father's health failed. Denying Charlotte was the right thing to do, but it had left him off-kilter and unsettled. Charlotte was dangerous, and vindictive. No matter what he chose, he knew he'd be damned.

Charlotte's face contorted, as if formulating an argument, but she said with a cracking voice, "I'm sorry." Her eyes shifted down to a wooden box sitting in her lap. "Won't you come sit down? I have something for you."

William had no intention of leaving the door, and stared at Charlotte with crossed arms. She asked again, "Please? I'm here to make peace, William. Honest." She blinked away a tear, and looked away as if ashamed.

He closed his eyes tight, reminding himself that Charlotte knew exactly what she was doing — she calculated every movement precisely. This knowledge, above even his sense of moral obligation to Mr. Jacobs, made William most weary of her propositions. She was beautiful and tempting, but also cunning. He'd been watching her manipulate her parents since she was a child.

His stomach knotted. *Listen to her so she can leave.*

He crossed the room to the chair that sat just beyond the edge of firelight. Rather than share the glow with her, he sat back into the shadow, letting his dark hair and stubble meld him into the darkness. He did not speak, nor spare a glance at the wooden box. Instead, he leaned back in the chair and rested his chin on his interlaced fingers.

What would Mr. Jacobs say if he knew his daughter visited William's house in the middle of the night? He forced down a shiver.

Charlotte proceeded. "It was wrong of me to come on to you yesterday, and to act the way I did. And I shouldn't have accused you of watching me. I convinced myself that you wanted what I wanted..."

William bit the inside of his cheek to keep his silence, remembering how she had twisted his nightly walks into something perverse. An accusation like that would most definitely place his years of dedication to the farm in jeopardy. Beads of sweat blanketed his body. Temptation and conflict gave way to fury.

"But I *do* watch *you*," she continued. "And try as I may to ignore my feelings, I'm drawn to you."

William gave no response. She blinked again, and tears streamed down her cheeks.

She whispered now, "I've decided to move to New York to stay with my aunt, so I've come to say good-bye. My birthday is coming up soon, I'll be nineteen — maybe I'll find a nice man and be married soon..." she shook her head. "I know I haven't made things easy for you lately, so now I will be out of your hair. I brought this as a peace offering, but I admit, it's also so you will have something to remember me by." She managed a chuckle, and pulled a wet handkerchief from her sleeve, making a fruitless attempt to dry her eyes.

William didn't know he'd been holding his breath until it rushed out at Charlotte's announcement. If she moved, William could go on with his life on the farm in peace, without her distraction or the worry over what Mr. Jacobs would do if he found out about her proposed liaisons. Although William had never once been inappropriate with Charlotte, until her actions yesterday, he walked a fine line between respecting her as his boss' daughter, and firmly standing his ground that he wasn't interested. Life on this Nantucket farm provided all he could ever ask for, and he'd be damned if Charlotte was going to lose it for him.

"I wonder, does anyone else know you have such a skilled hand at carving wood?" His heartbeat picked up a notch. No, no one was aware, and she could only know about it by peering in through his windows at night. He had never shared his hobby with anyone; he only carved wooden pieces to pass the time before falling asleep.

But again, William did not respond. His only motion was to steady his breathing, as he willed himself to appear unaffected by Charlotte's confession.

"I thought you would appreciate the carvings on this music box," she continued. "I'm sure you could do a much better job of it yourself, but when I saw it..." her voice trailed off. When she regained her train of thought, she smiled and finished, "I thought of you. Go ahead, take a look. Please?"

Take it and let her be gone, he thought. Shifting in his chair, he took the music box from her. In the poor light, he couldn't be sure the type of wood, but he guessed pine. His fingers ran across its indentations, tracing a leafy pattern, and he looked up to see if his mock interest had satisfied Charlotte.

She watched his every motion, until realizing he had stopped to look at her. "Oh, go on," she said, "It plays a lovely tune. Open it up."

William sighed. Surely there couldn't be much more to endure but a dreamy melody, so he opened the box. In ink on the underside of the lid, Charlotte had penned the day's date, *April 19, 1781.* His fingers searched around the sides and bottom for the spinner to wind it, but found nothing.

Charlotte reached around the top of the box and pointed inside.

"It has a key," she offered. "It fits there on the side..." Her eyes flickered wildly back and forth from the music box to William.

Just as Charlotte had said, a key rested in the bottom of the music box. Forged from polished metal, and somewhat large for a key, a four-leaf clover decorating one end, and three small prongs reached out from the other. William inserted the pronged end into a small opening on the side of the music box and directed a deliberate look at Charlotte. He gave the clover end one turn, and then another.

The tune began, but a sensation of pressure built in his head, instantly drowning it out. His eyes were forced closed, and his body buckled under a mysterious weight that pressed upon him from every angle. Breath disappeared from his chest, but then, when panic threatened to consume him, the pressure lifted. His eyes flew open, wide and searching for explanation. The light from the fire and flashes of lightning were gone. Darkness surrounded him. The tune from the music box had vanished, replaced with Charlotte's gasps for air.

Within seconds, William's vision returned, and soon he could stand without any disorientation, save for adjusting to unanticipated new surroundings. Charlotte stood a few strides away from him, going through the same process of acclimation.

The sky hadn't fully darkened, the sun glowing in pinks and reds just below the hill in the distance. They were outside, but the rain had ceased. He searched around, hoping for a point of reference, but all he could tell with any certainty was that they were still on Nantucket. They stood in the middle of a windswept moor, with tall grasses swaying with the salty breeze. The few visible trees twisted up from the earth, molded by the relentless Nantucket winds. Warmth hung in the air between gusts of wind across the moor; at odds with the rain-soaked chill he still held from the weather outside his cabin. He spun around, taking it all in. How could so many changes happen in such a short amount of time?

With mouth agape and eyes wide, Charlotte stared in the direction of a cottage in ruins across the moor. Her breath, only having just returned, started to catch in her throat like a case of hiccups. Was she scared?

"Charlotte," William tried to control his voice. "Are you alright? Do you know what's happening?"

She responded with a simple shake of her head.

"Where are we?"

She didn't look at him or give an answer. Instead, she began moving toward the cottage, first at a hurried walk, then picking up her pace until she ran at full speed. William followed, running as well. Their strides cut straight through the moor, the tall grass whipping at their legs. He caught up to her easily, but the sight of tears marking her cheeks stopped him dead in his tracks.

Her tears were legitimate, lacking the staged effect of her earlier performance. The fact that she wouldn't look at him twisted William's stomach. What were they running toward?

"Charlotte!" He caught up to her once again and took her shoulders in his hands. "Charlotte, what is it?"

She tried to move forward, ignoring William's calls. Her sobs magnified her tired breathing. Why would she be crying? He spun her around, forcing her eyes off the ramshackle cottage to look at him. Her stare landed far beyond him, and though she tried, she could compose no understandable words through her tears. Her head sank in defeat.

"Charlotte, what is it? What's in there? Why are we here?" He shook her, ignoring his harsh reaction to her unusual behavior. *"What is happening?"*

"I don't *know!*" She squirmed out of William's grip, falling over her dress as she moved away from him. For a moment, she sat, wiping her tear-streaked face and breathing deep to control her hysterics. When she finally calmed down, her eyes met his, yet she still held a vacant, pained expression on her face. Finally, she spoke, "I don't know, William. But the answer is in there, I suspect." She got to her feet and walked again toward the odd place, this time with slow, purposeful steps.

Baffled, William walked briskly after her, catching up again without effort. Charlotte's tears had stopped flowing, and her eyes narrowed, searching the cottage. She slowed as they approached what now became visible as an old rock dwelling that had been fixed with wooden beams and thatches for a roof. Firelight gleamed through the cracks and openings, but he and Charlotte did not enter. Charlotte found a window-like opening in the rocks, and gave a short, bemused laugh at something inside.

William didn't know whether he should be more concerned with Charlotte's unexplainable behavior or the unknown presence in the little rock room. She nodded toward her window, which he took as a signal to find his own opening to look through. Inside he saw a man, dark and heavily dressed in skins and furs, with a painted face.

He moved around with great effort, struggling between his small stool of a seat, and over to a table along one of the rock walls on which there were countless glass jars, tin boxes and objects William couldn't discern. He mumbled to himself as he took items from the table, and returned to his stool, where a smaller table sat in front of him. After laying out the items, mixing some in a bowl, and uttering his inaudible words, he struggled to get up and over to the wall table, retrieving different items before returning again to the stool.

Built into the wall behind him was an alcove for a fire, in which wild flames filled the area completely. Pots of all sizes hung along the rock sides, framing the fireplace, and one large pot hung directly over the fire, its contents boiling to the top. Above the alcove were dried bunches of herbs and roots, and William noticed that when the flames blazed powerfully, reaching up past the boiling pot, subtle scents of thyme and lavender permeated the house and beyond.

There were no adornments on the walls except various bundles of dried flowers, peppers, and more herbs. William searched the room for a bed, and finding none he wondered if the man lived there, or if he only performed his mysterious incantations in this strange rock cottage.

William motioned to Charlotte. When her eye caught his movements, she turned her head to him and gave an annoyed look as if he had interrupted her from the entertainment inside the rock house.

He tried to whisper as softly as he could, making exaggerations of the movements of his mouth as he spoke so she could read his lips, "What is this?" He gestured toward the man inside as if Charlotte might not have known what he referred to.

She looked down to William's hand, and pointed to what he held in it. He brought his hand up to the light showing through the window and could see that he still had the key to the music box tight in his grasp. In all the commotion of this odd and unpredictable visit to the rock house, he hadn't noticed he still held the key.

Charlotte looked back into the opening and watched again as the man began chanting louder. William's fists clenched. Charlotte knew as much to point out the key, but didn't bother offering any insight as to what that meant or why they were there.

He marched over to pull her back from the wall so they could talk about this strange phenomenon they were experiencing. He stopped short, though, when he caught a glimpse of the room through Charlotte's vantage point.

There, in plain view, stood Charlotte. He looked back at the spot she had just been standing, to find her still there. He took a few more glances back and forth. Now he couldn't help himself, grabbing her by the arm and tugging her as he walked away from the rock house to a safe distance to talk.

She put up no fight, walking obediently along after him.

"That girl in there. Who is that?" he asked, hoping against hope that her answer would be a relative that struck an uncanny likeness.

"That's me," she answered, eyes lowered.

William paced, searching for words while Charlotte stood, wringing her hands. He circled around several times, arms motioning wildly as he attempted to ask a question or pose a statement, but came up empty every time.

He lifted the key again and held it out to Charlotte, shrugging his shoulders, asking his question by that one gesture. She sat down squat on her legs, almost amused by his antics.

"William, I don't exactly have the answers you're hoping for."

"Not exactly?" Under normal circumstances, he never would have spoken to her in the manner rising in him just then. Their current situation, however, had left the subservient, obedient farm hand mute, replaced by an enraged and reckless William. "Well give it a shot, however imprecise your answers may be, because it's a hell of a lot more than *I've* got," he replied.

"Well, I don't know — I'm — let's say I'm just as shocked as you are to be here right now."

Her evasive answer danced around confirming the truth. "And where is 'here?' What is this place, and why are *you*," pointing to the Charlotte inside the rock house, "*there*? And why are *we*," pointing now to the both of them where they stood, "*here*?"

"Like I said, I don't know," she stood and turned toward the cottage, "but I think we should go back and have a look so that maybe we can understand?" She didn't walk away immediately. She waited for him to agree. When he threw his hands up in the air in resignation, she turned back to walk toward the ongoing mystery inside the little room, and William followed. This time he stood with Charlotte so as to see both participants involved in the peculiar ritual.

The Charlotte inside had stepped forward, and William could now see that she held the same music box in her arms that she had given him earlier that night, although she wore a different dress entirely. The Charlotte inside placed the music box on the small table in front of the man's stool, then pulled over a chair from somewhere behind her, and sat across from him. William couldn't see her face very well from the angle and the faint firelight, but she definitely looked smug. Whatever the reason she had come to this place, her self-righteous air indicated success.

The contrast between the two Charlottes' expressions in front of him screamed in alarm. The Charlotte inside resembled the same Charlotte that had presumed William's interest and thrown herself at him, making up her mind that he lusted for her, too. The charismatic, confident Charlotte — the only one he really knew. The Charlotte outside, however, had lost her haughty appearance, as if her façade had been washed away and William now looked at her in the flesh for the first time.

The man got to his feet and placed the music box in Charlotte's hands, motioning for her to stand as well. As she stood, he reached down to the table and took a small herb-filled bowl in one hand, and the key to the music box in the other. Charlotte opened the lid of the music box for the man to place the bowl inside it. He turned his back on Charlotte, focusing his attention on the fire behind his stool. As he thrust the pronged end of the key into the flames, he spoke loud and clear:

"The man you desire has denied you;

You wish him to regret."

He turned back around to face Charlotte and the music box, the key glowing orange with heat.

"Now you give this gift to him.

The effect you seek is set."

He dipped the smoldering end of the key into the bowl inside the music box, catching the contents on fire and producing a thick gray smoke, through which the man could barely be seen. His words, now louder, continued,

"Turning the key will lead him astray,

For years he shall wander in vain.

Searching, for the one who'll end

This life that is now his bane."

The smoke permeated the small room and escaped through the openings where William and Charlotte stood watching the ceremony. Needing no excuse to make his exit, but also unable to breathe through the smoke, William backed away from the house. His hands trembled as he ran them through his hair, struggling to process what he had witnessed. Could this man be the reason he found himself there that night?

Had Charlotte cursed him when she gave him the music box? To be sure, she could be crazy enough to seek out such ridiculousness, but there simply could be no truth to it. There may not be another viable excuse, but he couldn't bring himself to accept something as implausible as a curse.

Charlotte remained frozen in her position where she continued to watch through the opening in the rock wall. The smoke had thinned enough to tolerate, but William abandoned hope of understanding what had occurred, and turned back in the direction from which they had come. It was time to go home.

Without looking back or including Charlotte, he set off in search of the Jacobs' farm. It couldn't take long; William could cover nearly the entire island of Nantucket on foot in a day. He would surely soon run into a landmark or area that could tell him what direction to take.

He lengthened his stride and ran swiftly to the highest point, frustrated that dusk had turned to darkness, complicating his ability to see even the smallest distance in front of him. As he closed in on the top of a hill, however, the feeling of pressure all over his body once again brought him to his knees.

Trying to distinguish landmarks in the darkness of the moor proved effortless compared to the penetrating darkness he felt after the invisible weight had forced his eyes to close. He had started to breathe harder during his jog uphill, yet now he could feel no air in his lungs at all, and panic soon set in.

Seconds after the sensation crashed down on him, though, it lifted, leaving no traces of what his body had just gone through. He sat by the fire again, across from a drenched Charlotte. The music box played on, perched on his lap with the clover-ended key suspended mid-turn. The rainstorm churned outside, just as before, with frequent streaks of lightning lighting his cabin as bright as day.

Charlotte drew in a breath as if she'd just surfaced from being underwater, her eyes wild with astonishment. She sprang upright, sending her chair careening to the floor. Pacing around the room erratically, she breathed heavier and heavier until adequate air escaped her completely.

William couldn't fathom the idea of Charlotte hyperventilating in his house at this hour, so he set down the music box on the table near his chair and threw the key beside it so he could get some water to calm her. She took the water with shaky hands and tried to sip, but the water sloshed over the sides of the mug and down her hands and arms.

"All right," William started, "Let's have it. How did you orchestrate that nonsense back there?"

She didn't speak, instead taking a few minutes to steady herself, carefully sipping water and staring out the window at the flooded fields. As the tune from the music box finished, William took to pacing around the living area of the little cabin.

When Charlotte finally spoke, words flowed from her almost of their own accord.

"So if he will not have you,
No one he will have.
Though, be warned, my lady, for you shall find:
a curse always has two halves."

William had stopped pacing to listen to her strange words, then said them over in his head another time or two. "What is that? Did he say those words after I stepped away? What does it mean?"

"It means he warned me, and I didn't listen," she said as she returned to the seats by the fire, picking up the chair she sent flying to the floor. She set it upright, taking her time to place it precisely where it had been before. She did not sit, but stood behind it with her arms gripping the back for support. "I wasn't supposed to be there. I didn't know what would happen, but it wasn't supposed to be me." She looked up at William, a hint of regret in her eyes, and whispered, "It was only supposed to be you."

"But what — what *is* it all — what *was* that, Charlotte?"

She stood, contemplating for another long moment, no doubt wondering where to start. "I went there a few weeks ago. You *upset* me so, William. Here I am, *throwing* myself at you! And you just ignore me..." she trailed off, sighing. "I had heard of him... people said he worked with dark magic...just rumors, really. It made me curious, though. So I went to see him. I told him," she looked up at William, her face tortured with guilt. She turned away from him as she continued. "I told him of my situation with someone I felt had slighted me. I wanted revenge. Something you would remember forever. I wanted you to regret denying me."

So far, nothing of Charlotte's story surprised William. She was angry and disillusioned, and it was well within reason to think she would seek out such foolishness. He couldn't see any truth to this as an explanation of what had happened, however. There had to be some sort of realistic rationalization for what had actually transpired there tonight.

"So you went to a, what is he, a witch doctor? A sorcerer? You tried to *curse* me? That is absolutely ludicrous, Charlotte!" He wanted to believe his words, but the fact remained, something *had* happened. Something that he couldn't explain.

"I knew it was extreme, if it worked, which I didn't think it would. That's why I didn't give it to you before. And I thought maybe you were just being noble — maybe you were too afraid of what my father would say. So I came here yesterday, *knowing* I could convince you." She stopped, waiting for him to chime in. When he didn't, she pressed on. "So I got mad. All over again mad. I came back with the music box, and you know the rest. I'm sorry. Really, you have to believe me."

Was he really hearing this?

"Look, can I?" Charlotte stammered, pointing to the music box, "Can I see what happens if *I*...you know..." Before she clarified her intentions, she rushed to the table and took the music box up in her arms.

"I need to know why it happened to me, too." She worked herself back into a state of panic, her hands massaging the carvings on the music box, and making attempts to pace the room, but turning around with every step. Her eyes fell to the key on the table, but William reacted one step ahead of her, grabbing it up before she could take a step toward it. She yelled at him, fiercely, "Give me the key! I have to see what happens!"

"I'll be damned, Charlotte, you're not sorry for any of this, you only apologized because you're wrapped up in it now, too. What did you think, you'd sit back and watch me be cursed with...with what? A case of scabies? Impotence? Or better yet, struck dead when I turned that key? What did he say back there? 'Be warned, a curse always has two halves?' You missed that part when you were in the middle of your little dark magic gathering the first time around? Probably too excited with the thought of your revenge to catch that. But you did this time, didn't you? Sounds like you cursed yourself just as much as you cursed me. Congratulations, well done."

She made a grab for the key, but William struck quicker, dodging her hand and pushing her aside. "Forget it! It doesn't matter, I don't know what the hell happened here tonight, but it's not going to happen again, because I'm getting rid of that thing. Curse or whatever ridiculousness you think you arranged for me, I'm not having any part of it." He lunged at Charlotte, grabbing for the music box, but she stepped back just in time. She saw too late, however, that backing away from him put her directly into the corner of the little cabin, and William knew he had her trapped.

She protested, "No, no! William, please let me see what happens if I turn the key — I've got to know!" She dropped to the ground, transferring the music box to under her backside, putting her body in front of it. Without care or worry of hurting her, William yanked her by the arm and threw her out of the way. She stumbled over chairs and tables as she hurtled across the cabin, and the music box sat, now unprotected, in the corner on the floor.

Even as quick as he reacted, seizing it in his arms, Charlotte moved like the lightning outside. With a flash, she jumped on his back, screaming uncontrollably and reaching around his head for the music box. He didn't have a plan for disposing of it, but throwing it in the fire came to mind, promising a hopeful end. When he moved toward the fireplace, Charlotte's screams became feral.

"Please, William," she sobbed, "Please, don't!" She continued in vain to take it, but he held it out of her reach and in two steps had covered the distance to the fireplace. He tossed the key in beside it, and with that it was done, and Charlotte knew it. She slid from his back, collapsing on the floor with her head buried in her arms; her dark curls bouncing as she stifled her cries.

THREE
HERE COMES THE HOTSTEPPER

Just as quickly as the relentless feeling of constricting pressure came on, it lifted without a trace, and aside from the obvious confusion, I felt fine. My senses returned to me one by one, though, making an agonizingly slow process of becoming aware of what had just happened.

I had already felt the key in my hand and had taken inventory of my body parts, which were all intact. I could also feel that I was standing, rather than sitting on my outdoor patio like I had just been moments before, and around me a dim light glowed with a brighter area up ahead, like a tunnel. My arms instinctively wrapped around my body, uneasy with such a perplexing phenomenon, and I realized even the clothes I had been wearing earlier had changed. An over-sized silky fabric now hung loosely over a long-sleeved shirt, and loose-fitting, high-wasted jeans and tennies replaced my skinny jeans and Vans.

Familiar smells wafted through the broad hallway: popcorn and Friday-night-cheese, like you get on nachos at the concession stand of a high school football game. Further observation confirmed more concession stand smells: jalapenos, mustard, hot dogs, and beer.

Isolated jeers and whistles passed by my hiding spot, then disappeared and were replaced by different ones, but I could tell that beyond my tunnel thundered a deafening roar. I concentrated on hearing through the riotous noise, and just when I had picked up an intermittent voice above the rest, a buzzer sounded, cutting through it all.

As I struggled to comprehend my surroundings, I unwillingly accepted that for some reason I was now in what seemed like a coliseum or stadium. When my eyesight returned at last, it only validated what my other senses had already assumed. My silky loose shirt was a jersey: blue, accented with orange, with a large number 33 across the front. The letters across the chest were exaggerated and stretched, making it tricky to read upside down, but I could make out K-N-I-C-K-S.

The Knicks? Not that I'm not a basketball fan, but I'm not the type to sport a jersey at a game, and I'd never even been to New York. I thought back to the journal describing the clothes that were appropriate to the climate, no matter where the writer happened to be. If I now wore appropriate clothes for my surroundings, then I must be at...Madison Square Garden? I looked down at the key again and considered the likelihood that I had just been sitting in my teacher clothes on my patio with a beer and a music box, and moments later I'm in a Knicks jersey at The Garden. Not likely.

But wasn't this exactly like the journal? I understood more now why the traveler appeared to be lost. Even with all evidence pointing to the conclusion that I emerged in New York City, though, my logically sound mind went through an emotional separation between realistic possibility, and the current reality that I apparently faced.

I didn't get scared until I realized this. Now that I accepted what had just occurred, my pulse quickened at the thought of what would come next. Could I be stuck here? The writer of the journal never mentioned how he arrived or left, but I supposed if he had wrote, "I turned a music box key and was sent to the Eiffel Tower for twenty minutes, this is what I saw..." I would be looking at the situation with whole new eyes anyway.

One of the entries flitted through my mind; something he described to be like a movie theatre, although he didn't seem to understand that concept. When approached by a man asking for his ticket, the writer, unaware, was surprised to check his pockets and find that he did in fact have one.

Wanting it to be true, and seeing how under the circumstances, nothing could surprise me anymore, I checked my pockets. The left was empty, and the right...was empty too. My heart sank, knowing with no ticket I might be stuck in the tunnel all night waiting to see what would happen next. I entertained the idea for a while, until I started thinking that if I was at Madison Square Garden, it would be pretty lame to say I didn't see any more than a custodial tunnel.

Slowly inching toward the light of the outer hall, I noticed my hands shaking. I don't know what I was afraid of; for someone who had just traveled by way of music box, you'd think being seen by New Yorkers or getting caught without your ticket wouldn't even move your give-a-shit meter. People walking by didn't even glance in my direction, and when someone did look my way, their gaze didn't linger long, which I took comfort in. Hopefully that meant I wouldn't attract any unwanted attention.

I took another two steps, which put me right at the corner of the wall to my tunnel, and the wall that lead to everything else: vendors selling novelties, concessions stands, entryways to the arena, bathrooms. Briefly, I considered finding a bathroom so I could look in a mirror, curious if I still looked like me, but I could feel my hair, my nose, and nothing out of the ordinary; just ordinary me.

Another buzzer went off in the arena, and now that I had left the cocoon of my tunnel, I could hear the announcer's voice proclaiming it to be halftime, with a score of Knicks: 42, Celtics: 50. Soon the arena would empty with fans filtering into the halls for more beer, or to pee in order to make room for more beer. My palms began to tingle from the involuntary tight grip on the key, and afraid I might lose it in the crowd of people about to flood from the arena, I decided to slip it into my back pocket where I usually would keep my cell phone.

The key brushed up against something else in the pocket, first with resistance as the three prongs caught an edge, and then with a snap as it broke free. I whipped my head around to examine my ass as I pulled the pocket open, finding a thick piece of paper with torn, perforated edges slightly bending around the shape of the key. A breathy half-laugh escaped me as I marveled at how the music box had, in fact, prepared me properly just as it had the journal writer.

The ticket had several different things printed on it, and I had to search the whole thing over to find pertinent information. I spoke aloud as I read, "Use club entrance...New York Knicks vs. Boston Celtics...Madison Square Garden...January 9, 1996...."

Oh my God. 1996. My head jerked up to check out the people that had started to file out of the arena. Oh, wow, they definitely had the 90's look. The jeans were awkward and cut differently at the legs. The haircuts on men were tight on the side and longer on the top, and the women all looked like they went to their hairdresser and asked for something like one of the *Friends*. Even though I'd blindly trusted the journal writer, wanting to believe that something truly amazing and unfathomable had happened to him, in the back of my mind I still dismissed all of it as something I would end up figuring out. Eventually, logic told me, I'd find the reason he thought he was traveling through time or space. But this defied logic.

I stared down at my ticket again, looking for a seat. "Gate 65, Section 77, Row D, Seat 2," it said. That meant nothing to me, as I had never been there before. I skimmed left and right down the corridor where banners were hanging. I could see 60 immediately to my right, and 59 was the next one past that, so I looked left to see if 65 was in view. Because of the curve of the arena, though, I could only see to 63. Fighting the crowds in the hallway didn't seem ideal, but that meant the seats would be nearly empty, so I could easily find mine.

Like a stoplight had turned red, I noticed a lull in the flow of traffic right in front of me. Ticket in hand, I darted out and down toward my gate. I tried to look normal, like I belonged there, but I think the simple act of *trying* to look normal probably made me look like a suspicious dork. My head darted back and forth, my eyes wide open and alert, as if someone would grab my ticket and proclaim it as theirs. I speed-walked on down, passing t-shirt vendors and concession stands, wishing there had been money in my pocket, too; I could've used a beer.

Gate 63 passed, then 64, and finally, I arrived at 65. I concentrated on breathing in deep, calming breaths as I sauntered up coolly to the attendant checking tickets. I nearly lost it when he said to me, "Hey, how *you* doin'?"

"Um, great, thanks." I showed him my ticket, hoping for less talk and more leave me alone.

"Nice seats, you all by yourself?"

I considered telling him I was meeting friends, but decided the less I say, the less I have to explain, so I just nodded and held my hand out for my ticket. Behind me, I could hear a couple arguing. I couldn't hear what they were saying, but their tone was hostile to one another.

The attendant gave me back my ticket, and I happily left the heated exchange behind me as I walked through the tunnel and into the arena. It smelled like basketball leather and tennis shoes, and it was completely breathtaking. Even though this was technically an arena from decades in the past, it struck me with awed reverence. Concerts, sports, politics — for any major event, this was the place it all happened. Talk about star power, too; anyone who's anyone has front row seats. I craned my neck to see who was in attendance tonight. I tried to remember who were the big names in the 90's - the cast of *Seinfeld*?

The teams must have been in their locker rooms, because on the floor were kids' basketball teams performing dribbling tricks for the dwindling halftime crowd. I perched for a while right at the top of the seating sections, laughing at the music playing for the little athletes:

Ini Kamoze's "Here Comes the Hotstepper," followed by Rednex's "Cotton Eyed Joe."

As the dance team soon replaced the kids on the court, I realized more people had filed back into the arena, including the arguing couple from behind me in line. If I didn't make a move to find my seat now, I could miss my opportunity for an empty row.

I found section 77 and worked my way down to row D, which graciously sat empty. I could see the couple in the floor seats not too far from me, still very much involved in their disagreement. The man sat stiffly with his arms crossed without looking at the woman, and she smirked as she goaded him about something, her dark mass of curls bouncing vigorously as she spoke. I'm an admitted people watcher, and these two definitely intrigued me. Even with my limited view, I could see they were beautiful, both of them, and they seemed absolutely unimpressed by the aura of The Garden. The man watched a fixed point in space across the arena, like he only wanted to be somewhere else, but the woman eventually left him alone and began cheering on the dancers. Maybe she won the argument.

The teams soon returned to the floor for a quick shoot-around before the second half started. Without knowing how much time I would be present in 1996, I tried to appreciate it to the fullest. I danced in my seat, wishing Tucker and Nora could be with me. I enthusiastically cheered for the Knicks, but also quietly for the Celtics (I'm Irish). I did the wave. I rooted for the little racing dot on the Jumbo-Tron. I would have drunk with the best of them, if my pockets had provided me with any money. All in all, I thoroughly enjoyed myself.

As the minutes passed, however, I started to wonder how I would return from 1996 New York. I had assumed I didn't need to worry about possibly getting stuck here because the writer of the journal had described visit after visit, which I understood to mean that he returned from each of them. I mean, when you've already accepted something like traveling through space and time when you turn a music box key, why bother questioning the details of how it works?

Quickly regretting getting caught up in the frivolity of the experience, a maddening need to understand and control how to get back home grew inside me. I should never have loosened up. Look what it got me.

What if the writer knew the way to return, and it was so trivial, so menial that he didn't even see the point in describing it? He never mentioned the key or the music box for the same reason, probably. I took the key out of my back pocket, and looked it over again, hoping it would show me insight that it hadn't before. The same key as always, with no distinctive traits, sat in my hands offering no help or advice. Convinced I would need to do something to initiate my return, I got up from my seat and tried to find my way back to the spot in my tunnel from where I had previously appeared.

I tore out of my seat without fear of stepping on someone or putting my ass in their face. The poor old man next to me got the full frontal and a spilled beer, due to my lack of concern. Clutching the key to my chest, I ran out of my section and through Gate 65, ignoring the overly friendly attendant calling at me wondering where I was off to. The corridor was nearly empty again with the game in full swing, and I retraced my steps to the quiet and dimly lit tunnel in which I had spent what felt like an eternity earlier. Standing at the banner for Gate 60, I looked in on my tunnel, and could see from this new vantage point that there were double doors at the end, probably for the maintenance or custodial crew.

I turned the key over and over in my cold and clammy hands, thinking maybe if I moved it just right, it would have the affect I so desperately needed. It wasn't that I wanted to leave this phenomenon I'd gotten into. It didn't seem dangerous, until you calculated the possibility that I might not return, in which case I would probably bum cab money to a diner where I'd beg to wash dishes or wait tables until I had enough money to get myself back to Texas. Then, back home, I guess there would be a young version of me and a future version of me, and that would really freak the young me out.

Shut up, breathe, loosen up, it's okay, I told myself. I walked right back into the tunnel and shut my eyes as tightly as I could, waiting to be taken back home. A good solid minute passed before I gave up because nothing had happened. Adding insult to injury, I had squeezed my eyes so hard for that long minute that I'd made myself light-headed, and once again had to rely on my other senses because my vision was blurry.

"Fucking key, you can bring me here, but you're not taking me back?" Good thing city people are used to crazy muttering loonies, because I'm sure that's what I looked like to the few unfortunate passers-by.

All sensible thoughts left my head with each passing minute the tunnel held me hostage. I finally took to waving the key in the air, hoping to catch some portal that brought me here. I flailed and flapped around, like "Kung Fu Fighting" was in my head, and when that didn't work, I took to making stabbing motions all around the tunnel. I had just thrust myself forward and jousted toward the doors, when they both flew open and a cart full of trash bags on wheels charged, sending me flying.

"What the hell are you doin'?" The woman yelling at me was so short that I hadn't even noticed her behind the mound of trash. I lay sprawled flat on my back, and my legs had just returned to the ground from over my head when she came to stand over me with her hands on her hips. She was very displeased; whether at my odd behavior or that I had gotten in her way, I didn't know for sure.

"Well, are you gonna get out of my way, *m'lady*, or do I have to challenge you to a duel?"

Choosing to just get out of the way rather than exchange polite explanations, I logrolled until I rested against the wall. I didn't see the point of getting up, even as she wheeled her bag of trash past me without a care. Humiliated, but now too deeply worried about how to get home, the waterworks began. My hands reached for my eyes to wipe the first of my tears, when the pressure formed again, curling my arms inward to my chest.

The first time I had felt that sensation, I was alarmed and scared and didn't know what in God's name could be happening. This time I was so relieved that my tears nearly continued despite the invisible force that clenched my eyes shut as my body buckled and contorted. Rather than panic, I held on to the tiny thread of relief and hope, so that even when my lungs burned for air, I knew soon I would have it.

The darkness, the pressure, The Garden; it all disappeared in an instant, and I collapsed on my outdoor sofa exactly where I had sat before. The music box rolled over on its side and rested next to me as the tune played on, and the key rested secure in my hand.

I remember hearing David Bowie again in the distance, and then smiling and pulling the blanket onto me, and without even spending a moment thinking about what had just taken place, I closed my eyes and fell asleep more soundly than I had in a very long time. An immediate and intense deep sleep then overtook me. The kind where you wake up with drool in your ear.

I probably would have stayed there until morning, or whenever the odd spring chill finally froze me awake, but instead, it was Tucker's gentle nudges and dulcet voice that brought me out of it.

"Dude," he said, grabbing my beer bottle, "is this your first or your last?"

"Both," I answered, disoriented. How long had I been asleep? Alarm marked his face, confused why he would find me passed out like that. I must not have been sleeping for very long, because the skies had only just begun to turn orange, and the playlist inside hadn't even finished. The temperature had dropped a little with the sun sneaking behind the trees, and I was thankful I had thought to put the blanket over myself.

"Are you okay?" Tucker asked, guardedly.

The memory of Madison Square Garden brought me back to my senses with a bolt. "Oh my God, Tucker, guess what!! My mom brought over Grandma's box of stuff — I called you earlier to tell you, but — anyway, you didn't answer, and guess what!!"

"I know, Rynn," Tucker rested a hand on my shoulder, "Nora

told me you went through that stuff. That's why I'm here, I — we wanted to make sure you were okay after looking through it."

The tirade almost continued, but my insecurity stopped me short. I wanted to tell Tucker about what happened with the key and the music box, but as I formed the words in my head, they just sounded unbalanced. I felt my face flush as I stammered, looking for alternate words.

"Um, I'm good. Thanks for checking on me though."

"You don't look 'good'," his eyes searched my face for something to give me away, but I shied away in fear he'd see more than lingering childhood trauma.

Tucker sat down, pulling me to lean on his shoulder and hugging me with both arms. I let him assume the resurfaced thoughts of Grandma had shaken me, hoping it would satisfy his concern and close the door to prying questions. My eyes closed and I nestled closer to the crook of his neck, still groggy and sleepy, but also trying to buy time for me to think up something reasonable and believable to tell him.

FOUR

EXPERIMENTS

William stirred awake sometime in the early afternoon, groggy and dazed with hazy memories of the night before. Upon returning to his cabin, the weight of sleep enveloped him so completely that he could barely make it to his bed. The rain continued now, although the sun peeked through the clouds in fragmented pieces. His body felt heavy after the dreamless sleep, and it took all his might to force himself up and out of bed, dragging along into the living area. He wanted to confirm that the events from overnight were in fact visions or dreams, perhaps brought on by overworking.

He would have no such pleasure, however. In the corner of the living area near the door, sat Charlotte. She'd curled herself up, cradling her legs with her chin resting on her knees, stark awake and staring at the fireplace. William followed her gaze, and feigned no surprise at what he saw. He wanted it to be his imagination, or maybe Charlotte getting to him, but the proof was there, in the fireplace; the music box sat among the ashes and embers, untouched by the flames.

His eyes closed as he slumped against the wall for support. Clearly, he remembered taking the music box and throwing it in the fire. He watched as the flames consumed it from all sides. Even if

Charlotte would have risked burning herself to take it out of the fire-place, burn marks should have marred it. In fact, it revealed no evidence of damage whatsoever, still as pristine as the night before, when Charlotte had presented it to him.

William relived the night in flashes. The strange pressure after turning the key. Visiting the rock cottage. Listening to the man's incantations. Smoke filling the rock house. Yelling and fighting with Charlotte. From the corner, he could hear her rustling to her feet. William willed his eyes to stay closed, afraid of what he might do if he chanced even one more look at her.

With three weary steps, he reached the fireplace, staring at the damned box, which he lifted out of the ashes and tossed onto the chair beside him. Charlotte froze in the corner, afraid of coming any closer. With the fire stoker, he poked around in the ashes, feeling for the key. When metal hit metal, he looped the stoker through the clover end of the key and held it up in front of him.

He had no choice but to come to grips with Charlotte's apparently successful curse. William knew nothing of what a person in his predicament should do, but if he never saw that music box again, he would be satisfied with that. The swish of Charlotte's dress announced her approach, but William would have none of it.

Loud enough for her to hear, yet still in total control of himself, he uttered two words, "Get out." He did not chance a look in her direction, but stared intently on the now empty fireplace and the key on the end of the stoker.

"William. I watched it all night. I never took my eyes off it. It sat there in the fire. Everything else burned down to ashes, all of it. But it never moved. It never burned." She moved forward once more. "What's done is done," she sobbed. "We can't get away from it now."

His back stiffened. "Charlotte, I have asked you to leave. If you do not, I *will* throw you out. And then I will go to your father. Now...get out."

Charlotte did not risk speaking again or coming closer. Rather, her footsteps led her to the door, and without further argument, she left. Though relieved at her departure, he feared the possibility of truth in her last words.

He carefully felt the key, knowing it should be hot enough to burn him. Like the music box, though, it remained unaffected by the fire. It was cool to the touch, as if it had sat on the table all night as opposed to buried within the burning ashes.

"Well, what did you expect?" he asked himself aloud with a sigh.

Determined to return to the normal life that should be waiting for him just beyond the door, he left the music box and key by the fire, and stepped out into the rain. Blue skies were visible all around him now, and the few stray gray clouds were moving over him with the last of the shower. He trudged off through the mud, eager for his tangible duties to take his mind off Charlotte's havoc.

He hoped to leave all thoughts of the music box behind, but as he walked, he mulled over the options of what to do with it. It couldn't be destroyed by fire, so could it be destroyed at all? An ax or hammer came to mind, but he wasn't keen on the idea of beating it to pieces and having it pop up again the next day completely intact. Perhaps he could give it away. Or send it off to sea.

When he reached the stables, Mr. Jacobs had already come to check on the horses as well. While gracious for the company and comfort in the usual tedium of their work together, being around Mr. Jacobs caused William's insides to churn. So much had happened overnight that he felt like he had lived a year of secrecy, and yet, no matter how furious Charlotte made him, he knew the night's events would never be something he shared with her father.

"Well, hello there, William!" Mr. Jacobs greeted him warmly. "Looks like everything's fine in here, but I did notice the roof of the chicken coop got torn up a bit last night."

"I'm sorry I hadn't been out yet to see that, Mr. Jacob's. I'll get over there right now."

Mr. Jacobs waved him off, "No, I'll come, too. If I hadn't been so tired of being stuck inside, I wouldn't have gone out myself. No need to apologize!"

They started off toward the chicken coop, with tools in hand to mend the roof. On a normal day, William would have brought up a million things to discuss with Mr. Jacobs about what would need tending when the rain cleared, but at the present, no conversational words came to him. Instead, verses filled his head from the night, *"turning the key will lead him astray, for years he shall wander in vain...searching, for the one who'll end this life that is now his bane."*

He had no intention of ever turning the key again, particularly if it would 'lead him astray.' However, 'searching for the one who'll end this life that is now his bane,' begged the question, is there someone that could put a stop to this? However, if the 'one' is someone who'll 'end this life' literally...could death be the only way out?

"You alright, there, William?" Mr. Jacobs had probably been expecting William's usual chatter.

"Oh, yes sir. Still shaking off the storm, I suppose."

They soon reached the chickens, and Mr. Jacobs pointed out the spot that had been damaged and twisted by the strong winds. They set down their tools, which disappeared under the standing water. "It certainly was a good storm." Mr. Jacobs noted, "We'll be swimming for a few more days, from the looks of it!" The two of them were soaked through already from the light precipitation falling from above as well as from wading up to their ankles while they worked.

The roof took about an hour of quiet solid labor to mend, but that one peaceful hour had a lasting effect on William. Simple work on a beautiful piece of land. That's all he wanted. While they worked, the rain had eased up gradually until they realized it had altogether ceased.

Mr. Jacobs lifted his head to the sky and smiled. "Why don't we get on some dry clothes before we get on with the rest of it? I'll let the horses out on the way, and then I'll meet you down at the barn, alright?"

William opened his mouth to answer, but no words came out. Without warning, an unyielding weight pressed down upon him from every direction, crushing his lungs and incapacitating him.

Breath fled from his lungs, total darkness surrounded him, and when he emerged from the sensation this time, an enraged growl escaped.

If this happened even without having turned the music box key, he was significantly more concerned with the seriousness of these circumstances. Indifferent to his surroundings, he barely noticed that he wore different clothes and no shoes. As he stalked through a tropical jungle toward a sandy beach unlike any he'd ever seen, he realized he didn't even know what to look for or what to do.

There were people lying on the beach, all of them wearing very little clothing. His rage turned to confusion when a perplexed face wandered toward him. She dressed in the same attire as the others on the beach, but a puzzled look that mirrored his announced that she did not belong there either. When her eyes met his, her shaky fingers fidgeted with a shiny object in her hands. She made to move it behind her back, however the sun caught the silvery object. The clover ended key.

William's fists clenched, which had come to be an automatic reaction around Charlotte. Her eyes darted around, contemplating: to stay and have it out with William, or to run away. He approached before giving her a chance to decide, striding up to the spot where she stood, torn between what to do.

As he closed the distance between them, it became apparent to William that Charlotte wore what looked like undergarments. Another glance at the people populating the beach confirmed this as the norm, and not a single person seemed to be bothered by their lack of coverings. He had never seen Charlotte, or anyone for that matter, like this.

Charlotte noticed William's eyes lingering on her curves, and responded by making her best attempt to be seductive. Her back arched as she brushed her ebony curls back, exposing her shoulder to him. Her figure turned with purpose at the hips, accentuating the line starting at her stomach and running down the length of her legs. Voluptuous and impressive as she might have been, however, William remained focused on questioning her.

"What did you do? Why is this happening again?"

His harsh words shook Charlotte out of her state of temptation, and with a mocking show of hurt feelings, she put her hands on her hips and answered, "I told you I wanted to see what would happen if I turned the key. Although, from the looks of this place, I'd say no harm done." She made a dramatic sweep with her arms at the expanse of the beautiful locale. "I wouldn't mind visiting a place like this more often...with a handsome man like you."

He followed her hungry gaze down to his own body, which he now realized was as bare as everyone else on the beach. William never gave himself much thought, but from the way Charlotte bit her lip as she stared, he understood he must have held some element of attractiveness. He had always been strong, but trim, which he attributed to the hard work on the farm. The labor involved with lugging around equipment, feed, and animals had developed his muscular physique back in his teenage years.

Beads of sweat had formed all over his body, dripping from his dark brown tousled hair and down his uncovered chest, resting finally in the waistband of the unfamiliar red trunks that wrapped around his bare abdomen. William looked down at himself, nearly exposed in front of all those people, wearing clothes that were not his own, and in such a vibrant color of red that he'd never seen on anything but flowers. Charlotte's eager stare moved up and down as if she would pounce any second. Though he had grown accustomed to her propositions by now, it was a different situation entirely when they were both half naked.

"You're unbelievable. Give me the key." He kept his voice low, careful not to cause a disturbance that would attract attention from the patrons at the beach. Charlotte demurely hid the key behind her back, grinning as if he were playing a game with her.

"William, look around! How much time do you think we have here? Last time it seemed like only a few minutes..." She trailed off, looking around the shore. "Have you ever imagined such a place?"

William had more pressing matters on his mind than the beauty surrounding him. He contemplated the fact that when the key was turned, and it didn't matter who turned it, both he and Charlotte "jumped" to an alternate place... and time? He spun around and trekked back to the spot where he had been when he came out of the strange feeling of pressure and darkness. Not expecting to find answers, but hoping maybe to initiate the return to the Jacobs' farm, he marched in circles until he finally gave up.

Charlotte followed, watching William search unsuccessfully for answers. "Aren't you the least bit intrigued?" she asked. "We must be in a time of the future, don't you think?" She looked appreciatively at her clothing, and smiled. "I like it."

"I'm going to look around." The thought of collaborating with Charlotte incensed him, but at some point they would have to figure out exactly what was happening, if not for the simple reason of deciding what to do about it. That could wait, though. For the time being, he needed to get his wits about him and gather his thoughts. His mind went back to the words of the man in the rock cottage. *For years he shall wander in vain.*

People greeted him with smiles as he walked along the beach, speaking familiar words, but in an unfamiliar way. He considered asking someone where they were, or what year it was, but he shook his head at the thought, deciding it didn't matter. *For years he shall wander in vain.* He would not wander for years, because he would not turn that damned key again.

A whisper in his head declared it wouldn't be so simple.

Charlotte pranced along, catching up with him and holding something in her hands. It looked like a book, but on the cover smiled a beautiful woman wearing odd, yet brilliantly colored clothes. With his eyes focused far in the distance, he asked, "What's that?"

Charlotte bubbled with excitement, "I heard some people over there talking. One asked the other if they had already read this 'magazine,' and the other answered that yes, they were done with it. So I asked if I could see it, and they were so nice, they let me have it! It has pictures of people, and stories; it's like a newspaper, but so much better! Take a look!"

William slowed down, losing the fight with his own curiosity. Charlotte handed him the magazine, and they found a spot to sit to look through it. It did indeed remind him of a newspaper, with vibrant colors, and it contained page after page of beautiful people and what looked like products for sale. Searching the printed words on the cover, he found at the bottom: February 1967.

"1967?"

"1967!" Charlotte squealed as she lay back on the sand like the rest of the people on their blankets. "I hope we get stuck here forever."

He looked at her without concealing his annoyance. "Maybe you can. Why don't you go tie yourself to a tree and hopefully when I'm pulled back to the farm, you can stay."

Charlotte clicked her tongue at William. "I saw you looking at me. I know thoughts went through your head, I could see it in your eyes."

"Yeah, it's just too bad you're like a poisonous flower — beautiful on the outside, but lethal on the inside." He wanted to walk away, but he saw no point in it, as she would just follow him. Although, he did embrace his newfound appreciation for allowing himself to tell Charlotte how he truly felt.

The last few months he spent agonizing over how to handle her without causing more damage ended the moment they materialized at the rock house. Charlotte no longer deserved his polite words and careful consideration. Perhaps he should make it his new objective to tell her off every chance he got. There could be no harm in it. She'd never dare tell her father, so she would either take the hint and leave him alone, or persist, and he would keep himself entertained by perpetually ignoring her.

"So you turned the key?"

"Yes I did. Are you going to be nice to me now, William?"

"No. So *you* were taken to the rock house with me when I turned the key, and *I* was brought here with you when you turned the key. Do you think that means that either way, no matter who turns it, we both 'appear'...somewhere?"

"That seems to be the case, but I think we'd have to try a few more times to be sure..." She rolled onto her side and stroked William's back with the key, and asked, "Are you willing to experiment?"

His hand reached behind his back faster than she could anticipate, and seized the key from her fingertips before she realized what had happened. "Wha —?"

"Yeah, we'll experiment, but we do it my way. First, you never go into my house again. *Ever*. Got it?" Charlotte didn't answer. William turned and looked her straight in the eyes and repeated himself, "Got it?"

"Yes, I've got it" she pouted. "Second?" She dropped back to her position of sunbathing and folded her arms over her eyes, whether to shade herself from the sun or to hide her disappointment, William didn't know, or care.

"Second, we'll turn the key a few more times to see that it's working the way we think it is. We need to make sure there's not something else factoring into these little trips we've been taking. Then, that's it. We're done. Third, — "

" — wait," Charlotte interrupted and sat up, "why stop? This isn't hurting anything! Look around, we've been given a chance to visit the most beautiful place, and almost 200 years from what we know. Imagine the opportunity we have here!"

"Have you forgotten, Charlotte? You *cursed* me — and yourself as well. This isn't an *opportunity*. You think we'll be so lucky next time? God knows where we might end up. It could be somewhere dangerous. Aside from that, I can avoid you back on the farm if I want to. Here, I'm stuck with you without a say in the matter. So, I plan on being done with you once we understand a little more about what you got us into."

He got to his feet to make his final point, and told her, "Third: You take me back to the man in the rock house."

"Well, that's not going to do you any good," she answered as she rose to stand in front of him. "I went back today after I left your house. I wanted to know why it happened to me, too, so I went for answers." She stepped past William toward the water, staring at the waves as they rushed onto the shore. "The place is empty, like no one had ever even been there."

William knew better than to trust Charlotte's word, especially when she had a vested interest in the matter. He would just have to wait until they were back, and he would make her take him, even if he had to threaten going to her father.

"Fine. When you were with him that night, the night we went back to when I turned the key, what else did he say? I want you to tell me exactly."

Charlotte spun around, annoyed, "I told you already. You denied me, and I wanted you to regret it." William stood, hands on his hips and eyes boring into her. Seeing that her simple answer had obviously not satisfied him, she elaborated. "I can't tell you much more. I went to him one day and told him about you, and that I had offered myself to you, which you turned down. He wanted to know more about you, so I described you — what you look like, that you worked for my father and what you did on the farm, that you like to carve wood when you're by yourself...stuff like that. He told me if I came back that evening, he would be ready."

"Where did the music box come from?"

"I don't know, he had it when I arrived."

Knowing there was nothing else he wanted to discuss with her, he opted to go somewhere he could think, without her trying to distract him. "*I'm* going somewhere else. *You're* staying here." He started to walk away, when it occurred to him that he didn't know how much time might be left before their bodies would be compressed again, traveling back to their lives. "Whenever this little trip we're on is over, you'll be in my house, I guess, right?"

Charlotte shrugged, giving him her pouty face again.

"Well, last time we reappeared as if we'd never moved from our chairs by the fire, so let's hope it's the same this time, otherwise your father's going to be in for a shock when I vanish right in front of his eyes." Charlotte sat down and leaned back, pretending to be too absorbed in her sun bathing to hear him. "So," he continued anyway, "if you return in the same place as before, you'll be in my house. When you get back there, I want you to leave immediately. Don't wait for me; don't touch anything, just get out. I'll be on my way anyway, because before you turned that damned key, your father sent me to change into dry clothes. You'd better be gone."

He looked down at the key he had swiped from Charlotte, and wondered if it would still be in his hands when they got back. On their previous trip to the rock house, it remained in his hand the whole time, so he couldn't be sure. Deciding it would be his first "experiment," he stalked off without a look back, to a quiet spot where he could be alone. He thought he heard Charlotte slump back down on the sand with a huff, but it didn't bother him in the least.

FIVE

PEACE TRAIN

Tucker let me nuzzle for a long time, never seeming to be impatiently waiting for me to get up. I felt guilty, knowing he was being extra sensitive because he assumed I was grappling with emotions from going through Grandma's stuff, but I didn't have any other recourse until I figured out what to tell him. I didn't want him to think I needed emotional support if I really didn't, but there was no way I'd be stupid enough to tell him that a music box had just magically sent me to a Knicks game.

My goal was to appear excited and proud of myself for finally going through her box of things. I wouldn't be feigning anything there, because the box truly did have me enraptured. I would show him the journal, and act just as puzzled as I had been before my recent discoveries, but the hard part would be making sure he didn't connect the key to the music box. Tucker's pretty sharp, but it would be a long shot assumption to associate the two items, so I just crossed my fingers that he wouldn't be as mesmerized and intrigued as I had been, and wouldn't feel the need to satisfy the same curiosities.

Without sitting up just yet, I squeezed his midsection and mumbled, "Thanks."

I felt his cheek rest on my head, and he squeezed me back in response. In moments like this, Tucker and I didn't need words — often just a look or touch summed up our sentiments, and I hoped like hell that I wouldn't lose that now that I knew about him and Nora, although I knew it would be different. There was so much I wanted to share with him about what I'd just gone through, and also loads of questions I wanted to ask about him and Nora, but I didn't want to fuck up the moment by talking.

When I did sit up, his eyes were searching my every move. If anyone could see through me, it would be him, so I just sighed and gave him a sheepish smile back. I always felt safe and comfortable around Tucker. Other girls might have been intimidated by his charm and flawlessness, but to me, he was just my best friend.

I don't know how I lived every day of my life alongside such perfection; yet never fell in love or even lust. It would have been easy; blonde hair that curls just a bit when it gets too long, sticking out at funky angles from under his favorite tattered baseball cap; scruffy stubble across his jawline; and his eyes, deep cobalt blue set in dark full lashes. But it was the way his cheeks raised and his eyes squinted when he smiled that I loved the most.

Tucker never fussed over his looks, far too comfortable in his own skin to worry about it. Nothing about him was calculated; rather, he was the ultimate take-it-or-leave-it guy. You pair his natural beauty and personality with a what's-so-special-about-me? attitude, and girls fall all over themselves and each other to catch his eye. It had been happening like that since we were in elementary school; girls always crushed on Tucker — even older girls. When we were younger he never noticed or cared, and he only dated sparsely even in high school and college. Looking back now, I guess it's possible he only had eyes for Nora and was just waiting for the right moment to happen. At present, though, I wasn't prepared to ask.

"So tell me about your finds," he said guardedly. I doubt he was actually interested in grandma's things, but was really just testing the waters, seeing if I was up to talking about it.

"Are you proud of me?" I laughed as I rolled my eyes. "I finally did it."

"Took you long enough. What made you go ahead and face it now?"

It was an honest question, and it felt like I had to recall years into the past to answer it; to the time before I had found the journal...the key...the music box. "Mainly the fact that my Mom showed up with it," I answered honestly. "I'd had a shitty day at school and then, *bam*, Mom's on the front step with this box — and I knew the box, even though I hadn't seen it in like, twenty years. I knew I couldn't avoid it. And my principal said something earlier, too, about me needing to 'loosen up.' Can you imagine? Me?"

He rolled his eyes, but not in the way that meant he thought it was as crazy as I did.

"Anyway, with you two, moving forward...dating... I need to face reality —present *and* past ...or else I'll end up left behind. You and Nora would be married with kids and I'd be all alone with only The Container Store and my label maker to make me happy."

"Ahh, drunk labeling night, huh? Isn't your pantry pretty much organized down to the phylum, order and genus already?"

"You know me," I admitted. And he did. "So I dove in, and before I knew it I had taken everything out and..." the next words could give me away, so I had to be careful, "I even found something I didn't realize was in there."

I reached to the table for the journal. I tried to be blasé about it, dropping it nonchalantly in his lap. He leafed through the pages, but didn't read any of the entries. "Was this something Grandma gave you?"

He didn't remember it either. "Look closely," I prompted, pointing to the bark imprints, "See the marks on this side?"

"Looks like, tree bark?" His words were vague, but I could see something spark in his eyes; something starting to surface in his memory. He turned it over, examining the other side, then squinted at me like he wanted one more hint.

"That day," I said. "The day Grandma had the stroke." Still nothing. "The three of us were down by the creek playing, and — "

His eyes flew open with understanding, as he cut me off, " — we found this — between the rock and the tree, the tree was like, growing around the rock! This is it! We were going to take it up to show her, and..." He stopped, knowing he didn't need to finish that part of the story.

I grabbed his hand and smiled, knowing he would be worried he had gotten too close to the sensitive subject of the day Grandma had her stroke. "It's okay," I encouraged. "I had to go there in my head already." He remained frozen and unsure of how to proceed. "Really, Tucker, I'm good. Okay, I did have a pretty serious panic building before I looked at all this, but I just pushed through it and I'm glad I did."

Squeezing my hand, then getting to his feet, he said. "I want to hear all about it, but first: I'm getting a drink." He hovered over me a little, probably determining if I was too unstable for one myself, so I rolled my eyes at him. "And Nora's on her way, too, so if it's okay with you, we'll wait for her before recounting all the gory details?"

"Yeah, okay — she'll be here soon?"

I heard him call "should be" as he ran up the patio steps and disappeared into the house. Now left alone with just my thoughts, I realized I was shaking. Between the unsteady feeling the music box induced when "transporting" me to the Knicks game, the excitement of the truth about the journal writer, the drugged-like sleep I fell into after it all, and hiding it from Tucker and Nora...I didn't know whether to scream, cry, or throw up. Secrets are safe, comfortable, but the vulnerability that comes with the truth is sometimes enough to suffocate you.

I heard Tucker rummaging around in my fridge for beer, then the drawers for the bottle opener. I lay back down to try calming my nerves, but luckily he took his time changing my music, and by the time I heard Nora's voice join him inside, I came to the conclusion that it didn't matter what state they found me in because they were already prepared for the worst.

Not surprisingly, Tucker switched my music, chosing the mellow Cat Stevens' "Peace Train." He was working every angle he could, and I had to hold my head in my hands, ashamed of my deception. I knew I should tell them the truth, but it was dizzying to think about embarking on that conversation. *Hey, guys, if you can't afford a honeymoon when you get married, I can send you somewhere for free! Just turn this key...*

They came out with beer and chips and salsa, Nora never taking her eyes off me. No doubt Tucker told her that I kept proclaiming I was fine, and he surely interjected that he didn't believe me. As if acting out a plan they had just devised, Tucker resumed his place on one side of me and Nora took the other, both putting their arms around me.

"Ugh, guys, I said I'm fine!" Even if I *was* trying to evade them on the journal/key/music box matter, I really was fine and it was starting to irritate me the way they felt like I needed babying. "Do you really think I'm that fragile?"

Over the top of my head, I felt them share a look. The remnants of my exhilaration spoiled more and more every minute this carried on. Deciding nothing I said would convince them and so it didn't matter anyway, I just started talking.

"I think I'm going to put Grandma's quilt over the couch, or maybe I'll just put it in the office for the guest bed. And the music box is way too 'authentic vintage' not to have it front and center, so I thought either the mantel or foyer table or something. Or I could use it in the kitchen to put teabags in, or pens and pencils, I guess."

I got up from my seat on the sofa and walked around the table to access the chips and salsa. I really just wanted to see their faces; it bothered me to let them continue making their subtle exchanges that I couldn't read. After a satisfying glimpse at their perplexed expressions, I munched on chips while rifling through the cardboard box again, hoping to get them just a little bit curious about my new treasures so we could move on from scrutinizing Rynn. Although I was careful not to linger too long on particular items so I didn't draw attention to them, Nora zeroed in anyway.

"So what's with this journal you were telling me about?" She plucked it off the table as she propped her feet up and relaxed into the sofa to read some of the entries. She flipped through quickly, only taking the time to look at one or two in full detail. Her eyes moved to mine, noticing my agitation. She was on to me, I just knew it.

"What about it?" Tucker jumped in. "You've looked at it already?"

Calm, cool, casual, I reminded myself. "Yeah, but, it's all a little off. Some guy writes like he's traveling to different places and times, but never knows where he is. And he writes from the late 1700's to the early 1900's, if his dates are accurate." That part was still a mystery, and I didn't have to mock my confusion about it. I now knew how he jumped to these places without a clue where he surfaced, but how he lived long enough to cover 3 centuries remained an anomaly.

Tucker let that sink in for a minute, and then responded with a very articulate, "Huh?"

In the midst of appreciating Tucker's comment, I caught Nora doing the same thing, except the looks on our faces were undoubtedly different. Mine translated to a "you're such a dork, but I love you anyway" look, whereas hers was clearly a "that's *my* dork" look of pure happiness. Unaware of why Nora and I were staring at him, he self-consciously asked, "What? That doesn't make any sense."

Nora scooted over to sit next to him, taking his hand in hers and answering, "No, it doesn't. So do you think there's anything more to it, Rynn, or the guy's just plain crazy?"

"Uh, I don't think there *can* be more to it, do you? He must be off his rocker. Crazy's been around a long time, you know," I added with a smirk. "It's just so bizarre that this whole time it was there in that box and I never knew it..."

"Yeah, but think about it Rynn, if you had looked at all these things way back when Grandma died, who knows what you would've done with them — we were kids, they'd have been scattered all over our rooms, or broken or lost. That's what happened to my inheritance. Except for the vanity, I don't even remember what I got, much less where any of it is."

She was right, and she was always good about spinning things in a better light than I had seen. "Yeah, so being a chicken this long is a good thing?" I joked.

"Absolutely. I'm still curious about the journal, though. You said there's a key or something?" She flipped to the section where the key formerly hid and showed Tucker, whose look of confusion grew deeper.

I had known the key would come up, but hoped not to dwell too long on it, especially now that the interest of both Tucker and Nora seemed to have piqued. I didn't remember putting the key in my pocket, but I'd already realized the need to keep it close, so it didn't surprise me to find it there. I reached across the table to give to her, and when it left my hand, I cringed, all of the sudden nerve-wracked at the thought of the key in someone else's possession. Thankfully, their eyes were on the key, and not my tormented face. Nora examined it thoughtfully for a few minutes, appreciating the clover design, looking for clues like I had done, coming up unsuccessful just as I had with my first look at it.

"It's not a key to a door, not with prongs like this on the end," Tucker assumed. "I wonder what could be so important that this guy would hide it in a journal like this, but then leave it behind...?"

I shrugged, figuring that was the safest non-committal response.

The two of them sat quietly for a while, pondering all the possibilities of why the journal writer hid a key within its pages, and what the key might have belonged to. I took a seat across from them, watching as they skimmed the pages of the journal again and again, and flipped the key between their fingers, hoping for something to appear that they hadn't seen before.

I had done these exact examinations not twenty-four hours earlier, silently interrogating the items that now lay before them,

hoping for something to speak. Would they find themselves as capti-
vated by all of it as I had? To keep myself from pacing or fidgeting
while they sat right in front of me, connecting the very dots I yearned
to conceal from them, I sat down and returned, now compulsively, to
eating the chips and salsa. I washed it down nervously with gulps of
beer much larger than I was used to, and I noticed all at once that I
had finished the beer, eaten an obscene amount of chips and salsa,
and saw that Tucker and Nora were staring at me. I swayed on jellied
legs.

"Okay, Rynn, what the hell?" Nora accused.

Stupidly, with a mouth still full of chips, I responded, "Wha' 'oo
talkin' 'bou?"

"You *have* been acting a little weird," Tucker answered. "I found
you passed out at 5:20 with drool down your cheek, — "

" — you went from talking a mile-a-minute on the phone, to...
vague, and dismissive now — "

" — you're fidgeting like crazy and you just downed a beer and a
bag of chips in 60 seconds."

My mouth hung open, dumbstruck and guilty. I hadn't bothered
chewing during their run-down of my peculiar behavior, so I took my
time finishing the mouthful of chips and raced through possibilities of
what could explain my behavior. If I told them the truth, the worst
that could happen would be that they didn't believe me, in which
case I could prove to them the truth by turning the key in the music
box again.

Now that I thought about it, though, I didn't have a clue for sure
if anything at all would happen if I turned the key again, nor could I
say what would happen to Tucker and Nora. Would they come with
me, or would they be left behind to watch me — and what would they
see if I were to experience another episode of time travel? Maybe I
should let one of them turn the key, but was that a safe assumption,
either? That it would work for them as well?

On the other hand, seconds slipped away and any time to make
up an excuse other than the I'm-just-shaken-up-from-going-through-

Grandma's-stuff bit slowly disappeared. I'd already let that one ride with Tucker, though I was far from proud of it. I didn't know if I could stoop so low as to continue that deception, nor did I want to.

I must have looked like a train wreck. The two of them sat across from me, watching with alarm, waiting for the squirrels in my head to stop squeaking long enough for me to give them a straight answer. Whether the answer would be truthful or not, I still couldn't decide.

Nora shot a troubled look toward Tucker before diving into the journal again, shaking her head as she found no obvious cause for my strange actions. "What am I missing, Rynn?" I could tell from the look on her face she was torn between throwing accusations and cradling me in case I really was just wrecked from reopening the long-closed wounds of Grandma's death.

My thoughts ping ponged to any possible conversation to draw attention away from the current topic, and some juvenile part of me decided to toss up a Hail Mary. "So when did you guys finally realize you had, you know...feelings for each other?"

Nora sprang to her feet, throwing her hands in the air, and setting about pacing around the patio. Tucker remained seated, staring at me through creased brows, questioning everything. I was busted.

"Rynn?" Tucker spoke softly, carefully, but his words pleaded for the truth.

I had to come clean. This was not at all what I had planned, but then again I didn't have a plan. "Okay, look, I didn't want to say anything because I don't want you to think I'm crazy." Nora had stopped pacing, and listened intently with her hands on her hips as if she had made up her mind to be mad at me no matter what I said.

I took a deep breath, drawing in as much strength as I could before retelling what I had gone through in the past twenty-four hours.

"So I fell asleep last night reading the journal. I was fascinated by it, because it seemed so odd, but I guess a part of me wanted it to be true." I stood tall, now, as if giving a speech. "There's something in this guy's writing that I want to believe, like if I could only figure out what happened to him, then maybe I could help somehow."

Tucker spoke first, "Rynn, this guy writing the journal, why would you think he needs help? Or that he's still alive?"

"I don't know...at first, I just thought the guy was nuts, but there was still something I found myself trusting about him. The way he described his surroundings was so, normal. Eloquent, actually. He was looking for someone, too. It was the reason he kept a journal, I think. The women he came across and the places he saw were detailed, and I think that was because he was trying to find a pattern or repetition that might lead him in the right direction. That's also why I decided it was a man, he paid attention to women, but in a respectful way."

Nora went back to sit on the sofa with Tucker, and flipped through the journal again, confirming my story. "And so what do you think he was looking for?"

Shrugging, I replied, "Answers?"

"Okay," Tucker chimed in, taking the journal from Nora, "but his journal starts in, what, 1790 or something? And continues through the 1900's? How is that?"

"I still don't know about *that*," I responded honestly.

"Well, let's be honest, Rynn, you don't know for sure about *any* of it," Nora said impatiently, "you're just guessing about what you've told us. Can you just consider the possibility that after going through Grandma's stuff, you might have been a little unsettled, and maybe you're just hanging onto this idea instead of facing your buried feelings about Grandma?"

I smiled, because she was right, except that she wasn't. "A few hours ago I would have let you convince me of that. I *am* only guessing about the things I've told you, but..." The moment of truth had arrived. "I can show you why I believe this guy isn't crazy." I held my hand out for the key, which Nora passed over to me. I felt better having it in my hand, despite the extremely uncomfortable situation I'd found myself in.

"I don't know how I came to hold both pieces of the puzzle, but I think you'll at least understand a little better after you see for yourself." I positioned the music box in front of them on the table, and held out the key. "Who wants to give it a try?"

Neither moved. They were surely debating silently in their heads if they should call a psychiatrist for me. "Just humor me, please?" I asked them.

"Are you saying *that* key, tucked away and hidden all these years in *this* journal," Nora pointed to the items as she spoke their names, "actually fits into *that* music box?"

I nodded.

"Rynn," Tucker began a careful argument. "The journal had to have been between that rock and the tree for God knows how long, and the music box had been in Grandma's shop for forever, too. I just don't see how the two of them could be a match..."

"I know, I didn't think so either, but take a look. It's a match."

Nora grabbed the music box off the table reluctantly and set it on her lap. Appeasing me, she took the key and wiggled it slowly into the hole on the side until it stopped. With a slight turn, the three prongs fell into place. She looked up at me in amazement. As Tucker reached to take it out of her hands to confirm for himself, Nora turned the key two full turns.

A few bars of the familiar tune played, and then Nora slumped. All of a sudden, my mind flew out of control. What if I didn't understand what would happen like I thought I did? What did I just offer my sister to? Within seconds, though, before the panic could rise to its' fullest potential, her eyes opened wide and fearful, and she gasped for air. Tucker scooped her up and yelled at both of us, "What just happened? What did that thing do?"

Nora grabbed him, pulling herself into his chest and began coughing, choking on the air pouring into her chest as the tune of the music box played out. After a few minutes under Tucker's watchful eye and my terrified remorse, she finally spoke.

"Holy hell," she said between breaths, "the writer's not crazy."

SIX

GOODBYE AND HELLO

William stayed as far away from Charlotte as possible in the few weeks since she stole the key and sent him unwillingly to the tropical beaches of an island oasis. Although he agreed they would experiment with turning the music box key, it was his first priority that Charlotte knew it would be on his terms, and making her wait was one way to make it clear to her that he was in charge.

Before leaving the beautiful 1967 beachfront, William had taken the key from Charlotte, initiating experiment number one: would it still be in his possession upon return? When he reappeared back on the farm, William did in fact have the key in his hands, so he concluded that the key would return with whomever is holding it at the time of return. This was good news in that it meant William now had the key, and he could keep it safe and hidden from Charlotte, however one question answered brought up more yet to be determined. If William took the key and therefore it returned with him, what would have happened if, say, it were to be taken by a patron of the beach? Would it have stayed on the beach, and potentially been lost forever?

It would also be assumed, then, that if William were to be careless and *leave* the key somewhere, it would most likely not make the jump back with him, and again, be possibly lost forever. No matter how badly William wanted to leave the key, to be rid of it and all related to it, he had a nagging feeling that if he *were* to lose it, more of a problem would be created in the grand scheme of things, even if he was temporarily relieved of it.

Another question that only occurred to him as he resurfaced from under the feeling of extreme pressure was how time passed while he was "gone." Time appeared uninterrupted when he and Charlotte sat by the firelight in the rain-soaked black of midnight, but they couldn't have been sure how much time had passed when witnessing the man in the rock house. Now that he had experienced the curse in the presence of someone else, it worried him considerably what Mr. Jacobs might have observed while William was on the beach.

As far as he could tell, Mr. Jacobs noticed William slump slightly when the pressure bore down on him, but he gave no indication that anything odd or out of the ordinary had occurred. William had already opened his eyes and assessed his previous surroundings before Mr. Jacobs had even studied him long enough to be bothered, and remembering he had just been told to return back home to change into dry clothes, he slipped the key nonchalantly into his pocket and ran off to do so promptly.

Admittedly, William couldn't carry on as if life resumed a sense of normality, but he did his best to try in those few weeks while avoiding Charlotte. The less he allowed himself thoughts of the curse, the more it seemed like a childish nightmare. If not for the fact that every day, the music box sat in plain view right where Charlotte left it on the fireplace table, he might have convinced himself that the whole idea was a farce. The other constant reminder, however, was the key, which he had started carrying with him at all times. He didn't trust Charlotte, and knew better than to leave it where she could get to it.

Charlotte's presence on the farm during that time of avoidance was nonexistent as far as William could see. He neither ran into her nor heard talk of her, which relieved him greatly. He would have been happy to continue as so forever, but after a few weeks of the false sense of hope creeping up on him, he decided to start their music box experiments. The faster he made his conclusions, the faster he could be truly free of her and hopefully, of the curse.

Choosing to forego the courtesy of informing Charlotte of his plan to turn the music box key, William settled in one evening after a long day of working the fields, and sat down in front of the fireplace. He had been burying himself with his former hobby of woodcarving every evening before retiring to bed, which without question helped calm him and perpetuate the feeling of hope that his world began to right itself again. On this night, however, it would be the key he opted to pull from his pocket, rather than his whittling knife.

It took a fairly long time for him to stare down the key and commit to what he knew he needed to do. It would be so easy to talk himself out of it and turn his back on the bizarre phenomenon, but a big enough part of him wanted to confront the curse head on, if only so he could know what he was up against. Words from the man in the rock cottage now disrupted his thoughts daily, *"Turning the key will lead him astray, For years he shall wander in vain;"* the redundancy of the words bothered him —why would he turn the key if it would only lead him astray or wander in vain?

The only answer he could fathom was in the next line: *"Searching, for the one who'll end, This life that is now his bane."* The hope, or maybe it was bait, that someone could end the curse. His head spun from confusion. Ready to stop over-thinking, he put the key into the side of the music box and gently turned the key two full turns.

———————

WILLIAM AWOKE on the morning of June 1, 1792, as devastated as he had been on the day he buried his own father. To lose Mr. Jacobs now, as well, brought about feelings of loss that he never imagined a man of his age would experience. His mentor, his father figure, his boss, and his friend — Mr. Jacobs had been an integral part of William's life in so many ways, and to think about moving forward without him was more than daunting. Before his passing a few days prior, Mrs. Jacobs had confided in William that her husband had thought very highly of him, and in his days of sickness, he had reflected on his life and what he would leave behind. Mr. Jacobs trusted and hoped William would continue working on the farm, she had told him, and that after settling his affairs and making sure his family would be well provided for, he would be leaving the land and business of the farm to William to do with what he saw fit.

William never wanted much out of life; happy with the choice his father had made for the two of them when he relocated them to the farm, hoping for a better life. After losing William's mother during childbirth, his father had always done whatever it took for he and his son, and William tried dutifully to make him proud, even after his death. Now, he woke up on this morning a landowner, with money to his name and a handsome suit to wear to the funeral for the second-most important man in his life. Grateful for Mr. Jacobs' sentiment, but sickened at the cost, he begrudgingly dressed himself and prepared to deal with what might very well be the hardest day he would ever face as a man. He didn't own a proper wall mirror, but in the reflection of his tiny, cloudy, shaving mirror he tried to smooth his hair, shave his stubble, and straighten his tie, which Mrs. Jacobs would no doubt have to fix.

Stepping out of his doorway felt different on this day; a tangible feeling weighed heavy in the air, all around him, grabbing him and pushing him forward like a gentle current in a shallow stream, leading him to what would be the rest of his life. It gave William no comfort looking forward to tomorrows that he would be assuming charge of this land alone. There were other hands on the farm, yes, and he would have someone to talk to if he so desired, but it had never been that way; he and Mr. Jacobs spent their days on the farm mostly in solitude, save for the company of each other. That, William felt, was because they were of similar mind when it came to the farm. It was not an occupation; it was not what they did to earn money. It was their life and ambition. This land was the truest family either of them had ever had, unfortunately for both of them, William never having had a family of his own, and poor Mr. Jacobs having a misfit of a daughter.

Charlotte had left Nantucket years prior, as she said she would on the night of her appearance with the music box; her plans of moving to live with her aunt only delayed a few weeks by the strange occurrence of the "curse." If there was a day she returned to visit, William was unaware of it, and happily so. It goes without saying that there was no love lost between the two of them, at least on William's side. It was a blissful life without Charlotte dropping in inappropriately, or turning his life on its end with her asinine attempts at revenge.

William could not deny that the curse she had set on him was legitimate, as much as he would like to pretend otherwise. They spent several months experimenting with the music box, which took them to extraordinary points in time, and all over the world, before William was securely convinced that he knew all he needed to know. Namely, he wanted to be sure that there was no danger lurking by turning the music box key. Although the two of them were sent to many various places he would never have dreamed of, there was never a time that threatened their lives, and by whatever magic or witchcraft the man in the rock house had imparted upon the music box, he and Charlotte were always prepared with proper attire for the climate or occasion, and at times even found items in their pockets that were necessary for their situation.

He also learned if he turned the key only once, the duration of the visit lasted a shorter amount of time than if he had turned it three or four times over. While the locations never presented a danger, they weren't always comfortable, so once he realized this; he made it a point to barely rotate the key, ensuring a quicker return. It also limited the time spent with Charlotte, as he never saw her save for these excursions. The less time away on an escapade with her, the less he had to be with her at all.

Charlotte had continued trying to capitalize on the sunny locales and desolate outposts to play the part of seductress, either flaunting herself to him or attempting the damsel in distress act. Luckily for him, they usually didn't surface from the feeling of pressure to find themselves in close proximity to each other in their new location, so Charlotte typically sought him out frantically, while William carefully strived to remain hidden. Not to be deterred by his obvious disinterest, she shamefully worked harder and harder each time to find him and win his attention, yet to no avail.

The most unappealing part of this already unbearable day was the knowledge that Charlotte would be returning to the island to lay her father to rest. Perhaps years of separation would offer opportunity for her to grow and mature, but he knew better than to believe it. If they could get through the day in a civilized manner, he'd consider it a positive note. Their last conversation had been tense and heated, with William asserting his desire to put an end to the saga of the music box. He saw no reason to continue, if nothing could be gained from it, and determined that life should move forward, rather than hang on the words of a witch doctor. Without question, she disagreed, begging William not to turn his back on it. Although the argument she presented was that they would not find a way out of the curse unless they continued turning the key, to find the "someone" mentioned by the man in the rock house, but in his gut he knew she only wanted to further her attempts to win him over. It was as if the curse had set a fire in her that would not be relinquished until she could claim William's affection, and so it was also for her sake that he wanted to get her away from the music box, hoping her obsession would dissipate, given enough time.

The memorial for Mr. Jacobs would be held at the southernmost tip of the property, with the ocean in view and the wind thoughtfully sprinkling sand from the beach across your face, just enough to remind you of its presence. William knew Mr. Jacobs walked to this point at the end of most days to watch the sun set over the blue-green waves before returning to the main house for dinner. It was only fitting that he could be laid to rest among the dunes that calmed him, where he could forever be among the waves and let the sand sweep across his grave.

William had intentionally arrived early, hoping to experience the same calm from the beach that his mentor had loved so dearly. He sat for nearly an hour, alone with only the sound of the wind and the waves around him, rooting himself to the spot and declaring in his own silent way to carry on like Mr. Jacobs had hoped he would. William was accustomed to diving into his work to take his mind off of life's complications, but that moment near the shore, lonely and isolated, he began to feel a peace with what his future held.

Soon, the funeral procession made its way down to the spot over-looking the beach, with Mr. Jacobs' coffin being carried in a horse-drawn uncovered wagon accompanied by his mourners walking alongside it. He knew most of them, having met different family members over the years when they visited the farm, and the friends and acquaintances were mostly business associates William had dealt with regularly.

Mrs. Jacobs and Charlotte walked in front of the wagon, leading the horses toward William, where he stood resolute in front of the opening in the ground into which they would soon lower the coffin. From behind the black lace covering Charlotte's face, William could see her ice cold eyes land on him, penetrating through him as if she were searching him over, looking for something. Her eyes grew wide, shocked, and confused. She lingered on his face, obviously surprised by something she saw in him, until her look ultimately turned to smug, which William had seen on too many occasions. It sure didn't take long for Charlotte to unsettle him, just like an old habit. He turned his attention to the funeral, focusing on his duties to perform in lying Mr. Jacobs to rest.

The wind picked up, swirling the women's hair around their hats and ruffling their skirts, as the crash of waves on the surf punctuated each of the clergyman's sentiments. During the short service, William tried desperately to keep his eyes away from Charlotte's, but his curiosity got the best of him once or twice. Each time he succumbed to glance at her, she seemed to sense it, meeting his eyes with her usual contemptuous arrogance.

After the burial, the procession returned to the main house, with Charlotte and her mother again leading the horses, but now with William following slowly behind, stung by the sight of the empty wagon. Most of the guests departed at that point, and goodbyes and well wishes were given as the friends and family were sent on their way. When the last of them were out of sight, William made his exit in silence; walking slowly and deliberately, making cuts across fields that took him off in a different direction just because he didn't have anywhere else to go. He walked across the moors and back down to the beach where Mr. Jacobs now lay before circling back toward his house.

As he drew near the humble cabin he called home, a movement on the front step caught his eye. Charlotte rose to her feet, looking as if she had been waiting for him there for quite a while, probably since he first left the main house for his lazy excursion around the farm.

"If I remember right, I'm not allowed in your house...so I waited..."

She spoke differently; softer, less assertive, almost like she was asking permission to even be on his front step. For the first time, she looked timid and nervous to be around him, and William thought optimistically that she might have actually grown out of her overly self-righteous attitude. It would be much easier to talk to her during this emotional time if he wasn't so enraged by her. As he got close enough to see her clearly, however, her appearance absolutely shocked him — her face, her hair, and her body — was exactly the same as he had last seen it years ago. It was not merely that she had "aged gracefully," as they say...it was as if she hadn't aged a day at all.

He didn't remember exactly how old she was; only that she was a few years younger than him. When he saw her last, she would have been in her early twenties, aglow with a youthful appearance. The Charlotte he now faced again for the first time in years, however, looked every bit as young as she had before she left the island.

William might not know much about women, but it seemed altogether strange that one could pass through her twenties and move into her thirties without showing more age. Her skin was tight, and absolutely glowing, accentuated by her rosy cheeks. Her eyes were stark wide, as brilliantly blue as he remembered, and surrounded by dark, full lashes. If anything, time seemed to have had the opposite effect on her: her dark hair looked fuller, shinier, curlier...her lips more round and red...and he couldn't help but noticing her curvaceous figure.

The shyness she had displayed seemed to lift as she noticed how long it took William to examine her appearance, appreciating the affect she apparently had on him. She stepped down to greet him where he stood, still amazed and confused by her.

"Well, William, I thought perhaps the years had just been overly kind to me, but maybe I'm not the only one," she whispered softly, as she was now close enough to study him.

William watched her eyes roaming over his face, then down to his waist as she lifted his arms out to the side as if she needed a better look. Not understanding what she meant, he stepped back, taking his arms out of her hands, and asked, "What's that supposed to mean?"

Charlotte giggled, and stared at him quietly for a moment before concluding he really must have been asking a question, rather than playing dumb.

She rolled her eyes, speaking sarcastically, "Are you kidding? I noticed as soon as I saw you. Maybe you couldn't see it in me with my face covered, but you see it now, I know you do." She waited for his response, which was more of a sneer at her, still wondering what she was talking about. "William, you can't tell me that you haven't seen it, too..."

"Seen what? What are you on about, now?" There it was, the familiar inflammation that always accompanied Charlotte's presence.

Soon his body temperature would start to rise, making it that much harder to tolerate her idiocy and drama.

Charlotte looked him over again, inspecting. The way he parted his hair. His handsome suit, foreign on his frame. His tie, still crooked because he forgot to have Mrs. Jacobs straighten it. Something satisfied her, though, and smiling wryly, she asked, "When is the last time you looked in a mirror?"

"A mirror, Charlotte?" he laughed. "I work on a farm, what good to would a mirror be to me? I don't need to see my reflection to know how dirty I am at the end of the day."

Charlotte walked backwards, still enjoying whatever amused her about William's appearance. When she got to the step, she reached for her small lacy handbag, pulling from it a shiny oval shaped object with a handle. Eyes narrowing, William watched hesitantly as she returned to stand in front of him, holding the item up to his face. Fine silver gleamed; ornate swirls decorating one side, with a mirror set in the other. When she angled it directly toward him, his flat disinterest turned to disbelief.

He looked back at Charlotte, clearly satisfied with his reaction. In fact, she glowed with excitement, although William couldn't imagine why this was something that would make her happy. Turning his attention back to the mirror, he studied himself more thoroughly, taking it from her hands so he could turn it and see all the way around his face, up to his hair and down again to his neck. One would assume after twenty years of living and working on a farm, he would be...worn. Being out in the sun and wind, the long days and restless nights would show their effects. However there in the mirror, a young, handsome face unexpectedly stared back at him. His skin was tight, his eyes brilliant. He thought for a moment about the last time he would have seen himself in a full-sized mirror, and concluded that it would have been about ten years ago at the Jacobs' house.

"So..." William tried to form a statement, but the questions and possibilities that had invaded his thoughts were swelling in his head and burning now like a fever. He knew the only reason for Charlotte to be pleased by this would be because she credited the curse for such an occurrence, and it was a sickening feeling to admit that he could find no other explanation for it either.

"So, you look as if you haven't aged, and so do I. I'd say we haven't gotten away from the curse as easy as we thought — or *you* thought, since *you* were the one that deemed it unnecessary to do any more exploring with the music box."

William handed the mirror back to Charlotte, and stared straight into her eyes. She was right. It would defy the laws of nature to live for ten years without aging, and there was nothing in the realm of reality that could explain it. The memory of that distressing feeling rang from within the once-closed corner of this consciousness, reminding him he had always known it wouldn't be that easy to turn his back on the curse.

It took every ounce of pride just to hold her gaze, yet after a few minutes of silence, he somehow mustered all the willpower within him to speak his next words to her. With his jaw clenched and his voice barely audible, he asked, "What do we do, Charlotte? What does this mean?"

"Well, I guess it means there's more to the curse than vacations any time we turn the music box key." She beamed with triumph.

William forced air through his gritting jowls to steady his demeanor.

Charlotte continued, "I'll bet you haven't been ill, either — or injured, have you?"

It was true, he had been in perfect health for the last several years, and he had also avoided any sort of injury despite typical close calls with the animals and equipment. None of it had occurred to him, however, as something to consider as anything but pure luck.

As his emotions rose to his skin, causing his face to flush, he stepped around Charlotte and stalked off into his house before she could catch sight of it. Inside, away from her, he paced back and forth across the small room where this grand misadventure had begun so many years before. He had long since abandoned the need to keep the key close to him, and had thrown it into a box where he stored keepsakes from his father and a few of his woodcarvings. With this new turn of events, however, he decided to bring it out again.

Charlotte lingered in the open doorway when William returned with the key. She hesitated before entering, still respecting his wish that she never come into his house again. He rolled his eyes as he shrugged his shoulders in defeat, motioning her in. Creaking wooden doors broke the silence as William reopened the corner cabinet for the first time in years, revealing the music box.

They sat stiffly in the chairs flanking the fireplace, reminiscent of the night of their first experience, as William peered into the box in his lap. It was an uncomfortable stillness for him, knowing everything he had worked to suppress and avoid was now thrust upon him again. Charlotte sat opposite him, smug in her satisfaction.

In her eyes, the curse was successful. His efforts to find "the one to end this life that is now his bane" would no doubt be matched, if not surpassed by her vigor to win his affection. He made up his mind in that moment, that he would turn the key time after time. Be taken to place after place. See face after face after face. And he *would* find the one he had to believe was out there.

Charlotte would follow, and watch, and he would look past her for the next hundred years if he had to. He would make every day of this curse a private hell reserved especially for her.

Smiling vindictively, and twirling the key, he asked her, "Ready?"

SEVEN

LOVES ME LIKE A ROCK

Nora convinced us that she was unharmed, and that she would tell us in detail what had just happened, but insisted she needed to lie down and rest first. Having just lived through the same phenomenon, I nodded to Tucker reassuringly, and we left her on the outdoor sofa alone. He held my arm firmly as we strode across the yard to sit on the back steps. Neither of us wanted to let Nora out of our sight, but respectfully sat out of earshot so she could sleep peacefully. Now that we were closer to the house, the music from inside broke through the bedlam in my head with Paul Simon's "Loves Me Like a Rock."

Tucker never loosened his grip on my arm, and as we sat, he watched her sleep until satisfied she was safe, at which time he turned his gaze on me, asking, "*What* is going on?"

"It's okay, Tucker," I promised. "I don't know where Nora just went, but I know she's okay."

"Went?" His pained expression turned tortured. I should have just told them the truth from the very beginning, and saved him this anguish. Paul Simon's words resonated from the house.

I sighed, wondering where to begin. "Remember the way you found me earlier?" I motioned over to the sofa where Nora now lay, much like I had been less than an hour before. He caught the connection I was trying to point out, nodding and taking a deep breath, then turning his body and full attention to me.

"I turned the key, and before I could even hear the tune, it was as if the whole universe caved in on top of me. Everything went black... and I couldn't breathe, I couldn't move, I couldn't open my eyes. It was so much pressure, and I didn't know what was happening. I started to panic."

I went through the whole experience for Tucker. How the sensation lifted and it took a while for my senses to recover, realizing I was in different clothes, the game, and the mania I created in trying to get back home. He studied me the entire time with furrowed brows, which I had to ignore, knowing that meant he couldn't possibly believe what I was telling him. In fact, he didn't even speak when I wrapped up the story, ending with my nice comatose nap like Nora had just succumbed to.

"Well?" I had to ask.

He opened his mouth a few times to speak, but not surprisingly, it shut with exasperation each time. Finally, he managed a slow and careful, "So..." He waited again, grappling with verbalizing the summary of my story. "So, you're telling me the box is like, what, a time machine?"

I knew Tucker, and as he got up to his feet, keeping his eyes on Nora even as he began pacing back and forth, running his fingers through his hair, I knew what he was thinking. There was no way that my account of what had happened could have been true, therefore he was dealing in his head with the more likely reality that I was crazy, as well as searching for possibilities that could explain what Nora had just gone through. I watched him struggle with this for what seemed like endless hours ticking away, wishing I could put his fears at ease, but knowing the only way to convince him would be to let Nora share her encounter with him, too.

When I could take it no longer, I hopped up and looped my arm in Tucker's, leading him back to the sofa to awaken Nora. He didn't object, but walked silently and chose the seat adjacent to where she lay. She woke easily when I leaned down to softly whisper in her ear as I nudged her shoulder. Her eyes were restful, but looked around curiously as if she wasn't exactly sure where she was. Whether that was because she had just woken up in my backyard, or because she might have been dreaming of wherever the music box had taken her, I wasn't sure.

"Hey there, you," I spoke tenderly, "Do you feel okay?"

She sat up and took a fulfilling deep breath before smiling and leaning forward to Tucker, kissing him gently on the corner of his mouth. "I'm okay," she said quietly only to him, before sitting again and addressing me. "So, Rynn, where'd you go?" she playfully asked. Tucker shot a look at Nora, confused that her question backed up my story.

"A Knicks game in 1996, where'd you go?" I answered matter-of-factly.

"I have no idea, but it was definitely tropical, like a rainforest."

Poor Tucker had had all he could take, "Nora, seriously — this isn't funny, did you two plan all this as a joke or something?"

Nora shot an offended sideways look at him. "I wouldn't dare! This is crazy stuff, I know, but what just happened was real. Maybe you should try it out yourself."

He stared at the music box as if it were gnashing ferocious teeth. Something in him must have resigned to the idea that Nora and I were telling the truth, because he asked her guardedly, "Tell us what happened when..." he motioned warily at the table where the music box sat, "when you turned the key."

"It went immediately black, like all the life and air...and all my senses had been sucked out of me. I didn't know what was going on, and I couldn't breath. I thought I was dying...but then out of nowhere everything came back. Blinding bright light, salty, wet air, heavy in my lungs and moist on my skin. When I could focus better, I could see a beach, and I then noticed I was wearing a bikini. So I tried to keep my head on straight, remembering the journal writer and the music box and key were the reason I was there. I thought about the guy being in different places and about him taking notes, and that from what you had said, Rynn, he never seemed to be worried, or even surprised by being there."

"It was such a beautiful place! I walked along the shore, with the wide-open ocean on one side and thick, dense trees on the other. I could hear animals in there, you know? Birds and monkeys, and sometimes it would be really quiet, but then I would hear a movement, like the bushes rustling as something ran through them. That part freaked me out," she shivered.

Tucker and I were on the edge of our chairs, leaning toward Nora as she recapped her adventure. Aside from the wildlife, she was alone on the tropical shore for the duration of the trip until just a few frightening minutes before her return, at which point the beauty of the surroundings became insignificant.

"I wandered for ages and ages up the shore. I was careful to stay on the beach away from the edge of the rainforest, because of all the animals and noises I heard. Gradually, though, the sandy beach had turned inland and had become more like a riverbank of a small canal. That's when I started questioning how to get back, and I had wandered into an area that had gotten too shady and before I knew it I felt like I was in the middle of all those noises I'd been hearing. So I turned around to head back toward the beach, and I ran right into this — this..." Her speech had revved up to an almost unintelligible speed and pitch. "This guy. An Aborigine. I don't know if he'd been following me, or if he had been there in the shadows and came out to see who I was. He just looked at me without speaking, for what felt like a long time, and I was too uncomfortable and scared to say anything. Finally, he says, in a thick accent, "You know, lady, these ain't the best parts to be hanging around. There's life in these trees... and what's worse, there's life in these waters. But you won't know it; you won't see it...until it's too late."

I couldn't believe I had so carelessly volunteered my sister for something I didn't fully understand. My previous efforts to keep the music box a secret, overridden by the excitement of telling them the truth and also proving I wasn't crazy had all clouded any potential judgment of the situation.

My level of guilt was outmatched by Tucker's unparalleled worry. He watched every word out of her mouth, terrified of the next. This was my fault, and whereas I had begun to think that the right course of action would have been to tell them the truth from the beginning, I questioned now that I should have done a better job hiding it and therefore saving them this distress. I was eager to apologize and make promises to keep the music box from causing us any more trouble, but I needed to hear the outcome of Nora's misadventure first.

"I thought the worst, of course," Nora continued, "but as much as he had creeped me out at first, I know he was actually concerned about getting me back to the shore. I smiled, and told him I had wandered too far, and then I tried to walk around him back the other way, and he grabbed me by the arm and stopped me. He says, 'You're willing to chance simply walking out of here, miss?' and then he turns behind him to look around. Then he says, 'I guess you're thinking right now that you must have just gotten lucky, making it in here untouched. Sorry, miss, but that ain't the case...' and with his thumb, he points behind him in the water. At first I couldn't tell what I was supposed to be seeing, but then I saw the water rippling around a set of crocodile eyes. My knees almost gave, and I didn't even think about it, I just grabbed the guy. He turned toward the crocodile, holding me safe behind him, and I peeked around his arm and saw the bodies of two more crocs rising out of the water alongside the one I had seen."

That's when Tucker lost it. He jumped to his feet waving his arms, then twirled away from us, throwing his head back as if asking the sky for the words that failed him. When he turned back around, is eyes were trained on me. The way he looked at me, like I had just sent his Nora into a crocodile pit, which technically I did, pierced right through my heart. I knew she was safe, because she was sitting here with us, but how many people can say they've lived through terror like that? And how many people have listened to their loved one's account of it? I tried to stand, but nausea roiled in my stomach, forcing me to sink back into the chair again.

Tucker's voice cracked as he asked, "What did you do? How did you get out?"

At that point, Nora blinked back a few tears, and she took a few minutes to regain her composure before answering. Succumbing to her emotions, though, she gave up waiting for it to pass, and instead spoke through them. "We waited for a long time." Her voice shook. "We just stood there. He didn't seem worried about himself, but he had a really tight grip on me. He made me turn around to watch behind us, but he never let go of my arms." A sob broke through, interrupting her, and she compulsively wiped tears from her cheeks, her eyes... "I don't know what happened after that. The feeling came back like when I turned the key, and it all went dark again," more sobs escaped, before she could finish, "I couldn't breathe — "

Tucker appeared at her side in an instant, with his hands on her face, wiping her tears. When she spoke again, it was only to him.

" — I couldn't breathe, but I could *feel* his hands, gripping me tighter as I slipped away." She buried her head into his neck, quietly weeping. "I'll never know what happened to him...he saved me, and I escaped — but I'll never know if he got away."

During her story, I had conjured the whole scene as if I were there, and now I understood why Nora had been so upset. I had assumed stupidly it was remnants of fear, but it was guilt. I pictured her savior, holding Nora safely behind him, all of a sudden left alone as crocodiles approached. I dropped my head and hoped like hell that he had been able to find a way out.

The three of us were wordless for a good long while, each of us processing our own understanding of the situation. None of us could have been thinking the same thing, which is what was so odd. Tucker hadn't experienced any part of the strange phenomenon, and no doubt he wanted to be a skeptic. I could see as he sat cradling Nora, though, that he was no longer thinking that we had punked him. In fact, he stared at the music box with careful curiosity, and I had a pretty good feeling he was fighting a sense of obligation to turn the key just to see for himself what would happen.

Nora, still affected by leaving behind the man that saved her life, continued to sniff, occasionally rubbing at her arms where red marks were now obviously visible. This would torment her, but I could see in her eyes, which were roaming over the table at the music box, the journal, and the key that she white-knuckle gripped in her hand, that she was trying to move on to making something of this. She grabbed the journal and began browsing again, looking for answers within it.

I watched the two of them, coming to grips with this new reality. A reality where truths exist where before there was fiction. A reality where a person's puzzling legacy has been left in my possession. A reality where it has become my job to seek answers to his century old mystery.

My thoughts went back to the beginning, before I had firsthand knowledge of the music box's...power? Surely that wasn't the right word. There was more to this; there had to be a reason that turning the key to a music box would send you through space and time, but what? I forced my mind away from the terror and guilt of Nora's unfortunate trip, and went back in time to the questions we were asking before she turned the key. Looking at the "facts," we knew the writer documented details of these odd excursions, for what seemed to be the purpose of finding someone. He noted the women, mainly, which would make one think he searched for...love? If this was true, that this man was simply looking for love, then the real question was why he was in this unique quandary in the first place. The other fact, using the term loosely, was that he wrote from the 1700s through the 1900s, which is another impossibility I formerly questioned, but after accepting time travel as truth, it's a slippery slope to eternal life, I suppose.

Tucker broke the silence, clearing his throat. "So, guys, seriously. What is this? Why is this happening?"

"Anyone have theories?" I asked. No one offered any.

"You said you went to a Knicks game, Rynn?" Nora confirmed. "What happened to you?"

I had forgotten she had been sleeping when I gave my account to Tucker, so I briefly filled her in with the same story as earlier.

"Hmpf," she scoffed, "Lucky. Were there any entries in the journal that were like mine? You know...scary, or...dangerous?"

I didn't recall any, but that didn't mean he didn't encounter them, it just meant he didn't write about it. "No, nothing like that. But we only know about what he wrote, so I guess it's possible he might have had experiences like that, but refrained from reminding himself of those unpleasant episodes?" I didn't know. All of it was guesswork at this point.

We sat for another few minutes, pondering. Nora turned over the key again and again in her hands, as if doing so helped her think. I didn't want to bring up my looking for love theory, because it just seemed too cliché.

"Rynn," Tucker chimed in, "This is the first time you've seen this stuff in, like, forever. Do you remember being told anything about it back in the days right after Grandma passed away?"

I thought about those days, and felt nothing accept the familiar sickness that accompanied thoughts of Grandma. "If anyone told me anything, I really don't think I would have been very receptive back then. All I remember is being in a fog, so...no. But maybe we could call Mom and see if she knows anything?"

Nora shrugged, "It's worth a shot. It's been a long time, though, even if she knew something back then there's a good chance she's forgotten by now."

Tucker got out his phone as he called Nora a "party pooper." After three touches on his phone screen, he waited for an answer. Had my parents always been on speed dial or only now because of their relationship status?

"Heyyy," he responded to Mom on the other end, then got right to it: "Okay, listen. We're over at Rynn's, and she was showing us the stuff from that box of Grandma's stuff you brought over...yeah...well, there's some little figurines, and the old quilt, and that music box... yeah, I know...huh? Oh, yeah, that's why we came over, to see how she was doing after going through it. Yeah, she's great, actually..." he stumbled a bit at this point, "anyway, that's why I called. We wanted to know if you remembered anything about this stuff? Yeah...uh huh. Right. So what about the music box, do you know any of its background? Well, it's just..." more stumbling, "it's so...unique, you know? Like do you know how Grandma came to have it in her shop, or where it came from? I know, it was a really long time ago...okay...oh, yeah?" Tucker nodded and "uh huh'ed" for a good while, listening. "Well that's interesting. Wow, okay. Yep, that's helpful. We might try to research it some more then. All right, we'll talk to you soon...thanks. Bye."

He had barely hung up when Nora and I were both demanding answers.

"Well," he began, "she didn't remember at first, but then she had like, a light bulb moment. She said Grandma had absolutely loooooved it, and considered it one of her most treasured items in the store. She," Tucker laughed under his breath, "she loved the beautiful carvings, but it was one of her favorites because, in true Grandma fashion, she always thought it had — wait for it — a story." Tucker said the last words dramatically with a flourish. "She remembers that Grandma came back with it from one of her trips, Nantucket, she believed. Wherever it was, it was a woman that gave it to her, not something she found at an antique shop or estate sale or anything."

"Did she say when?" I was extremely curious now.

"Sometime in the Sixties, she thought. She said Grandma had told her the story about the woman that gave it to her, though." My pulse rocked me, extending from my chest to the rest of my body as I waited to hear the origin of the music box. "Grandma had been going from shop to shop, just browsing, and she struck up a conversation with a woman in one of them. She remembered specifically because the woman was so attractive, with such an ageless beauty, Grandma thought she could have been a movie star. Grandma told her she was from Texas, and the lady swooned about loving Texas so much. They apparently talked for a while, and the lady told Grandma she had been somewhere that sounded a lot like our area back home. When she found out Grandma had an antique shop, she told her she had something she would love, and she apparently went home to get the music box and, for some reason, she gave it to her. Of course, Grandma said she could tell from the way this lady acted when she gave it to her, that the music box had a special story."

"Yeah, well, Grandma didn't know how right she was," responded Nora with a shaky laugh.

EIGHT
A TEXAS MEADOW

September 24, 1922

A charming creekside meadow – warmed by the sun, chilled by the breeze. Downstream, birds scatter from the trees as a half-dozen deer stop for a drink. I hear sounds like motorcar traffic just beyond the tree line across the meadow, and I'm confident there is a town there, but there's something so appealing about this very spot that I think I will forego my search just this once and choose to enjoy my surroundings instead.

William placed the pen in his pocket and checked his journal's cut out to be sure the clover-ended key was still safely hidden. Once satisfied, he secured the leather strap around it and placed it behind him on the rock where he had perched, knowing he wouldn't need to worry about it for a while because he had turned the music box key a full five turns, ensuring a lengthy trip into the unknown. It really was a beautiful place, and he was thankful that luck was on his side when he chanced so many turns of the key, but as much as he would have liked to explore and learn where they had landed this time, he had begun to grow weary of the search that was now sadly, well over a century long.

Leaning back against the tree behind him, he did something he rarely did when on an excursion such as this: he reflected on the positives. For so many years, William had become accustomed to working tirelessly to make the most of his circumstances, however today, for a change, he stopped to actually appreciate this life that he had done his best to command, rather than let it become "his bane."

Unfortunately, the quest to find the one that could possibly be the answer, or the end of the curse, had proven to be every bit the burden he had feared. William faithfully continued turning the music box key, allowing him and Charlotte again and again to be taken to places beyond time and imagination. Not sure what he should be looking for, in this "one," though, he scrutinized every face, assuming perhaps he might begin to see familiarity in them. It was a valiant effort, even if it had grown to be decidedly futile.

Never one to give up, William began taking notes in a journal to document the people, places, events, and curiosities that he had witnessed over the many years of traveling. He had been taken to surroundings he'd never imagined, and to times so far into the future that he often returned utterly dazed from the perplexity of it all. The journal helped him keep perspective in those early days following the death of Mr. Jacobs. Back then the world at large was still a mystery to him, being thrust into such peculiar places and times, so his notes allowed him to come to terms with his ever-changing world, even if those changes wouldn't take place for decades or centuries. Over time, and with help from occasional reflections of the notes in his journal, William began to find order in the patterns, and a peace in the intrigue of these days yet to come. He learned from everywhere he went, taking something with him from each visit, no matter how inconsequential it might have seemed at the time.

As was his habit, when not covering the expanse of space and time, William worked diligently on the farm, day in and day out from sun up to sun down. It was not only to keep his mind occupied, but also necessary to ensure all the responsibilities were met, which became increasingly difficult to do alone. Only a short amount of time had passed after he came to be the owner of the farm, that William had outlived the other hired hands, causing him to consider heavily the fate of the farm he loved so dearly. He knew he could not carry on relying on himself alone, but the simple fact that the curse hadn't aged him prevented him from forming anything but short-term working relationships with people.

It was in this state of mind that William came to realize the necessity of taking control of his own unique destiny. He had never intended to exploit his knowledge of the future for his own benefit; but then again, it was not by his choice nor by his doing that he was forced to live this way...perhaps forever. He turned to his journal once more, looking then for revelations, rather than faces. Looking for places, ideas, or anything that might invoke insight as to what direction he might turn with the farm.

For years that turned into decades, he had documented hundreds of visits to the ends of the earth within the pages of his journal. He was accustomed to browsing the accounts of his travels, analyzing faces and hoping to find someone that stood out, but he now directed his attention to the finer details to potentially be used for his own gain. Years of novel ideas jumped off the pages, but most would be of little use to him. Not only would it be nearly another century before some of the most amazing and lucrative inventions could feasibly come to fruition, but he was desperately alone in this venture and could only hope to find options he could carry out on his own. Tempting as it was to have a go presenting an idea that was not his own and stealing someone's thunder, William had no intentions of being dishonest; he merely needed alternatives to prevent losing the farm.

Inspiration finally reached out from the journal in an entry detailing a leap to the mid 21st century. He remembered a simple, yet beautiful wildflower farm, in which tourists and visitors sprawled across acres and acres of nature's bouquets. William knew then he had the perfect location, knowledge, and abilities to create something similarly fabulous. Pressing his memories, he conjured as many of the elements from the stunning expanse of magnificence as he could, blurring the outlines until the backdrop resembled his own Nantucket scenery.

Immediately, William set out on the path of planning and studying that would eventually lead him to transform the old farm into something new. Well aware the full transition could take several decades on his own, William took on the challenge happily, giving him something unique to explore every day. With each turn of the music box key, he watched the world around him with new eyes. Looking for trends in design, the use of natural elements, and even how the botanical world was embraced in products. His energy was renewed by the possibilities at hand.

Recreating the farm became homage to his father and Mr. Jacobs, but ultimately, William did this for himself. He enjoyed the creative aspect of designing acres and acres of beauty. He continued carving and whittling, however more seriously as art pieces and took his creations of wood to a larger scale, making giant structures and gazebos that future visitors would eventually appreciate.

As a matter of necessity as well as convenience, he sold most of the animals: cattle, horses, grazing sheep, and mules. Caring for them required more manpower than he could afford on his own, and his employees had already reduced to scarce numbers, occasional transients, mostly, to keep curiosities about the never-aging William at bay. Reluctantly, he kept the ornery chickens because they were manageable and could continue providing an income, and he kept his oxen only until tractors came to fruition at the turn of the century, because that was the one animal he would need to create the new outline of what would become Bennett Park.

With the money he received from selling the animals, he traveled to various places to gain perspective, ideas, and knowledge to use in order to transform his home. He began in the winter of 1809, gathering seeds and bulbs to plant when spring arrived. Many of the species of plants were native to the area and he had seen before, but seeing how this was an experiment he was willing to spend a lifetime on, he took chances and risks on unfamiliar and often exotic species, some of which paid off, and yet others became a learning experience. Every day, every month, every year...he etched away at the old landscape of the farm as it grew to hold the beauty he had envisioned.

Decades past swiftly, with some days spent traveling by the music box, studying faces and places, and with other days spent venturing to farms on the mainland or beyond for inspiration. By the time he found himself in the breezy meadow that day, William estimated a relatively short amount of time until Bennett Park would open to the public. As far as he could predict, the finishing touches on the land would be complete around 1930. However, knowing the Great Depression, followed by the second World War would coincide with his time frame, he assumed it would be necessary to wait for an upturn in the economy. He forced a laugh at the irony of waiting yet another few decades for his hard work to be shared with the public.

The sound of footsteps in the grass brought his thoughts back to the beautiful meadow, yet despite his good mood, William couldn't help his habit of sneering at Charlotte's approach. She had moved back home to help care for her mother after Mr. Jacob's passing, and in a few years, Mrs. Jacobs, too, was lost. But their coexistence on the farm was thankfully, purely, just that. Over the years Charlotte came and went, unnoticed and unannounced, and William eventually moved into the Jacob's house, leaving his old cabin untended but hospitable enough for Charlotte's occasional returns. They neither interacted with each other nor acknowledged the other's presence in their everyday lives. Charlotte had at least respected William on his own land, although quite the opposite was true when the two were pulled into the darkness that would lead to unknown destinations.

It was with renewed vigor, it seemed, that each time she found herself drawn out of her daily life toward unforeseen journeys, Charlotte set her sights on William, attempting time after time to entice him with her flirtations. William coldly and smugly ignored her, letting *her* spend eternity chasing after "one" that would prove equally as elusive as his own. Although he derived a certain passive-aggressive satisfaction from this perpetual game of cat and mouse, it was tedious and exhausting, nonetheless, every time she appeared.

"Oh, don't you just love the southern states, William? So charming!" Charlotte sauntered up, surveying the spot where William sat, appreciating the gentle trickling of the river.

William intended to once again gaze past her, but he found himself genuinely curious about their whereabouts. "So where exactly are we in the southern states?" he asked with mocked disinterest.

"We're in Texas! And just atop that hill there overlooks a quaint little town with a main street lined with shops and diners...it's magnificent!" She held out her hand to William, asking, "Would you like to go see?"

He remained seated, gazing toward the hill that Charlotte had described, considering taking a walk to see for himself, but he certainly did not plan on having company. As he stood and took a step away from Charlotte, she rushed up to take hold of his arm.

"Or we could just sit and enjoy the creekside?" She dropped her hand from his arm, hoping for him to stay. He turned, still deciding whether he was ready for a fight, or to just walk away. He was not in a particularly aggressive mood, while still uplifted by his reflections; but then again the mean spirit in him was so easily drawn out by Charlotte that he remained at all times prepared for an icy exchange.

An uncomfortable moment lingered between them, as they both stared at each other, waiting for the other to speak. It had gone through his head on so many occasions, that if only Charlotte could have been less...less spiteful. Less vicious, less self-absorbed...he forced a painful grin at the thought. In times like this, he truly felt the full weight of the curse. He had spent an eternity tied to someone so foul and reprehensible, and it was when his mind tried to frame possibilities of "if only's" in order to make the circumstances more bearable, that he realized how implausible those "if only's" actually were. If Charlotte had been the person he could have happily lived alongside all these years, she would never have been the type of person to attempt the cruel twist of fate in the first place.

It was a sadistic cycle that William found himself in on rare occasions, reluctantly admitting that even he had become lonely enough to open himself to ideas of giving in. As much as he had poured his heart and soul into Bennett Park, it was evident at moments like this that it was not enough to fill the void he pretended to ignore.

Rather than let his emotions go any farther down the path they were set on, he redirected them toward his frustration and anger at Charlotte, which was the more natural course. William had found throughout the years that he was able to tolerate most anything with ease, but nothing ignited a new wrath of fury like the feeling of vulnerability.

Charlotte knew the look in his eyes, and before he could unleash his sharp tongue full of hurtful accusations, she spoke to cut him off. "William, please! Have I not showed you my remorse? Day after day, I leave you alone because I respect your feelings toward me. I know you blame me for this, but –"

"— but what?! What, Charlotte, could you possibly say to end that sentence? Of course I blame you for this, you *are* to blame! Neither of us would be here if it weren't for you! We would be happily dead in our graves after having spent a long and full life with our loved ones if it weren't for you!"

His breath was heavy after the quick outburst. Unable to look at her, he raised his head to the sky and closed his eyes. His words had come so quickly from within, he had to take a step back and process them. It surprised even him that he spoke of the suppressed life he tried not to think about; the life that he had lost, and would never have. It infuriated him to have let that slip to Charlotte when he had managed fairly successfully to keep his mind from caving to that thought even privately. The last thing he wanted was to give her the slightest hint of his longing for companionship.

Desperate to change the subject before Charlotte could use it to her advantage, he prepared another hurtful rant towards her. Yet again, though, she spoke over him.

"Oh, William, we're only human! Who wouldn't want to spend a long and happy life with someone? I know I am responsible for taking that away from you, I just..." she stopped, as if choosing her next words precisely. Slowly she covered the short distance between them as she spoke, "I don't know why you don't see...that it could be me." Close enough now, she reached up and stroked his hair as she looked intently into his eyes. He tried unsuccessfully to steady his breath, which was made more difficult now by Charlotte's closeness.

He wanted her to stop talking. Blasted by the confusion of his emotions, he knew she was exploiting his unexpected display of weakness. Words failed him, though, and unable to put up more damaging defenses, he closed his eyes again.

Her touch sent shock waves through him, like he had never experienced before. Whispering softly, her breath lingered below his ear. "I would love you, William. I could be yours forever." His heart sped, and behind his closed eyelids were blurs of glorious colors moving in circles, dizzying him. All in one moment, as her lips touched the nape of his neck, he surrendered his grip on rational thoughts, feverishly gathering her up in his arms and pulling her full body into his. They were falling to the ground together as their bodies intertwined and their lips met for the first time.

In a way, William's anger with Charlotte fueled the strange passion that now overpowered him. At that moment, he lost himself in her, giving in to his more visceral instincts, as the meadow around them became a muted memory.

Charlotte's hands grasped wildly at William, as if he would come to his usual senses at any moment and break away from her. His mind did, in fact, wander toward resurfacing many times, but was pulled back under with Charlotte's surge of intensity. He knew he should stop; that this could only end badly, but reckless abandon ruled over him.

When he was finally able to pull away momentarily, allowing logic to claim control once again. He sat up, despite Charlotte's physical protests. She continued reaching out to him, searching again for his touch.

She began to speak, but her words were stifled by a familiar crushing sensation.

William sprang to his feet, fighting the weight boring down on him, reaching frantically for the journal he had left on the rock. Sightless, and competing with the relentless force upon him, his hands shook as they groped the rough surface for the leather of the journal. He brushed the edge of it, feeling it slip away over the edge as he was stripped from the meadow and brought crashing back to his house, with his screams finally escaping from under the invisible pressure.

NINE

COME ON EILEEN

Although Tucker and Nora had only been at my house for a relatively short amount of time, the events of the evening were still weighing heavily on all of us, and it was a unanimous decision to call it an early night. With so much new information to process, we realized that not long after Tucker had hung up with my mom, the three of us had stopped talking altogether, and were staring blankly off into the distance. With too many directions to go in our own heads, for the most part we were all dumbstruck, and agreed to sleep on it before exhausting our thoughts any further.

After waving goodbye from my front steps, I figured my mind would have been too busy to actually fall asleep, but in fact the opposite was true. I could feel my body dragging already as I locked up and shuffled to my bedroom. It was as if the deep sleep from which Tucker had awoken me slowly snuck up to consume me again, and I welcomed it. I looked forward to reflecting on the night's revelations with a clear head in the morning, not that I expected it to help. Does a full night's rest help you process that not only do you possess a time machine music box, but that back in the Sixties some gorgeous overly friendly chick from Nantucket insisted on your Grandma taking it home to Texas?

No sooner was I in bed that I was gone to the world. No dreams, no tossing and turning, just glorious sleep and a much needed break from over thinking. Even the morning wake up call was less bitter than usual, with Dexy's Midnight Runners singing "Come on Eileen."

Being so well rested should have made for a great day at school, but a tiny little conniving voice in my head sabotaged my good intentions. It was 5:30 in the morning...plenty of time to call in a sub, and my lesson plans and materials were, as always, prepared and orderly in case of emergency. Was this an emergency? I knew it wasn't, but the journal and music box were on my mind the second I woke up, and as hard as I tried to push them away to concentrate on school, it didn't seem to shake.

I'd never played hookie before, not as an adult or even as a kid. It had never occurred to me to take the risk. However, staying in my robe, drinking an entire pot of coffee, and snuggling up on the couch in Grandma's quilt while reading more of the journal tempted me to loosen up once again and chance it, because I gave in and picked up the phone to dial a sub.

Everything from the night before had been brought in and awaited me now on my coffee table, poised for my browsing and speculation. I don't know what I expected to find in the journal, as I had already looked through it thoroughly and still couldn't conjure up answers to any of it. The fact that the music box had sent Nora into such a precarious situation, left me not only extremely wary of turning the key again, but also with a major conflict ensuing within. One argument was that coming across this mystery made it mine to solve: dangerous or not, this was my inheritance and that makes it my responsibility. The other argument was that this, simply put, was none of my business. None of my business *and* dangerous.

It seemed like chickening out, though, to just step away and leave it be. Looking back, everything in my life had been so safe and careful, and as much as I hated to admit it, I think Grandma would have been disappointed that I didn't take more risks. I remember her telling us, in regards to the sacrifices she and my grandpa had to make in order to build up the antique shop's business, that you never truly know the value of anything if you didn't give your blood, sweat or tears for it. I didn't know what she meant back then at seven, eight, or nine years old, but I could see now that playing it safe and waiting for things to fall perfectly into place had thus far been grossly underwhelming for me.

So I knew two things for sure. One, that I could sit down and read every entry of the journal, but in the end, it would not give me any more knowledge than it already had. The writer only told of his experiences, and unless new light might be shed on his words now that I had an understanding of the music box, the journal was a dead end. And two, turning the music box key would very likely lead me to shed my blood, sweat, or tears...but ultimately, it was the only thing that could lead me to what I would value the most, which was answers.

Convincing myself of this was easy compared to actually moving forward, though. Genuinely worried about where I could end up if I turned the key again, I chose to put it off until later in the day and cozied up with my coffee, the quilt, and the journal. If this was going to be something I gave my blood, sweat, and tears over, I didn't want to go into it blind again. Knowing what the music box does and being prepared for where it might take you are two totally different things, so I reread each and every entry again with new eyes.

April 14, 1801
   Quite an event occurring, I've never seen such a large crowd in one place, and everyone so sharply dressed. A program in my seat says I'm in Castle Garden in Manhattan,

September 11, 1850. "Phineas T. Barnum presents the 'Swedish Songbird,' Jenny Lind" As I am unable to see any faces in the poor light, what am I to do but enjoy the show?

I MADE a mental note to look up both the Castle Garden and the "Swedish Songbird." Knowing we had both been taken on trips to New York was somewhat useful, meaning I could end up in the same place the music box had already sent one of us to. Not much help, necessarily, although it would be a pretty big bummer to end up where Nora recently left.

May 9, 1801

A perfect spring day on a university campus. I settled on a grassy area directly south of a grand clock tower, where many students have gathered. Many wear items of clothing that say, TEXAS. Some are studying, some are sleeping in the sun, and others are playing games of catch. A young girl closest to me wears an orange shirt with white lettering that reads, 40 ACRES across the front, and politely lent me her newspaper when she noticed me straining to read it. 'The Daily Texan' reported the date as March 10, 2010. My attention drifts towards the girl again, who is petite, and attractive with light brown hair and beautiful almond shaped eyes.

Holy shit. The journal fell from my lap as I jumped up to stand on the couch like I'd just been bitten by something. How in the hell did I miss this the first time I read through the journal? Were the pages stuck together? Had I skimmed too fast, or maybe read it as I was falling asleep?

That could have been any girl, I told myself. *You weren't the only girl on UT campus with that shirt. You weren't the only girl with that shirt that used to sit on the South Mall. You weren't the only girl with that shirt that used to sit on the South Mall that ever lent a guy a newspaper.*

That was me. The memory had faded, along with all my other memories of having near-conversations with beautiful boys back in my college days, but I knew that was me. I remembered thinking to myself that day that I should ask him if he had plans for spring break, but back then I talked myself out of uncomfortable interactions with good-looking guys.

The journal entry said the date was March 10, 2010, which would have been exactly the right timeframe for my memory, right before spring break. I read and re-read the entry again attempting to dispute the fact that I had apparently met the journal writer and never even known it, but I couldn't. It was him, right there next to me.

"Damn it," I cursed out loud. "He thought I was attractive!" Of course I would talk myself out of starting up a conversation with a gorgeous man and find out years later he thought I was cute. I paced the floor, shooting glances at the journal as if it had offended me. I didn't know what to do with this anymore. Bizarre and impossible seemed easier to comprehend than the possibility that I had come into contact with the journal writer, and let the opportunity to talk to him slip right through my pathetically insecure fingers.

As if talking to him would have done any good. I didn't know about the journal or the music box or any of this back then, and if he was only "visiting" my college campus that day he would have been pulled away at any minute to return to wherever he came from. We wouldn't have exchanged anything but courteous casual conversation. No phone numbers, no dates to follow, no discussion of his life and his curse. This chance meeting was just enough to plant vicious seeds of wonder in my head.

Wonder. Confusion. Curiosity. Frustration.

I wanted to believe in this, for the sake of the journal writer. I wanted to jump in with both feet knowing it was ridiculous to think any of it could be true, but because of my choice to accept it, that maybe I could make difference. The thing was, it was easier to do when it didn't seem to be connected to me. Now that I knew I had been involved, even in a small way, I felt like I *had* to accept it.

Time for a break. Anxiety made every cell in my body speed up, bouncing around inside me, so I decided if I was this worked up already, I might as well channel it into a nice long run, and hopefully afterward I could think better.

But there went the wheels turning, again. It was him. Right there, thinking I was attractive and had beautiful eyes. His face wasn't preserved by my memory; just the feeling of nerves in my stomach when I saw him. He must have been writing in the journal right there in front of me and I hadn't noticed. For the first time I wished I could know his name. "The journal writer" was now too impersonal, seeing how I'd actually met him.

Where was he now? Was he still alive? Would he be looking for the music box and key in order to continue his quest? Could he have found the person he was looking for already without the music box? Again, begging the question still as to why he was searching for someone in the first place? Only two possibilities of a motivation powerful enough to spend over one hundred years traveling through the history of the world for this person came to mind: love, or the promise of an end. Maybe it was both. Maybe the writer would find the person and fall in love, which would end the curse.

My heart rate sped too fast for the running pace I kept, which told me it wasn't helping to chill me out. *Constructive thinking*, I told myself. So what if he did find his someone? Maybe that would be best, because I could already feel myself getting carried away with Grandma-like fantasies, and I didn't like when I came up with those on my own; they never had happy endings like hers did. For fuck's sake, this was getting me nowhere. My mind had gone in so many directions, from jealousy that the writer might have already found the one he was looking for, to forgetting him and turning the music box key for my purely selfish sense of adventure, to longing to have that moment back in college again to talk to him.

While wanting to explore my more adventurous side, I didn't want to lose sight of my former goal to help the man in the journal. At the same time, however, and in light of new developments, I didn't want to lose my head over a near introduction that I interpreted to mean he's searching for me and we will fall in love and live happily ever after.

So I set my new priorities.

#1. Have fun, take risks, see the world, because Goddamnit I have a time traveling music box.

#2. Hope to find a way I can help the journal writer, who may or may not be alive, who may or may not need help anymore, and who may or may not still think I'm attractive. And if not, remember priority #1.

This was a rare opportunity for me to do something amazing, that I alone (and Nora, and the journal writer) would ever have the chance to do. I wanted to make sure I embraced this that was passed on to me from Grandma. Although she was never aware of it, she would have encouraged me to enjoy it like no tomorrow. She probably also would have told me that it would lead me to the man, though, Grandma would never have overlooked the possibility to make this into a love story.

For the remainder of my run, though, nothing could drown out the thoughts pounding in my head. The harder I pushed to stay focused on my breathing instead of my errant notions of absurdity, the harder my legs pumped. I sprinted towards home, where I succumbed to exhaustion and sprawled out on the floor to cool down before starting a bath. I then had to rely on my own willpower to keep my memory from getting tangled in my imagination, recreating "woulda, coulda, shoulda's" of the past. It was just no use. In my mind I was back on the South Mall on that Spring day, confident and willing to speak to the gorgeous stranger. We laughed and flirted, he told me everything about his curse and that he'd been searching for me all his life, and when it came time for the music box to take him from me, he reached out and grabbed my hand, bringing me with him.

I know, pathetic. I could wish and hope and dream all I wanted, but it wouldn't get me any closer to him. With a defeated sigh, I shook my head and resolved that at this point there was little choice but to go turn the key again and just see what happened.

Part of me couldn't wait, and the other part had performance anxiety. Only somewhat worried about danger, it was more about the growing pressure to find answers or something that could lead me to the journal writer. That's when I reminded myself of Priority #1. This was my adventure first, and my quest to find him second. After soaking my tired muscles in a bath and then meticulously procrastinating through my entire hair drying, make-up, and clothes picking routine, I finally arrived on the couch with the music box, the key, and the journal in front of me.

It was go time.

In a matter of seconds, I blacked out again, unable to breath and waiting anxiously to see where I would be when my eyes could open again. With blurred vision and a hammering heartbeat, I straightened up to see what looked like a private room on a train, but I could tell immediately it was not present day. The fabrics of the drapes and seat covers were rich and heavy. A hat stand in the corner held a modest black hat with a small arrangement of feathers and flowers on the band. Reminiscent of Mary Poppins, I half expected to find an upholstered bag that held the entire compartment's furnishings tucked away inside.

A ruckus on the other side of a door within the small room, followed by mumbling and cursing, announced that I wasn't alone. Before I could take a look down at my new attire, the door swung open to reveal a nurse affixing her facemask, who seemed startled to see me. She was beautiful, but something about the way she looked at me with her icy blue eyes set me on edge.

Pulling her jet black tendrils back into a haphazard bun at the nape of her neck, and securing her facemask, she said curtly, "It's all yours," as she exited the room, slamming the door behind her.

Frozen on the spot, I took a few minutes to compose myself. Instinctively, I suppose, I had held my hands behind my back, concealing the key. I tucked it into my bra, leaving nothing to chance. This didn't seem to be the sort of place I would be able to wander unnoticed. Walking over to a full length mirror in the corner, I could now see I wore the same nurse's uniform as my cold welcome party: a long and full skirt, covered with a simple apron, and in my pockets were gauze, a washrag, a cloth face mask, and a nurse's hat. So I was a nurse. I looked around the compartment for anything to give me context, and found a newspaper on the table near the window. The year was 1940, and even though the text was in Italian, the headlines and pictures were clearly reporting on World War II.

Fumbling, I tied the facemask over my mouth, as if that would make me less visible to everyone. I guessed the train was en route to a wartime hospital, but even that was highly suspect. Carefully pulling the door open just a crack, I peeked out and through the hallway.

"Haaaw, jeez," I mumbled behind the facemask. I wasn't on the way to a hospital...I was on one. Beyond the corridor, were two rows of beds in which an occasional injured arm and leg stuck out at odd angles. Bandaged heads and faces lay still under light blankets, while lab coats and petticoats hurried from one bed to the next.

I decided it best to lock myself behind the door until the duration of the trip was over, however, some jackass doctor noticed me and motioned me over to him. *Damnit. Damnit. Damnit. What am I going to do now?*

Securing my facemask to hide as much of my face as I could, I slowly approached the doctor. "Thank you," he said as I reached his side, "could you change bed 8's dressings, please?"

Looking around as if another nurse would come to my aid and take over, I caught the eyes of no one. Nodding nervously, I figured the worst I could do would be a poor job, and then maybe someone really would rush over and let me off the hook. When the doctor was out of earshot, I bent over to the barely conscious patient and whispered my apologies. As I unwrapped the man's shoulder, I looked around for clues as to what in the world I should be doing.

There were three other nurses that I could see, and all but the snotty one that greeted me were busy working and quietly assisting. She instead, stood at the head of the bedding area for a while, studying each bed and patient before resting her eyes on one, staring intently at him. Her eyes cut to mine, and I froze again, sure that I was caught. Sneering, but dropping her gaze, she strode off toward the bed of the man she had been watching, who lay quietly sleeping. She must have been the head nurse, which was decidedly not the person I wanted to piss off.

As soon as her attention was transfixed completely by the patient she now sat next to, I slipped off toward the direction of the first compartment I appeared in, with the brilliant plan of hiding until the music box whisked me away from this rather unpleasant and fruitless adventure.

TEN

INTO THE MYSTIC

Just as it had been after my first music box trip, a deep sleep crept up again. With no one to stir me awake this time, I was shocked to see that it was 2:00 in the afternoon by the time I came around. My stomach responded by growling angrily, so I figured as long as I was playing hookie, I might as well make it good. On a special occasion, there's nothing I liked more than sushi, and I could easily argue that this was definitely an occasion of some sort.

I slid the journal into my purse, then found a ribbon from my school craft closet to make into a necklace on which the key could dangle under my shirt. I wanted to feel it against my skin and know that it was safe. Within a half hour I had arrived and walked up the creaking wooden steps of Kyoto, my favorite sushi restaurant, and ordered a starter of miso soup and ginger cucumber salad.

Some people are too self-conscious to go to restaurants alone — afraid people would judge them for not having a date, or at least a friend to accompany them. I am not one of those people. For one thing, I could give two shits about what people think about me, and another thing, I love time to myself, especially in a restaurant as fantastic as Kyoto. Between the aroma of tea and broth, and the lighting that is just a notch brighter than a romantic dinner setting, it allows for a perfectly comfortable and serene experience. It is always calm, too. Even on their busiest nights, the wait staff appear to float from table to table, meeting the needs and requests of every blissful diner.

As if all of that weren't enough, Kyoto has the most celebrated sushi menu in the city, and for good reason. The warmth and richness of the miso soup, the crunch and crispness of the cucumber drenched in ginger dressing, and the pure explosion of flavors and textures in the sushi. I couldn't help the contented sigh that escaped from me as I delighted in the whole scene. It was almost enough to erase the frustration of the whole morning, but with a renewed annoyance that my trip to the hospital train wasn't more helpful, I turned my attention once more to the journal while I waited for my food.

A tingling spread in my stomach as I flipped to the last page I had read; the page that included me. Considering the number of women he would have observed in all of his travels, he was sure to have been attracted to many of them. That was okay. It had to be. I couldn't be jealous of practically fictitious women that might have caught the eye of a 200 year-old man I'd never officially met. Yet nerves shook my hands as I focused on the man's swirling handwriting in the next entry.

May 10, 1801

I'm on a crowded bus traveling through the dessert. We have passed signs reading Route 66, and others with Arizona state road numbers. Everyone around me is sleeping or has large bands around their heads with ear coverings I'm assuming to be used for listening to music.

Well, that was harmless enough. But from the perspective of the writer, it was just as pointless as my trip to the hospital train. I could imagine how infuriating it must have been for him to turn the key day after day for as long as he did, having no choice but to force himself to believe he would eventually find what he was looking for, though it appeared that on several occasions, the music box led him to nothing notable whatsoever. It was all just details to him that would hopefully add up to mean something in the end. However, considering how long the journal, the key, and the music box had been in my family's possession, I wondered if "the end" might have already passed for him. The only reason I chose to believe he might still be alive was his already documented life span. If he wrote from the 18th century through to the 21st, he had defied more than just the space and time continuum.

I turned to the next entry. Whereas the last two records were only a day apart, there was a long gap to the next one by nearly six months. No doubt, he likely found it pointless and difficult to continue his trips into the often useless unknown. The distance between the entries was probably evidence of a patch of frustration, or maybe he did turn the key but found himself in a place that offered no information. *Ugh*, I rolled my eyes. I had no idea, and my compulsion to figure this out when it was next to impossible spurred my annoyance once again.

November 1, 1801

A definite first for me. I am suited up and fashioned with skis on the top of a snow covered monstrosity. Thankfully, I was able to make it downhill to a large house, that once I finally was able to get the overly secured equipment off my feet to go inside, I could see was a warm shelter selling food and drink. As there was no money in my pockets, I satisfied myself with observing from the corner of the room. Red noses and wind-blown hair seem to be the norm...not altogether unattractive, in fact the sporting way of these women is quite

intriguing. Under all the heavy coats and gear, however, they
look a little like they've just bathed in snow.

That was a pretty accurate description of snow skiing. Any time I'd ever been, I had looked like a million bucks when I left the condo, and came back with no make up left on my face and a tangled mess of wet hair swirling around my ear warming head band. Oh, and the red nose, which is the cornerstone of the skier's look.

The next entry was over a year later, but remembering the notebook covered a time frame of about 130 years, it would have been impossible to have accounts for every day in that range, and that there were likely to be many long stretches with no entries. I flipped through the rest of the pages, and sure enough, there were some entries that were over a decade apart. Having that kind of time eternally present and looming over him must have been mind numbing, and given that he never spoke of anyone else in the journal, I had to assume he was alone. I doubted that I would have been strong enough to live like that, which led me to wonder if he might have ever tried to find a way to end his life. I shuddered to think of the place one would have to be in their head to seek out such measures.

Drastic as that sounds to a normal person with a normal lifespan, I could also empathize with what it would be like to live every day with no end in sight, and be forced to search unending possibilities for something, or someone, and all the while, not even sure of what or who he was hoping to find. And to make matters worse, and assuming the journal writer was still alive, he had been without the journal and key since the last journal entry in 1922 that documented the meadow by the creek where he lost, and we found, these mysterious treasures. This meant he'd now had close to a full century without even the option to keep his search alive. At least before losing the journal and key, he had a way of moving forward and the hopes of finding enlightenment. Now...there'd be no way to be sure of any of my speculations, but I could see that I would have lost hope long ago if I were in his quandary.

My food arrived, and with good timing, as my anxiety and worry spiked off the charts for this person that in just a few short hours, had become the only thought in my head. As I ate, the fixation on the journal writer began to ebb away, yet I knew I would come back to him in good time.

Yellowtail pieces, salmon pieces, and several rolls later, I was satisfied, but not necessarily over my mania. My watch read 4:00. I planned to return home, read some more of the journal entries, and then later in the evening, turn the key once more. Knowing how the music box travels knocked me out, I decided it would be best to do right before bed, otherwise I might end up sleeping all day and awake all night.

When evening arrived, and the time came to prepare for another trip, my hands were shaking with nerves. As I fumbled the key into the slot, it occurred to me that when the writer had spoke of "only one turn, so it won't be long," in one of the first entries I had read, perhaps the number of times he had turned the key dictated how long he was gone. I hadn't kept track of how many times I'd turned it on my own excursions, but I'd guess it was about two or three, and I'd been gone for roughly thirty minutes to an hour. For the argument of going big or going home, I took a risk and turned they key until my hand muscles groaned from the motion; about eight turns. Then, with a deep breath, I waited for the unknown.

The tune began, followed by the black hole compression, taking away my strength and breath just long enough for me to regret the eight turns, and then it was gone. Sucking in air as if I'd been trapped under water, I noticed an echo around me. Even without my eyes fully focusing yet, I could tell from the sounds bouncing off the walls that I was in a very small room. Slowly, as my vision cleared I could make out dark wood all around me, but thankfully, seeing an opening above my head, I knew I wasn't completely enclosed. I turned on the spot, feeling my shoes glide over soft carpet beneath, and then saw that behind me was a toilet. I was in a bathroom.

The key was still in my hand with the ribbon dangling from it, so I draped it around my neck for safekeeping. I reached for the neckline of my shirt to tuck the key necklace under it, but instead of the shirt I had just been wearing, I felt only my open chest. *Ummmm...*

I threw my head down as I groped at my body, relieved to see and feel that I was not, as I had feared, naked. However, I was not in clothes that I would have ever in a million years expected to wear. The fabric was silk or satin, and cold against my legs as it gently swayed with my movement. The dress reached almost to the floor, hitting the ankle of a pair of substantial strappy heels. The empire waste also marked the ending point of a very revealing plunging neckline. I cupped my breasts, wondering how in the hell they seemed so secure and confident in so little fabric. The top fit more like a triangle-topped bikini with haltered straps around my neck, leaving my back shamefully exposed.

One can only feel their way around an outfit like that so much in the stall of a bathroom before having to just go check it out in a mirror. Although no one appeared to be in the bathroom with me, I craned my neck all directions as I cracked the door to have a peek. My eyes carefully took in the room beyond my stall, confirming that it was in fact empty. I could also see a side room to the right of the sinks that looked like it had a few lounging chairs and a larger mirror. I flinched as I approached, thinking I'd run into someone else on the other side of the wall, rather than my own reflection. My hair was swept back from my face into a high but loose bun, save for a few sexy soft curls around my face and ears. The dress, I could now see, was gold, and the strappy heels, jewelry, and the shade of makeup I wore were all complimentary. Wow. I admit, I took a few extra long looks at this person that I'd never known was inside of me.

It really was me, and I was hot. I probably would have stayed longer, but my eye caught a shiny sequined purse resting on the lounger behind me. It was gold, too — no coincidence, I was sure.

Assuming it to be my last accessory for an evening destined to be eventful, I slung it onto my arm and put the ribboned necklace and key inside it as I practiced my strut out the door. Before closing the clasp, I noticed a small cardstock paper inside the purse.

Stepping through the bathroom door, I entered a large corridor with elevators, and just beyond appeared to be the lobby of a grand hotel. I paused at a beautiful granite table that set in the middle of the elevator waiting area, letting an oversized flower arrangement that adorned the table conceal me as I pulled the cardstock paper out of the purse. In elegant calligraphy, it read:

You are cordially invited to the marriage of
Diane Elaine Barnes
and
David Robert Valenzuela
On the Thirty-first of July,
Nineteen hundred Seventy-six
Reception held at The Fontainebleau Hotel,
Miami Beach

Hell yeah! I was about to crash a Miami Beach wedding! A sign near the elevator entrance stated that the Valenzuela reception would be held on the Ocean Lawn, with an arrow pointing in the opposite direction from where I stood. Taking in a breath that drew me up to full height, I headed toward the Ocean Lawn with a sense of calm security in the unknown ahead of me.

Under the stars and stretching to the shore, the Ocean Lawn was just that, and so much more. Dressed as a ballroom, there were tables covered in candles and towers of floral arrangements set upon mirrored glass; outlining the open center were pergolas gleaming with crystal chandeliers; and interspersed between the tables in the center were opulent marble columns with twinkle lights wrapped in translucent fabric stretching from one to the next, forming a spiral around the dance floor.

I froze, rooted to the ground below in utter amazement. I couldn't imagine a more luxurious setting for a wedding known to man. I threw my head to the sky and smiled, remembering my eight turns and hoping I was right that it would keep me here longer. And then, I attempted my best Travolta strut around the whole damn place.

Not a single person knew me, but I could feel eyes following me. Whereas in my last trips I did my best to stay under the radar, afraid to be discovered as an outsider, I felt no need to be hidden here. I smiled excitedly at the friends and family of Diane and David, not caring if they wondered who I was.

The pergolas opened up to a low marble-columned wall that separated the wide open ocean beyond and the outdoor ballroom behind me. As I caught the eye of a lone gentleman staring out into the distance, I reveled so enthusiastically in the scene that I couldn't help beaming at him. His crooked grin gave me butterflies, but not intending to waste a good dance floor, I gave him a flirty cut of my eyes and trotted off back in the direction of the wedding party.

The closer I got to the dance floor, the clearer I could hear "Mustang Sally," and thankfully, there was already a crowd dancing madly, meaning I didn't have to be the only one letting loose. Hands in the air, hips groovin', and lost in carefree bliss, I danced until my heart was content. Rod Stewart rang true with "Maggie May," and the whole crowd sang along to "American Pie." I must have arrived after all the announcements and introductions of the bride and groom, because they were among the gyrating hoard of people sweating, laughing, and loving every minute.

I danced through "Oh What a Night," and sang at the top of my vocally challenged lungs to "Sweet Caroline." Determined that I couldn't top that if I tried, I made my exit and found an empty table to rest my happy but aching feet.

A friendly face from the dance floor followed me, grabbing two glasses of champagne off a waiter's tray, and sat down next to me. Smiling wryly, I accepted the glass and held it up to his.

"To the beginning of forever," he toasted.

"Or to just enjoying one day at a time," I retorted. My new friend gave a quizzical look, though, so I corrected quickly, "And the beginning of forever." *Clink.*

Satisfied with the toast, we drained our glasses and he introduced himself warmly, "Hi, I'm Darren."

"Rynn," I answered.

"Rynn? Interesting name. So, are you with the bride or the groom?"

Thinking on my toes, I came back with, "Neither. My date's a cousin of the groom, but he's a dick, so I ditched him."

Darren's eyes flew open, and his Adam's apple started to twitch nervously. "Nice to meet you, Darren. Thanks for the toast." And with that, I dismissed myself to the cake table.

Conceding to the ladies serving cake that I didn't plan on deciding between the groom's cake and the bride's, they politely placed a little of both on my plate, and quizzically watched me walk away. I headed back out to the area beyond the party, to eat my cake in the sand. Surprisingly, the gentleman I gave my flirty eyes to was still there, sitting now on the steps that led to the sandy beach.

"Excuse me," I pardoned myself. "Could I...?" I motioned toward the steps.

"Oh, sure, sorry," he apologized as he stood to move out of my way. He backed down the few steps and ended up in the sand as well.

I could feel rambling idiot mode coming on, especially now with the nervous awareness that this man was even more handsome than I'd realized at first sight earlier in the evening. Despite his suit typical of the 1970s style, including the shirt with awkward ruffles trimmed in a dreadful reddish brown color that perfectly matched the jacket and pants, he was nothing short of breathtaking. Saving me from myself, he extended his hand to help me down the steps, and I graciously took it. That gave me just enough time to compose myself for a real conversation.

"I decided I wanted to feel the sand on my toes," I told him. I suddenly wished I didn't have two pieces of cake on my plate. I set it down on the steps as I slipped my heels off, then added, "Can I join you?"

With a smile, he motioned to the steps and we both sat down with our feet in the sand. "I feel like I should offer you some cake," I laughed, "I *do* have two pieces here."

"I noticed..." he responded, laughing as well. "That's okay, I already had some. Cake is my first priority at weddings."

"Good plan. So at some point tonight you left your spot here to get your cake, huh?"

"Actually, I got the cake first and then found my spot," he answered matter-of-factly.

"Well, I guess if you were going to spend all evening in one spot, this is the one to choose," I agreed. "Although, it *is* a wedding...one might mingle...or dance?"

"Noted. I'm mingling now, aren't I?"

"I suppose." I took a bite of cake and chewed slowly. "And the dancing?"

He didn't answer right away. The sound of the waves was now audible from this close to the shore, punctuated by the celebratory screams and occasional musical notes from the dance floor. Probably Darren and a new friend.

"Not much of a dancer," he answered, shrugging his shoulders. "But maybe if the right song..." He must have decided to change the subject, because he then asked, "So are you a friend of the bride or the groom?"

"Um," deciding against my earlier answer choice, I said, "both. We go way back. You?"

"Uh, distant relative. Barely know either of them." He laughed, like it was a joke. "I'm William."

"Rynn," I offered.

"Rynn," he repeated thoughtfully.

Everything I thought I would ask during a normal introduction to a handsome man didn't apply here. I wanted to know where he was from, or what he did, but I saw no point in asking any of these things because in just a short time I would be gone and he would be a memory. Handsome as he was, I knew I should go finish my evening on the dance floor rather than stay there, creating a connection with a man I would never see again.

"Well it was nice meeting you," I said truthfully. I started to get up and grab my shoes, and he stood as well, out of politeness, I suppose. As I turned, I offered, "Enjoy your spot."

He didn't answer, but smiled and nodded as I walked up the steps. A waiter came through clearing scattered cake plates, taking mine before I even reached the top. With one last look back, I moved out of eyesight and found a bench overlooking the low columned rail to slip back into my heels without the interfering nerves from the dreamy man in such close proximity.

The reception raged strong behind, and I fully intended to rejoin the group as the life of the party eventually, but I decided to soak in the shore for a little longer. I'd never been to Miami, and I wanted to remember it's every smell and sensation. After a good ten minutes of smiling and breathing in the salty air, I heard the beginning of Van Morrison's "Into the Mystic" on the dance floor. I sighed, wondering if this single moment in time could possibly get any better...and mere seconds after that, I felt someone standing close behind me.

I recognized the familiar voice before I could turn around to see who it was. "So I'm not a dancer, but if I were, I would probably dance to this song..." he said quietly. I stood to take his outstretched hand, and he guided me around the bench and rather than walking to the dance floor, he pulled me toward him right there under the stars.

With my arms around his waist and my head resting on his chest, we moved slowly back and forth, to the memorable tune I had listened to hundreds of times in my lifetime. He squeezed me close to him and I could hear him quietly singing about a gypsy soul and then unexpectedly, he threw me out for a twirl move I wasn't prepared for.

Grinning at my surprise, he pulled me back toward him; I joined him in singing through our laughter. Another playful twirl, and he responded to the strum of the guitar with more exaggerated dancing.

Our hips rocked animatedly to and fro as the iconic melody took us around the area we now claimed as our own private dance floor.

As the song continued, we swayed together, occasionally amusing one another with a surprise spin. When the song unfortunately came to an end, he swung me back to his embrace one last time, and I couldn't bring myself to step away.

"Thank you," he whispered in my ear. His voice vibrated the hair on my neck, sending a trill down to my toes. I was suddenly keenly aware of his hands near my hips, resting on the delicate fabric of my dress, the only thing separating his tender touch from my flesh. "It's been a..." he paused, "a very long time since I've danced."

I smiled at him, knowing that any further conversation would just make it harder to let go of once I returned to my own life in the 21st century. I looked up into his eyes. "Best dance I've had all night," I replied truthfully.

We were so close. His breath seemed to catch as I moved my arms to rest around his neck. *What could it hurt?*

I acted before talking myself out of it. As I launched myself higher on the strappy heels, he sensed my movement and met me halfway. His lips fit into mine as if a magnet locked them together. Energy surged through us, connecting us, like the blue streak that forms when you touch a plasma globe.

His hands lifted to the back of my neck, his thumbs reaching around to brush my cheeks. We parted, and his forehead rested on mine. He hadn't opened his eyes. I knew, because mine were wide and searching for why the hell we had to stop. We did, though.

"I'm sorry, I don't know what came over me," he lifted his head, but his eyes were still closed.

"No, it's okay. My fault." I waved my hands to excuse his apology. "Actually, I think I'm going to be leaving soon...so..."

"Actually, me too." He stood straight, as if he wanted to say more, but he sighed instead, shrugging his shoulders and resting his hands in the pockets of his burnt sienna tuxedo trousers.

Walk away, I told myself, and unwillingly I obeyed. I pointed my feet to the dance floor, and with each step closer to the music, the more pep in my step I noticed. A voice on a mic announced that a few more songs were lined up before it would be time to send off the bride and groom, and I spent the rest of the night with the wedding party having the night of our lives.

Nearly an hour longer must have passed before the tugging sensation of the black hole pulled me away from the most amazing night of my life, and back to my reality. I had a feeling, however, as I inventoried my simple pajama pants and t-shirt, that even though my real life was nothing like what I'd experienced in my night in 1976, I would probably never look at it — or myself, for that matter — as mundane ever again. Some of that foxy lady from the mirror in The Fontainebleau bathroom was still in me, and I was so glad that I'd found her.

ELEVEN

DRINKS ARE ON PEARL

Smug. I woke up smug the next morning, and it didn't go away all day.

The grin I fell asleep with appeared to be a completely involuntary action, as it was present in the morning as well; so prominent, in fact, that I could feel it before even looking in the mirror. Remnants of the kiss permeated my before-school routine. The Travolta strut hadn't worn off, either. My coffee tasted better than usual. I looked different. I felt different.

Everything about the night before had lifted me to a whole new level; yet, I couldn't tell anyone about it, which must have been the explanation for my pompous attitude. Secrets often do that to me, especially good ones. Something about being the only one privy to such knowledge seems to give one an imaginary edge.

I found myself staring into blank walls and blank faces, seeing only the magnificent setting of the wedding on Miami Beach. Memories of the dress, the dancing, the William, the night of all nights...the memories were nearly as entertaining as real life the night before. For the first time since I couldn't remember when, I'd let go of my reservations, and I really liked the carefree, magnetic version of myself.

Receiving attention was always accidental in my mind, so I made sure I never looked like a girl that needed it. I dated, but never chased. I was a well-protected girl with all her walls up, so to date me guys had to try really...sadly...embarrassingly hard. It's a wonder I ever did find a date, and no wonder nothing ever lasted.

The girl that emerged from the bathroom last night, however, was not protected with fortress walls and I knew the attention I received from William, Darren, and the whole reception was not an accident. I also knew I was no more or less attractive than my usual self, even with the great dress. Rather, I had allowed something inside me to shine through like I'd never done before.

Halfway through the school day I realized my co-teachers were staring at me, no doubt speculating that I'd gotten laid or something. Knowing they'd be whispering behind my back all day made me once again radiate with continued smugitude.

I had a sneaking temptation to keep this a secret from everyone, including Tucker and Nora, but remembering how that turned out the first time easily persuaded me to rethink. They might not care about all the fantastic details of my night, but I would at least tell them about my near introduction to the writer back in college and about the trips to the hospital train and Miami Beach.

I sent each of them a message to meet me after school, and they both responded that they would be over after dinner. *Must be date night*, I rolled my eyes. Eager to tell them the latest news, I nearly tackled them when they knocked at the door.

I couldn't help jumping up and down once they were in the house, "Guys! Guess what!"

"Chicken butt," they both answered. They settled in on the couch, nervously eyeing the music box on the coffee table, then giving me the same concerned look. I know they were trying to keep up with all this craziness and what it had brought out in me, but they could catch up on that in their own time.

"Shut up and listen," I pretended to scold. "You're never going to guess what I found in the journal."

Tucker's ears seemed to perk. "Something useful? Do tell."

I grabbed the journal off the side table and flipped to the page that documented the writer's visit to my college campus. "Here, see for yourself," I said as I held out the journal for them both to read.

They skimmed the page quickly, both making a face around the part where he referenced the "40 ACRES" shirt, and then looked up at me, puzzled when they were finished.

"It sounds like..." Nora half-pointed at me.

"That's because it is," I answered. I sat down in the armchair, watching them put it together.

Tucker spoke up to clarify, "So this was campus, back in 2010 when we were all there, and he was there, too. Are you telling me that was you?"

"I didn't believe it at first, but it *is*. I hadn't remembered the encounter until I read this, but I do now. He had been looking sideways at my newspaper, probably trying to see the date, and I offered it to him. It was a completely ordinary interaction, so I had forgotten about it. But I rarely read the paper, so I know I'm not confusing this with just any other day." I didn't want to admit to them that I clearly remembered the butterflies that kept me from confidently striking up a conversation. "He was right there!" I continued, "I *met* him. Well, kind of..."

The two of them remained as if permanently struck by confusion. Staring at me, then at each other, then at the journal entry. They seemed to have no words. Nora finally broke the silence, "This is...really weird. Am I the only person who thinks this is weird?"

"I don't know what to think," Tucker answered Nora. "You think it's just a coincidence that he was there on the South Mall that day, and so was Rynn? And now she has all these things that were his... that can't be just an accident, can it?"

"Okay," Nora stood and started to pace as she spoke, "since we're just thinking out loud, let's just go ahead and say what we're really thinking. Nothing that we have to go on is fact, so there are no wrong answers to any of our speculations, right? *So what is really going on here?*"

Even though Nora's words were encouraging that we shouldn't be embarrassed by our ridiculous ideas, no one offered any for a while. Nora continued pacing, and Tucker and I sat, staring downward as if the answer was engrained in the wood floors or the patterned loops of my rug.

"Well," I broke the silence, "if we are accepting this as truth, and since two of us have experienced it for ourselves I guess we *have* to... then we might want to determine if it's..." I felt like a 6 year old discussing the fantasy world we were about to enter. This time, though, it was in reverse. Instead of creating all the details of magic and fairies before the game started, we were actually living it first and then struggling to know what to call it afterwards. I sighed, "I've been thinking of it as a curse. I can't bring myself to use the term magic. But...whether it's black magic, voodoo, or some mind-bending trick being played on us...it *is* something that's not an accepted truth for anyone else."

"I can't believe I'm having this conversation," chimed in Tucker, "but I know what you mean. You know how in books or movies, at the end the character wakes up only to realize it was all just a dream? Maybe it's something like that, where the episode of travel you guys experienced was really a fantasy or idea planted into your subconscious? Nora, when you turned the key, we saw you slump and then rise up again. Maybe everything you saw and felt was more like a virtual reality."

Leave it to the dude to find a scientific explanation for this shit. Apparently Nora thought the same thing, because the look she gave him with her arms crossed unsettled even me.

"Tucker, you weren't there," she said, "you couldn't possibly understand what it was like. It couldn't have been virtual reality — it *was* reality."

"I know, but I just can't wrap my mind around all of it. I mean, look, even if it was some fantasy planted in your brain, that begs the question of how it could be done. And by whom? Look, I really *don't* think this is a conspiracy theory sort of phenomenon. But...I just had to throw out something a little more plausible than a curse or magic, even if it still isn't all that plausible at all."

I then remembered that we had been so engrossed in our brainstorming, that I hadn't told them of my day of hookie in which I spent time in the World War hospital train and the wedding. The words began to form in my mouth when Tucker scooted over, squaring himself up in front of the music box. "Where's the key?" he interrupted.

I didn't answer, not sure why he needed it. He zeroed in on the ribbon around my neck, despite the fact that the key was hidden under my shirt.

"I see it. You're wearing it right now on that ribbon." Seeing the defensive side of me raring up, he added, "Look, I'm on the outside here. How am I going to know what it's like just by hearing about it from you two? I'm not saying I'll be able to figure it out just by turning the key for myself, but I *do* want to understand. Let me see with my own eyes."

It was like we were kids again, fighting for our chance to play a new game. Just as it was fair to take turns back then, it was fair now to let Tucker know exactly what the music box did. I couldn't expect him to stay on the outside much longer, listening to our accounts of these mysterious events. I unenthusiastically slipped the ribbon over my head and pulled the key from under my shirt. I had to tell myself that if I were brave enough to turn it myself, then Tucker would definitely handle himself fine. He held out his hand, and I placed the key in it.

Nora looked as if she considered arguing, but must have come to the same conclusion that I did and decided instead to sit and wait by his side. Tucker took the key and slipped it into the pegs.

"Hold on," I protested as I joined him on the couch. I wanted to be sure he looked me in the eye and heard me clearly on my only request. "I figured out that the number of turns is related to the length of your trip. I turned it about 8 times last night and I ended up at a completely amazing wedding reception for for*ever*. I got lucky, though, so just turn it once, okay? I don't want you to be somewhere dangerous for very long." Nora shivered.

He nodded, turning his gaze to the music box that was about to send him into the unknown. With a deep breath, he went for it. One quick turn, followed by the now familiar pings of the tune, and then Tucker's eyes closed as he hunched over as if experiencing a painful stomach cramp. Instinctively, Nora wrapped her arms around his shoulders, but in an instant he rose up from the sensation with wide eyes.

He emerged safe and sound, but shook his finger at me with an irritated grumble, saying, "Only one turn. Last time I listen to you..."

Nora and I exchanged a shaky giggle. Tucker lifted his feet over my head and laid them on the couch behind me, leaning back on the pillows behind Nora with one arm around her waist.

From under his other arm covering his face, he sleepily told me, "Rynn, grab your laptop — I need to look something up."

In the time that it took to go into the office for my laptop, Tucker had fallen completely under, while Nora moved to the armchair to watch him. Reminiscent of Tucker and I monitoring Nora sleep while we discussed what could have happened during her own music box excursion, she and I took to quietly speculating what Tucker could want to look up. Quickly coming to the conclusion that we would just have to wait and see, we moved to the kitchen in order to leave him undisturbed.

It occurred to me that this was the first time Nora and I had been alone since the announcement of her new relationship status with Tucker. I felt like such a shitty sister, not having had a chance to gab about this new excitement with her until now.

"Nora, I'm sorry I've been so wrapped up in this music box stuff to make time for you. Tucker's gonna be out for a while — tell me all about you and him."

She didn't seem bothered at all by my admission of self-interest.

In fact, she almost blew me off with a shrug. "How could you not be focused on this? I am, too."

Finally having the time to ourselves for girl talk, she shared that it had been a mutual acknowledgement between them that their feelings for each other were growing beyond that of friends. Apparently it all started one day when they casually exchanged a hug, but neither one of them released the other. The moments stretched, and when they caught each others' eye, he pulled her in tighter and met her questioning gaze with the charming smile that she'd known for years, although never like that. That evening they stayed up until four o'clock in the morning, admitting years' worth of denied or hidden longings to be more than friends.

"I think we both knew those feelings were there, but had never entertained them until that hug brought them to our attention. Then we couldn't hold back, and as we talked it became clear that there was so much more; deeper even than the curiosities we were already aware of and had suppressed. All of our memories from our whole life were laced with undertones of affection for one another."

As she finished her story, she looked at me once again as if her explanation might have sparked a new disapproval of their relationship after all.

"I love you," I told her, "and I love Tucker. I couldn't dream of a better person for either one of you than each other. Just promise me," I pleaded honestly, "that you won't leave me out of *every*thing. I won't be a third wheel all the time, but you can't ditch me completely, okay?"

She smiled and hugged my neck. I took a few minutes to recap my own adventures to the not-so-exciting hospital train and then the overwhelming Miami Beach wedding.

"Wow," she said, "guess we know you're the type to kiss and tell, huh?"

"Totally," I shrugged.

"Too bad you couldn't keep the dress..." she said dreamily.

I looked up to the same spot where she stared, imagining me

looking all Seventies sexy. I envisioned my reflection again in the Fountainebleau bathroom. "Yeah," I sighed, "too bad."

A rustling on the couch signaled that Tucker was coming around again. He stood up, barely steady, and stretched as he turned to locate us in the kitchen. "Jeez, girls. That's some crazy stuff. And you," he pointed to me again, "just had to tell me only one turn, huh?" He opened the laptop and rubbed his face as he waited for it to load. He massaged his groggy eyes, and I wondered how he had managed to wake himself in the first place.

"So I take it you didn't go anywhere dangerous?" Nora asked, clearly comforted by his display of attitude.

After a few keystrokes, Google brought up a page and Tucker read quickly through it before he turned the screen to us. He read aloud the highlights of an online article about Janis Joplin. "The Harvard Stadium," he read, rubbing his face awake. "Janis Joplin's last concert. 10,000 people expected to attend, and 40,000 showed. I was at one of the most historical concerts ever, but only for about half an hour thanks to your one-turn-of-the-key rule." I thought he really was upset with me for a minute, but then he continued. "It was amazing. I could go on all night, but there's more...there was a chick that was *really* interested in the key."

"The key?" Nora and I both asked.

"Yeah, when I finally was able to see straight again I started asking the people around me where I was and what year it was and stuff. I could tell that wouldn't be out of the ordinary, there were so many potheads all fried up...and this girl overheard me and zeroed in on me. I thought she was an undercover cop or something, but then when she got right in front of me she saw the key in my hand. Her eyes were crazy, like she knew what it was."

I hung on the edge of my seat. "So what'd she do?"

"She just stared at it for a really long time, and it freaked me out, because I didn't know what she was going to do. I mean, we don't know what we're dealing with, and it got me thinking about the whole conspiracy theory side. She freaked me out. Then she asked who I was, where I was from, trying to sound casual. I played it off like I was a student, but acted like I was a real stoner to cover why I was asking weird questions."

"Did you tell her where you were from?" Nora questioned.

"Nah, said I was from Boston. By then I put it around my neck and had it tucked under my shirt, but I still saw her eyes flickering down to where it hung. She stayed close by the whole time. I kept feeling her eyes on me, and I'd look up and she'd be staring at me. If I had turned the key more than once, maybe I could've talked to her or something. But to be honest, she didn't seem like the type that would be helpful. She had these eyes...they were like a white-blue color, and there was something cold in them."

I thought briefly of the cold eyes of the head nurse on the hospital train, but dismissed it, still wanting to hear more from Tucker. "So was that it? You watched the concert until you were brought back here?"

"Yeah. But right before I was sucked out of there, she came over to me again and asked if I wanted to go backstage, said she knew a guy or something. I told her 'No thanks,' and she turned to walk away, but then she looked back and said, 'You sure? Drinks are on Pearl...'"

Confused, Nora and I thought about that for a minute. "What's that mean?" she asked finally.

Not knowing the answer, Tucker grabbed the laptop again and spoke as he typed, "Drinks... are... on... Pearl..." When the page came up, he read from it, "In the last weeks of her life, Janis Joplin had prepared a will, and $2500 was set aside for her friends to throw a wake in the event of her death. When she passed away a few months *after* her final concert at Harvard Stadium," Tucker paused momentarily for dramatic effect. "Invitations to some 200 special guests read: 'Drinks are on Pearl.'"

TWELVE
MUSICAL MONTAGE

On that night, following Tucker's trip to Joplin's last performance, the three of us agreed that maybe we should give the music box a rest for a while. With the eerie woman we began referring to as "Pearl," lurking in plain view at the concert, it raised further questions of just what we were up against.

Naturally, since we agreed to put away the key, I turned it as soon as they left. I had a feeling that neither Tucker nor Nora actually believed I would store it away, or else they would have taken it themselves for safe-keeping. To be honest, I think they were both a little too freaked out, and legitimately so, about what we had landed ourselves in the middle of.

As for me, I bucked against the new change of atmosphere this Pearl character had created. The confidence I'd uncovered on the Ocean Lawn of Miami Beach was not going to be overshadowed by fear of someone like her. I didn't have a clue as to who she was or why she was there with Tucker, but with reckless abandon, I continued turning the key, ignoring any feelings of doubt or insecurity Pearl might have posed on my own music box experiences.

Days and weeks passed in a blur, as I turned the key as often as I could manage while still maintaining my daily responsibilities at school. I found myself exhausted, but unwilling to forfeit a single night's trip to wherever the music box fancied for the evening.

CALIFORNIA REDWOODS. I had never been there, so I couldn't be sure, but the towering colossal trees led me to that assumption. Outfitted with proper hiking boots, a baseball cap, and warm loose clothes, I followed the trail through fern-lined pathways until reaching an overturned tree trunk that invited me for a sit. The massive backpack I carried beckoned, and proved to be just as nicely equipped as my attire, complete with the trail map, water, light snacks, and even an early generation MP3 player.

"Score!" I said out loud, placing the earbuds in my ears and pushing play, unsure of how to browse the music selection. Billy Joel tinkled the ivories to "You May Be Right" while I browsed the trail map. Assumption correct, the map showed the coastline of the Redwood National Park, but I had no clue as to where on the map I actually was. After rehydrating with water and with new pep in my step from Billy Joel, I continued down the trail, hoping it would lead me to a beautiful view of the Pacific Ocean that the map promised lay just beyond the trees.

The trail was empty, foggy, and slippery. Yet each step took my breath away. I felt as small as a mouse, dwarfed by the ever-reaching height of the century-old trees. Moisture hung in the air and I drank it in with each breath, too inspired to feel the fatigue that should have set in after nearly an hour of hiking. Shards of sunlight broke through occasionally, blinding my view momentarily, but also giving hope that the sun remained steadfast above.

Only a single fellow hiker crossed my path as I approached the break in the trail I'd been hoping for. Beyond seeing he was an older gentleman, I barely noticed him, for the cliffs below and the ocean beyond were finally revealed to me and I couldn't take my eyes off the glorious sight.

I stood, committing every detail to memory, and waited there until my time came to and end.

———

VEGAS, baby. People everywhere, buzzing and chattering. Blinking lights and electronic chimes surrounding me. Even if I had been lucky enough to have money, though, it would do no good to gamble, since I doubted I'd be able to bring my winnings with me when the music box yanked me out of there.

So rather than saddle up at the slots, I turned for the strip. The voice of Elvis appeared in my head, singing "A Little Less Conversation." When I got outside, I could see that I had been in the MGM Grand. I'd only been to Vegas once, when Nora insisted on celebrating her twenty-first birthday in style. New York-New York was across the street, but from left to right, the strip blinked with signs inviting me in. I didn't have a plan in mind, but I figured I couldn't go wrong with wandering and people watching.

Focusing now on the passersby, I could see it must be sometime in the Eighties. Big hair and mullets dominated, and serious high heels and miniskirts were rampant. *Oh shit*, I thought, as I realized I probably looked just like them. Ugh...yep, walking the strip in the shoes I now saw (and felt) on my feet made me look like the city's most novice hooker.

"Hey," an irritated male voice called behind me.

I turned to see a stranger looking very put out with me. Staring quizzically back at him, I slowly pointed to myself, questioning, "Me?"

"Yeah, Sweets," he responded. He held up a waitress tray and shook it at me, spouting off gruffly, "Ya think ya just gonna walk outta here when ya need a break? This is Vegas, honey, I *own* you. Now get back in there."

Options went through my head in hyper speed. I could tell this guy to shove it, and walk away, but he seemed serious — and mean. I didn't want to chance what his reaction might be. I could go back in and quietly take the tray, but I didn't know where to go after that, which would probably make Mr. Nice Guy react badly as well.

I would just have to fake it and hope for the best. With a shrug, I walked back to the door and squeezed myself through, battling for any space not taken up by my apparent boss. Assuming being sassy wouldn't help my situation, I stood quietly and waited for him to point me in the right direction.

He thrust the tray at me, and shook his finger behind me. "Ya customa's are waiting..."

Not sticking around to hear any more, I turned on the spot and took off. Quick thinking told me to just look for someone dressed like me and follow her until she lead me to the bar. I could handle it from there, surely.

IRELAND. Scotland. England. I didn't know, but it looked like a rugby match at the center of a stadium, where I now joined massive drunken men cheering on their team. I tried to think back to my college days. We had friends that played rugby, and I did make it to a few matches, but the only things I could remember about the sport, beside the crushing tackles, were scrums and hat tricks. That, and the fact that our rugby chums and his teammates really enjoyed being drunk, rowdy, and naked. Often all three at the same time.

Taking a few scrutinizing glances at my fellow fans, I was comforted somehow by the fact that we were in a time of the past, as if this crowd was less threatening or likely to discover the intruder that I was, merely because they were not from my world. It was like a scene from a movie, everyone dressed in drab browns and greys, topped with Oliver Twist hats.

I weaved my way through the onlookers to search higher ground for a new vantage point that better suited me where I could follow the nasty blows uninterrupted by large mens' elbows cheering and jeering in my way, or coming dangerously close to my face.

Feeling ballsy, I found a less vigorous spectator, and asked who was playing. He looked at me quizzically and carefully responded, "Ireland & the Scots."

"And you're cheering for....?"

He looked at me and exasperatedly responded, "You jokin'? Ireland!"

"Cool! I'm Irish. I mean, I'm not *from* here, but my grandparents were. I'm really proud of my Irish heritage. Yep, I'm a fan."

The poor guy looked like he wanted to walk away from me, a gibbering lunatic.

"Yeah, well, thanks." I decided to let him off the hook and turned my attention back to the game.

The pitch was muddy, and so were the players, making it difficult to see the jersey colors that discriminated the teams. But it felt good in a cannibalistic sort of way to watch the mayhem caused by the sporting rage down below. Who would've thought?

I KNEW THIS PLACE. I came here my senior year of high school. Stratford-upon-Avon: the birthplace of William Shakespeare. More specifically, I was right outside the Holy Trinity Church, where Shakespeare had been baptized and buried. I shivered with the overwhelming scope of such a place...possessed by the history and legacy of the greatest poet and playwright of all times, but it also brought back a flood of wonderful memories of my own trip to London.

The quaint little riverbank was lush with green grass and cascading flowers, contrasted beautifully by the otherwise ordinary brown stone of the church. If I remembered correctly, the body of Shakespeare was buried just a few feet away from me, inside the church some twenty feet under the ground. The extra protection of depth was to make sure his body would not be moved, whether for examination or to be moved to Westminster Abbey. I drifted inside to read again what my memory now failed to provide; the humorous words on his epitaph.

GOOD FREND FOR JESUS SAKE FORBEARE TO
DIGG THE DUST ENCLOASED HEARE.
BLEST BE YE MAN YT SPARES THES STONES AND
CURST BE HE YT MOVES MY BONES

Thankful that my eyes could see such a blessing again, I turned back out toward the garden. On my first trip to London, I was one of 200 American students that made up teams of academia nerds. It was like a backwards "British Invasion." Our teams had each won academic competitions in our own areas and continued to an international showdown. As amazing as it was to compete internationally, I felt like the rest of the trip was the true reward. In addition to the attractions in Stratford-upon-Avon, we were able to tour Windsor Castle, the Crown Jewels and Trafalgar Square, just to name a few hot spots. We also had a New Year's Eve party on a boat cruising the River Thames, and enjoyed The Buddy Holly Story at the Strand Theatre. I had to suppress a snort, remembering being one of the only ones that knew the words to Buddy Holly's songs, thanks to my Grandma's influence.

With a sigh of satisfaction thanks to yet another amazing trip, I almost completely forgot about the journal writer.

I EMERGED FROM THE DARKNESS, surprised to find I still seemed to be in darkness. With blurry eyes still struggling to clear my vision, I could see a strange glowing area far away, but I couldn't make it out. I had no idea where I might have been, so I centered my attention within a closer proximity.

Wind whipped at my shoulders, indicating that I had surfaced outdoors. As I turned around to look over the scenery behind me, a voice startled me, asking in a thick accent, "Miss, you need something?"

Everything came into focus with a snap. The voice belonged to a waiter, and behind him what looked like the rooftop of a bar or restaurant, in faint glow of moonlight, with an occasional twinkle of a table candle.

Looking now to the friendly voice, I asked the waiter, "Can I ask you a weird question?" He smiled like that wasn't the first time he'd been asked that, nor would I surprise him with the weirdest question he'd ever heard. I continued, "Where am I?"

He answered me casually, "Bangkok."

Bangkok. Huh. There was song about Bangkok, wasn't there? Addressing the waiter again, I asked, "What, uh...what year is it?

"1991," he answered with eyes narrowing.

"So you know that song, something about one night in Bangkok?"

"Yes. I lived in America when that came out," he shook his head with a slight eye roll, I must not have been the first American to reference the song.

"Oh, sorry." I'm not sure why I felt the need to apologize. Remembering the indiscernible glow from my first moments here, I looked back toward that direction. Even now that I could see clearly, it didn't help me recognize what I was looking at. The tall illumination resembled a shorter, squished Eiffel Tower that radiated with yellow gold, surrounded by smaller golden points.

"What's that over there?" I asked.

"That's what everyone here came to see," he lackadaisically waved his arms to point out all the patrons that were turned to face the golden tower. "Wat Arun. Temple of the Dawn. Major tourist spot." Apparently satisfied that he had answered all of my crazy questions, he bowed slightly and walked away from me.

I sat alone for several quiet minutes, taking in the skyline of this unexpectedly beautiful city. Reflected onto a river that ran between us, the Wat Arun's light fractured into billions of flurrying fireflies by the occasional passing boat. It entranced me as I waited for the reassuring heaviness on my body, bringing me back to my own world.

I absentmindedly toyed with the key around my neck. It seemed to have absorbed the gold from the Temple across the river, gleaming with a lustrous metallic light. The hair on my neck stood on end as I caught the gaze of a woman sitting in the deck above me, her eyes trained on the key as well.

Tucker hadn't described her, but I knew it was her. Pearl. She had a wild hunger in her, with eyes darting back and forth from me to the key, and back and forth. She looked like she might jump over the deck railing and pounce on me. I didn't cower from her gaze, though, determined to let her know she didn't scare me. I took her in, just as she seemed to be doing with me, and as I looked her over, I became eerily aware that I had seen her before, too. She had the same icy blue eyes I saw from behind the nurse's mask on the hospital train. And her hair: jet-black tendrils. I remembered them from the train, too... but from somewhere else as well. Angrily shaking, like Medusa's snakes swirling with their poisonous gaze.

The basketball game. I had stared at the back of her head and watched her arguing, entranced by her bouncing locks. I didn't get a good look at her face then, but as I put all the pieces together now, I knew it was her.

Logic protested in my head, pointing out that if she knew something of the key, and she obviously did, then maybe she could help me learn the truth about the journal writer. But a more powerful instinct was also present, and it knotted in my stomach with fear.

Pearl had no intentions of helping me. She would not lead me to find the journal writer. And I had a feeling she would not be letting me joyride through the music box any longer.

THIRTEEN
YOU ARE MY SUNSHINE

On a Saturday morning following weeks of nonstop travel to worlds near and far, present and past, I woke with a jolt, unsure of where I was or who was with me. Messages had gone unanswered from Tucker and Nora, or responded with simple texts that I was in meetings, or tired, or busy. In reality, though, the music box journeys were starting to catch up with me.

Although I knew the trips left me in a near-coma, and I only turned the key when I was ready for bed already anyway, there seemed to be a cumulative effect happening now. Once reoriented to my own bed in my own house, I still struggled to make sense of my surroundings, like I'd spent more time gone than home. A stranger in my own sacred space, I felt as if I needed to be reminded of where my things were and what direction the bathroom was.

My depth perception was wrong, too, as I bumped into tables and tripped on rugs. Hopefully, I decided, a hot shower could remedy my music box vertigo, and if that didn't do the trick, then I'd move on to massive amounts of coffee. Honestly, I'd drink massive amounts of coffee anyway; that was the perk of Saturday for gripe's sake.

Steeping in the unrelenting burn of hot water, purposely turning up the heat to my threshold, I found I could still feel the icy cold chill of Pearl's stare. Better on my feet or not after a hot shower, I had a feeling that something in her eyes would not be washed away with the water. It pissed me off. It scared me. It confused me. The roller-coaster of feelings toward the music box churned in my stomach. I had pitied the man in the journal, then obsessed over him, given him up temporarily to party like a rock star across the globe, and now I had to deal with *this* chick?

This wasn't *my* music box adventure, though. It belonged to someone else before me, and I had to acknowledge that I had put all my eggs in one basket thinking it was the writer's alone. Could it have actually been Pearl's adventure? Pearl's journal? Did I take it from her? There's nothing like thinking you have it all figured out, only to have your legs taken right out from under you by something unexpected. One thing was for sure, I needed a break from the music box.

Because I was in no hurry to see how close I would come to Pearl the next time I turned the key, and because I genuinely felt like a visitor in my own life, I forced myself to step away. It had started to be easier, gallivanting across the universe instead of just being me. I couldn't recall what I would have been doing on a typical Saturday afternoon before the music box came along. Come to think of it, I didn't even know what I'd been doing on my Saturday afternoons *since* the music box's appearance. Going through the motions, sleeping off the hangover from the trips, staring at the wall lost in memories of my travels...I must have been a walking zombie.

Worse yet knew that I'd totally blown off Tucker and Nora during my dawn-of-the-dead state. They had to have known why I was acting so strange, I just hoped they weren't too miffed at me.

I chose to come out with the apologies and self-deprecation right off the bat. My text to the both of them said, "I'm an asshole. I've been in a music box coma for a few weeks even though we said we'd table it for a while. I'm ready to come back to reality, if you'll have me. Plans today?"

Looking around the house, I was shocked to see complete cleanliness. I figured after experiencing what can only be described as a fugue for the last few weeks, my house would have been in disarray. However, laundry was folded, dishes were washed, floors were swept. Obviously, cleaning house would not be keeping my mind occupied while guiltily waiting for the other two to text me back, so I filled my coffee cup and sat down on the couch to see if the TV could offer better distraction.

The usual Saturday morning infomercial crap wasn't on, which I found odd. I flipped through the channels for any explanation of the programming change, but didn't see much until the date on the guide caught my eye: Sunday, 4/23. Sunday. Holy hell, I had slept through an entire day, totally unaware.

As much as I hated to think of putting the music box aside, I knew I would have to limit my excursions from now on. Maybe once a week...I could do that. I would have to. I needed to force a detox from the music box.

Nora's ring brought relief from the unfortunate conflict in my head. Eager to get my mind onto something else, I answered, hoping to hear a happy tone on the other end.

"Hi!"

"Well, you've surfaced?" She tried to sound mad, but she couldn't pull it off.

"I'm sorry, I've been really out of it, I didn't realize..."

"So it *is* the music box, then? Rynn, should I be worried? I will come over there and take that damn key if I have to — "

" — No," I interrupted. "I know it's been a little too high on my priority list, but I'm going to *self*-regulate, I promise." She sighed on the other end. She was debating on heading to my house right that minute to steal the key, I just knew it. "Nora, it's okay. I'll be honest, I turned the key every night before going to bed for about two weeks now, and I thought it was okay because I would just fall right asleep afterwards, but...I barely remember the last few weeks. I even woke up so confused this morning that I had to think for a long time about where I was. I've been to so many places, and seen such amazing things, but it's really started to take its toll on me. I woke up so confused this morning...that...I thought it was Saturday. I must have slept all day and night..."

Absolute silence echoed on the other end now. I knew I'd been careless, but Nora's disapproval turned me automatically defensive. After all, I *was* coming clean and being honest about it. Now that I knew I could literally lose days of my life after too much travel, I would be responsibly scaling back.

"Ooookaaaayyy...so exactly how will you be self-regulating?"

Relieved that she was speaking again, and it didn't sound like she'd already hopped in the car to drive to my house, I answered reassuringly, "I decided once a week. That's fair. I think — I mean — I could probably do a few more times a week, but — "

" — Rynn, stop! Why do you even have to turn the key anymore anyway?" Now she was probably getting in her car.

I didn't have an answer to that. She was right, I didn't actually have any compelling argument for why I didn't just box it all away again. "I don't know, Nora...I guess I have a *few* reasons. One, being... it's fun. Who else in the world gets to experience anything like this?"

"I hope that isn't the only excuse you have. I'm sure there's a lot of things that are 'fun,' but that doesn't mean you should do it. Hang on..." She fumbled around a little, then I heard some noises and then a knock on my door.

"Ugh! Is that you?" I demanded. She hung up. I opened the door and she walked right in. My look of exasperation was obvious, to which she shrugged and responded, "What? I happened to be on my way over here already. You didn't ask what I was doing, or I would have told you. Anyway, the last time I had a real conversation with you was weeks ago, so I decided to pop in."

"Where's Tucker?" I questioned.

"Working on a project for work. Now, I think you have a few more justifications to give me of why you feel like you should continue with this whole music box mess?"

Defensive, I coughed, "Mess! What's a mess?"

"You lost a whole day of your life because of the strain these trips have put on you. It could be *harm*ful, Rynn!"

"I'm fine, I just needed to catch up on sleep I guess. That's why I won't do it so often anymore. I'll continue with my reasons, now, if you don't mind. Two: I still want to figure it all out — who the journal writer is, and if he's alive and out there somewhere. And Three: Pearl. She knows something, and she was there — I saw her. I did consider the journal being hers, but what I know of her doesn't seem to jive with the words of the journal writer. I still believe it was a man, I just haven't found him yet."

Nora's head perked at the mention of Pearl. "Ok, I want to know about Pearl, but Rynn, can I just ask why you think this guy's still alive?"

It was a valid question. In all honesty, it only came down to my stubborn belief that he was alive. I did my best to answer her with something more concrete. "I just do. Look, we know he broke the laws of physics by traveling with the music box because we've experienced it first-hand. We have accepted that he lived for well over a century because that isn't so crazy any more after the time travel idea. There was a reason he used the music box, and there was a reason he was *alive* to use it for so long. His journal is incomplete — he never wrote of finding what he looked for. He's still out there, Nora, but we have the only tools to continue his search."

"Fair enough, I guess," she sighed. "So Pearl? She was there? How do you know it was her?"

"Her eyes. She stared me down from a deck above, so I couldn't talk to her, but she was definitely watching me. She had those crazy blue eyes, and they were focused on the key. When our eyes met, it was like she had this nasty...grin. It froze me from head to toe." Nora was processing, but didn't seem like she knew what to say to this further development with Pearl, so I continued, "There's more. It wasn't the first time I'd seen her. When Tucker described her eyes like a whitish-blue color, I had a flashback of a nurse on that hospital train. Something about her unnerved me, even then, but I just assumed she was the nurse in charge or something, and she acted snotty to keep people in line.

When I saw her last night, though, I could see her whole face, and her hair. Her hair was so dark, it blended in with the black night. But these curls, black that almost shines blue – it's the same hair as the nurse and also the same as a woman I noticed on my first trip to Madison Square Garden."

Nora remained still, listening. Finally, she verbalized a question, "So that's three times that you think she's been with you...and once with Tucker. Do you think she was there with me? I didn't see anyone else except the man..." Her voice trailed when she spoke of the man that very well might have saved her life on her one trip via the music box.

"I don't know, but it's possible she's been there. Maybe she's been there on all of the trips. I know sometimes I'm in a crowd, other times it seems like I'm all alone, but I guess just because I haven't seen her doesn't necessarily mean she hasn't been there."

We paced, lost in our speculations about Pearl, without speaking. I returned to the couch, and Nora followed.

She rested her chin on her laced fingers in silence for a few beats. Finally, she asked the biggest question of all. "So do you think that means 'he' has been there, too, all along?"

I thought back to all the faces I'd seen over the course of my adventures. None had repeated like Pearl's, but that didn't mean he wasn't there. "I want to think so," I answered. The memory of my first trip played like a movie in my head. "At Madison Square Garden she was arguing with a man, and it definitely wasn't a stranger. Maybe that was him?"

We sat for a few thoughtful moments in silence. The weight of our speculations and realizations was immense. "You want some coffee?" I offered.

She shook her head "no," but then she answered, "Yeah, okay."

I left her on the couch while I fetched her a cup and stirred in some sugar. My own cup had gone cold during my phone-conversation-turned-random-pop-in with Nora, so I started over fresh and returned to find Nora still as a statue in her spot.

We sipped for a while in silence, before she finally spoke. I had expected her to try to convince me to store away the key and music box, but instead she said, "Whether he's there or not, Pearl is part of it all, too. I know you're not going to give up on this, so make two promises to me, Rynn: Do NOT turn that key more than you can handle. Once a week is more than enough, I think. And, be careful. Pearl might be a piece of the puzzle, but...there's a reason we're all creeped out by her. If she planned on being helpful, she would have shown that by now. Just watch out."

Acknowledging my agreement to her terms with a nod, and knowing I would have to wait an entire week before coming face to face with the music box again, I proposed a change of pace. "Let's get out of the house and do something. Will Tucker be working all day?"

Smiling, she answered, "Yeah, probably. What do you want to do, just the two of us?"

My spirits were lifted already. Even if we were the three musketeers when Tucker was with us, there's just nothing that can equal time spent with your sister. It had been a long time since we'd had a day together, just us. I was already smiling, predicting the fits of giggles and near-peeing-your-pants laughter we would experience today.

"We should start with lunch, for sure. Then, I don't know, a movie, shopping? Both?"

Nora shook her head, "Actually, I think Mom and Dad wanted to have us all over later, didn't she call you?"

"Um," I stalled. I had no recollection of a call from my parents. Did I miss it during my two-week hangover? Maybe she didn't call. I got up to go check my phone. I pulled up my missed calls, and sure enough, "Mom," listed in red.

I clicked on my voicemail: "Hey Rynn," came the voice through the speaker. "Dad's grillin' tomorrow and we wanted everyone to come over for dinner. Haven't talked to you in a while, so call me. Or, hopefully we'll see you tomorrow? Okay, bye."

Ashamed, I dialed my mom. I looked over to Nora, who squirmed with anticipation to hear how I would explain myself out of trouble.

"Well, hello," my Mom answered.

"Hey, Mom."

Annoyance was present in her voice, "Rynn, where've you been?"

"Yeah, sorry, Mom," I defended, "Um, my phone was dead yesterday and I didn't realize it, — "

"Uh, I don't know if I believe that. Look, it's my fault, I should have checked on you sooner. I worried when I gave you that box of your grandma's stuff you might not deal with it well, are you sure you're ok?"

I rolled my eyes. A music box getaway looked like an even more enticing escape right at the moment...

———

OUR "JUST THE two of us time" was cut a little short with the invitation to our parents' house for dinner, but we still had a nice lunch and some shopping at a trendy little market area in town. Tucker met us at Mom and Dad's, which was a little different, since it was the first time he and Nora were around everyone as a couple. Nobody really missed a beat, though; it was as if my parents had expected this to happen all along. That impression made me wonder what they might have expected to happen for me, and catching Mom's concerned stares in my direction didn't help, even if she did quickly turn her troubled expression into warm smiles when she met my eyes.

I left their house at a sensible hour so as to get home and in bed early, especially when I shuddered to think of the reception I might have waiting for me at school the next day. It could be possible that I had held the same level of responsibility at school as I did at home, but even in the best possible scenario, I was sure I must have screwed something up. Confident that I could have managed on autopilot with the kids, it was the adults that worried me. I began to pray that the zombie-me was at least smart enough to avoid people, and all I would have to do for damage control would be to make up some story about something that was bothering me.

My sleep was restful, and while I did get a few awkward unreadable smiles from my co-teachers, I had resolved to worry little about what might have transpired in my "absence." It couldn't have been that bad, and even if it was, I would deal with it. I had better things to think about, like getting through the week without being able to turn the key until Friday. I had chosen that day so that in the rare event that I needed two days to recover again from any possible music box episode, I would be covered. Each day was painful, as I waited for it to end and move on to the next. I poured myself into school, staying as long as I could before going home; cleaning obsessively, planning way too thoroughly, organizing and categorizing items in my classroom, completing lesson plans for the entire year, adding educational links and personal pictures to my teacher webpage.

Reluctantly heading home when amber skies turned black, I would then busy myself with the same mindless tasks as I had at school. I was running out of things to label and color code by the time Thursday night finally ended, and the next morning, I sprung out of bed of my own accord...TGIF!

After the school day mercifully ended, I went to the grocery store and then home, so I could perform the last duty of the night: a very involved and labor-intensive dinner of honest to goodness homemade Chicken and Dumplings. Anyone can use pre-cooked chicken, store-bought broth, and throw in some veggies, but I went for the "no shortcuts" recipe. During the few down times while cooking, I browsed the journal with a glass of wine. I knew the little book forwards and backwards, but I couldn't help wondering if there could be a mention of Pearl that I hadn't noticed before.

As suspected, the journal offered no reference to anyone's regular presence. I continued leafing through as I ate, pondering what Pearl's involvement could truly mean. I had to assume she was on the same trips as I was, even if not in view. If I were accepting this as truth, I could expect to see her tonight, and no amount of thinking on what I should do in that event could actually prepare me for our encounter.

I ate slowly, processing the conflict between looking for a familiar face that could be the writer, but not letting that put me in danger if Pearl appeared. This was getting tricky, and a world of unexpected possibilities spiraled out of control in my mind's eye.

I stared at my half-eaten soup bowl endlessly, consumed with daydreams of potential scenarios. Finally, I shook my head clear and cleaned up the kitchen. At 9:00, I sat down on the couch facing the music box, key in hand. A little early for the slumber that would be brought on after my return, but I honestly couldn't wait any longer. If I thought any more about it, I might start thinking clearly enough to fear the danger Pearl could pose, and I didn't want to chicken out. I was going to have to meet her head on if I wanted to learn anything more about the journal writer.

I took a deep breath, partly because I knew I would lose it soon enough anyway, and partly because I was nervous. The key turned over in the music box once, twice, three times. Darkness consumed me in the usual exhilarating way, as I fought back the panic that inevitably followed, and in mere seconds I was breathing in the air of my new surroundings.

I smelled barbeque. Car horns honked and people chattered nearby. It was hot and bright, like summer in Texas. Just like home. After a short time, my eyes were back to working order and around me I could see a dirt road that led to a small highway, and coming my direction was the beginning of a parade. Red, white and blue flags checkered the crowd, and spectators sat on tailgates or in folding chairs alongside the road. Small children waited eagerly to wave at the rodeo queens and catch a windfall of candy.

I knew I was smiling, because this very well could have been a memory from my own childhood. Like small-town Texas at it's best. I thought back to before I left my living room couch and was overjoyed that I turned the key three times, and wished I had gone for more. I briefly remembered that Pearl should be around here somewhere, but at that moment I just wanted to sit and wave like the rest of the parade-goers. Older model trucks with business advertisements passed, along with glittery floats carrying the County Fair court of royalty, youngsters on go carts and four-wheelers, and the whole fleet of Volunteer Fire Department vehicles, which added up to one pumper truck and a small rescue SUV.

I waved and cheered along with the other locals, embracing the emotion swelling in my chest brought on by this visit down memory lane. With the parade over in just minutes, I faced the possibilities ahead of me now: I could continue enjoying the festivities like everyone around me, or I could search the crowd for Pearl.

There weren't that many people in attendance, a few hundred faces, maybe. Probably a good sized turnout for a tiny little town like this, but not so many that the kids couldn't run around and still be found quickly by their parents.

The parade goers seemed to be migrating toward the other side of a slight hill, where I could hear young voices singing "You Are My Sunshine." Once I topped the hill I could see a metal building with a band on a stage, tables and chairs as well as auction items set up all around it, and food lines near a giant barbeque pit. Scanning the handful of people who must have hopped in line early and had already sat down to eat, I could see that none of them were familiar. Beyond the covered seating area in front of the stage, there were more tables scattered amongst oak trees providing nice shade from the sun. Still, I saw no Pearl among the group.

Making sure the key was well hidden under my shirt, I decided to cruise around and see what there was to see. Cute little Grannies worked the iced tea stand and sold meal tickets, and families strolled along holding hands until the kids spotted their friends or cousins and rushed off to join them.

"Adorable little place, isn't it?"

It was her. That voice had the same chill as her stare, and it disturbed me knowing I now had more to bring home with me than just the memory of her gaze.

"I've been dying to meet you, you know. I took me a while to figure out who was turning the key, especially after that *boy* had it, but I watched for a long time and...you keep turning up."

Speak now or forever hold your peace. I turned to face her. "Yeah, I've been noticing you, too," I said casually. Nice, like I want to ask her out on a date. *Be mean, bare your teeth.* "Who are you, and what are you doing here?"

"Ha!" she laughed. "If anyone's going to be asking questions, I think it'll be me."

Don't back down. "Oh? What do you know about the key anyway?"

She laughed under her breath like I was the only one not in on the joke. Her confidence unsettled me. I knew she had every bit of authority over me when it came to the music box and key, I just didn't know why.

"Look," I tried from a different angle. "I inherited the music box, and I know it used to belong to someone who wrote about it in a journal. That's where I found the key and I figured out that they worked together. I just don't know how you fit into any of it."

"And I suppose you're going to just keep turning that key until you find out?"

What a bitch. "You could be helpful, you know."

"You know by now I won't be helping you." Her smile was vicious. "Consider this your warning. You'll keep turning the key to find your answers, but just know that every time you do...I get closer to what I need, too."

My insides churned. I wanted to stay and keep her talking, but I had a feeling I would become less involved in the conversation and more invested in holding back angry, frustrated tears. Cutting my losses, I tried to come off as confident and carefree as I could. My parting words to her were, "Then I'll see you next time."

I turned and walked away, just praying she wasn't going to follow me for a come-from-behind attack. Struggling to keep my pace calm and untroubled, I walked to the far side of the area without looking back even once. For all I knew, she could have circled the other way and I would run right into her in a matter of steps. To avoid that risk, I threw myself down on the end of a nearly empty bench and craned my head behind me to make sure I was safe for the moment.

"Are you okay, darlin'?" came a voice from the other end of the bench. It was a sweet old man with a caring face, and I nodded appreciatively to assure him that I was all right. Such sweet people here, I really hoped they didn't have to witness my murder.

Everyone at the table redirected their attention back to each other again, continuing with the conversation I must have rudely interrupted. I could still feel one pair of eyes on me, however, from straight across the table. Ready to beg for their pardon, I looked up to speak my apology.

He was looking at me; knowing me, remembering me. I knew I didn't look the same as when he had seen me last, but he was perfectly unchanged. Perfectly.

He smiled wide before finally speaking. "I wanted it to be you," he said simply.

I couldn't speak. I wanted to, but before I could find the words, the darkness returned, and pulled me away.

FOURTEEN

THE SOUND OF SILENCE

I sunk into the couch under me, with one image in my mind's eye: William. I had done it; I had found him, and I ached for another immediate glimpse of him. Knowing all I had to do to was to sit up again and turn the key was helplessly tempting, but with the approaching shroud of sleep and the promise of seeing William again, I let the memory of the Miami Beach evening lead me into my dreams.

As I sunk fully under, triumph over what formerly seemed impossible spurred my slumbering imagination. Even in my subconscious, I could see his face and hear his words as if we were still on the Ocean Lawn. Dancing, laughing, enjoying a deliriously enchanting evening with a perfect stranger that I'd apparently known all along. My two encounters with him melded together, until at the end of our dance, instead of parting, he spoke the sweetest words in my ear, "I wanted it to be you."

The scene played out over and over in my head until the uninvited daylight warmed my face, thieving me from my paradise. Initially, it was upsetting to be brought back to my living room all alone, but my mind was made up without hesitation that I would forego my week's wait, and turn the key again instantly. There was no way I could spend the next seven days without seeing his face and finding out his story, not when I had invested so much time and emotion seeking him out.

Springing from under the blankets that I must have unconsciously found during the night, I straightened my couch-hair and wiped the sleep from my eyes. Unconcerned for the most part about my appearance, as it didn't matter; I could very possibly wind up arriving under water in scuba gear, I thrust the key into the slot and gave it five anxious turns.

As usual, the darkness descended and the air was siphoned from my lungs, and upon the return of my senses, I was instantly hit with a blustery wind and deadening cold. Foolishly thinking I would have surfaced staring face to face with William, I stared at a frighteningly vast expanse of white snow and ice, peppered with frosted trees. There was not a soul in sight, not human at least. Not that it was comforting to think of what possible animals might be lurking near.

Within seconds of my appearance in the icy terrain, it was clear that I would be far from comfortable on this trip. While well equipped with layers of downy comfort covering my entire body, my fingers and toes were already throbbing with numb pain. *Get moving,* I thought. I needed to get the blood flowing as well as look around for William. It was a cloudy, overcast day, and yet still, my eyes stung from the radiant snow; a situation not helped at all by the relentless wind.

I walked out into the open, assuming that even if I was unable to see him at this point, at least I could make myself visible. Minutes ticked by, with only the sound of the wind tearing through the trees as it raced toward my raw face. Considering how long my five turns should give me, I fought back against the thought of time running out before finding him. I called out his name, time and time again, and waited.

They had to be here, both of them. I had momentarily forgotten about Pearl, with my mind so consumed with William. Part of me felt more self-assured now in the event I would meet with Pearl before, or even instead of William today. It was more than she had anticipated, no doubt, that I had even reached this point of enlightenment. In a way, I had already beaten her – but I knew what they said about winning battles...and losing wars.

As I wandered, inch by burning inch, the pain stretched beyond my fingers and toes and into my hands, feet and legs. The more I tried to stay in motion, however, the harder it was to will my limbs to move. Not even my warm breath was a comfort, with the speed in which it turned to frozen ice crystals. I estimated about thirty minutes to have passed, and so far I had only managed to identify the freezing point of human tissue. I was getting nowhere fast, and at the rate I was going, frostbite would prevent me from even moving my eyelids.

There were plenty of options for a sheltered spot to pass the remaining time, if it came to that. I could stand here in the open and wait to be seen while freezing in the process, but my body wouldn't take much more of it; I would have to cuddle with a tree eventually. After another few minutes passed it was all I could do to twirl slowly on my spot while training my eyes on the surrounding trees' edge. Defeated, I pushed myself toward a patch of trees, and backed myself into the most enclosed space offered by the lower reaching branches.

Without much left to do but curse my fucking five turns, I watched and waited. Huddled in a ball, tucking my hands between my stomach and my legs, I thought for the first time about the danger this had put me in. I really didn't expect that I could freeze to death, but it sure as hell felt like a possibility as I sat there unable to feel either set of my cheeks.

Thinking back to Nora's experience, what would have happened if the man hadn't been there to save her from becoming crocodile chum? Death in the space and time of the music box would be permanent, or I would choose to accept it as such so as not to be complacent. Over-zealously turning the key five times might need to be replaced with a more conservative number just for cases such as the predicament I was in now. It was a distressing thought to ponder, cutting my time down to such a minimum, considering how long it could take to find William and how much we had to discuss.

The cold sunk deeper into my core, even slowing my thoughts. My breath as my only warmth, I closed my eyes and focused on the steam before it fleetingly disappeared into the frozen atmosphere. Delirium approached, as a rhythm strummed in my head...a familiar song, but I couldn't place it. I held on to it, so as to tether my consciousness to the here and now, and before long I was humming along as it materialized from just an echo into Simon and Garfunkel's "The Sound of Silence." Hello darkness...hello friend.

Fighting the darkness, I pried my eyes open, immediately wet with tears from the biting wind. Snow twirled in gusts over the landscape, blurring the horizon, but through the cloudy mist, I saw movement. Cautious not to fall for a mirage, though, I wiped my eyes and focused with all my strength on the spot that had been given away. Something stood out from the white snow, and after a few minutes of dedicated scrutinizing, my heart began to drum with excitement. The figure was too far away for me to determine whether it was male or female, but even the mere possibility that it could be William elevated my mood.

The rigidity of my legs was one thing to deal with, but after the careful rise to a standing crouch, I realized the absence of feeling in my feet was much worse. Each step reminded me of the T-1000 in the Terminator, his limbs breaking piece by piece as he stepped through the freezing nitroglycerin. The agony subsided as I drew closer, though, confident that it was him I was running toward. Emotion came over me, and I picked up the pace to a jog.

The pain, the anticipation, and the fear of the unknown ahead of me culminated, finally releasing in sobs. Tears dropped onto my cheeks, freezing instantly. As the distance closed, my body began to resist, the fire in my muscles consuming me. With everything I had, I coerced my legs to continue forward as I got near enough to see the shape running with the same ferocity towards me. Wiping frozen tears from my eyes, and awaiting our impending reunion, I ran to him with all my might.

Without warning, a flash of darkness came out of the trees twenty yards in front of me, stopping me dead in my tracks. Pearl now stood in my way, completely at ease and seemingly untroubled by the sub-zero temperatures that had nearly brought me to my knees. I looked over her shoulder and saw that William was still a good eighty yards behind her. Soon, the three of us would all be face to face...and then what?

Neither of us spoke. She looked neither threatening nor danger-ous, but instead appeared content, even smiling at me. It was not a warm, genuine smile, though. It was a "gotcha" smile, which rattled me. Only a short time prior, I had convinced myself that I had surpassed Pearl's underestimation of me.

Behind her, William had slowed, now walking with a more cautious stealth, as if he didn't want to be heard. I wondered why he would need to tiptoe around her; was I yet again taking for granted my understanding of the music box dynamic and those involved with it? Pearl continued her disconcerting stare, as I weighed my options. Try to have a conversation? Tell her off? No, I was much safer just waiting for William to arrive and I could follow his lead. Briefly, I lost sight of him, but then caught movement along the tree line where he was now quietly approaching.

The seconds slowly ticked by while I waited. "The Sound of Silence" reverberated again in my head. It all happened in an instant. I heard it first: the pops of the ice, followed by a nauseating rip as the instability gave way to shattering cracks running from the spot where I stood suspended over what I could now see was water below. And then I fell through.

I saw nothing on the way down, but I understood why Pearl appeared so satisfied, happily standing in my way. In my haste to reach William, I had failed to notice my path had led me over a semi-frozen lake. All she needed was to keep me there on that ice until my weight had proven too much.

And now I was looking up from what should have felt cold, but instead I was positive I'd fallen through the cracks of hell, because every piece of me was on fire. Looking up at the point above me from which I fell, I could see bits of ice, broken and floating along with the ripples I had created. Each piece bobbed and floated back to its original place.

As I stared, I realized I had forgotten to swim, and was sinking farther and farther from the surface. The burn was relentless, but putting mind over matter, I fought the tormenting sensation and pushed through the water. I would have to move the pieces of ice if I was going to reach the air, either by throwing them out of the way above me, or pulling them under.

My first attempt was to push them up onto the outside ice and snow, but as weak as I was, I could hardly push them up an inch without sending myself deeper under. Lifting them above the water level would be next to impossible. Frantically, I began pulling the smaller shards under and shoving them aside until I had enough room to at least poke my face through and steal a quick breath. Coughing and sputtering, I choked in as much air as my lungs could hold and afforded myself a look above. Pearl must have been just beyond view, because all I could see was gray skies. I sucked in one more deep breath and went under again to move a few more pieces out of my way so I could try to climb out.

As if being under the frozen tundra in an ice bath wasn't enough, pulling the ice under proved to be a bigger challenge than anticipated, and fear finally crept up from wherever I had suppressed it thus far. The buoyancy of the larger ice blocks prevented me from pulling them down, and the smaller chunks seemed almost too small to manipulate with my gloved bricks-for-fingers. In a turbulent rampage, I threw and scraped and pulled any and every piece of ice that would move at all. Adrenaline and panic were now on my side, and little by little, the ice was moved away from the opening, allowing room for my head and arms to break through.

Air rushed into my aching lungs, but as I coughed and gagged in relief, Pearl's outstretched hand appeared out of nowhere to grab by head and firmly submerge me once again. Her grip was secure in my hair, and despite my thrashing and spinning, she was clearly in control. I stayed as still as I could, thinking that maybe if she was trying to kill me, then I could at least act dead in hopes that she would let go. It wasn't long before I knew she wouldn't be so dense, and another surge of terror shot through me. I didn't know where it came from, but I decided if I was going do die, then she was going to come with me. I secured my grip on her hand in my hair, and then used my legs to push against the icy edge, bringing Pearl's hand down deeper and deeper, and ultimately pulling her toward the water.

The opening through which I formerly could only see daylight, became clouded with a dark shadow, as she came unwillingly close to the water. It worked. She released her grip, and backed away. Even with the assumption that I would not be able to surface again with her there, I watched the hole where she now crouched staring down at me, and brazenly swam toward her.

I didn't have a plan, but thought if nothing else, I could steal another gulp of air and pull the same thing on her if she grabbed my head again. Just as I got close enough to see her face clearly before I emerged, something large moved right through her like a train, throwing her from my view. I thrust myself up and out of the water, and it dawned on me that the airborne savior had been William. The two of them tussled about on the ground, and when I was sure they'd be at it for a while, I made my feeble attempts to climb out of the hole. My attempts, however, yielded nothing more than further spent energy: I was going nowhere. With nothing to do except keep an eye on the struggle between William and Pearl, I could literally feel my remaining energy leaving me, the strain of the last hour finally becoming more than I could bear.

William pinned her down and hastily shot a glance at me to satisfy that I was safe above the water. Although I had seen him before, on two occasions, I looked at him as if it were for the first time. He was amazing. Even with his faced contorted with fury, his features were exquisite and beautiful. Pearl appeared to have been putting up quite a fight of her own; every time William rose to walk to me, she grabbed his ankles or swiftly tackled him again. This went on for a surprisingly long time, and as I watched, tremors began to take over my body.

Whether from the freezing temperatures, or from overwhelming my muscle capacity, I had slipped down into the water again and held barely a fingertip onto the outer ice. I just wanted the time to run out. I didn't even care anymore if I got to see William or talk to him or touch his face like I'd hoped when I turned the key so anxiously. I wanted to be home, under my blanket. I didn't even take another breath before letting myself slide completely under again, and I sunk slowly down below.

I watched the opening get smaller as I descended, the sun shining through it just enough to light a path down into the deep. The song returned to my fading consciousness, again, in random phrases and beats. Hello darkness...hello friend.

I closed my eyes as I drifted. The pain was gone...the shakes were gone...the fear was gone. I let go.

Then the song went silent.

Nothingness surrounded me finally, and I imagined God lifting me from the water and pulling me up to Heaven. It was bright in Heaven, and breathing again flooded relief into my whole body. But then the pain surged again, which was disappointing, to say the least. Heaven should have been perfect.

Then God spoke to me. He asked loudly, and rather harshly, "Where's the key?"

I wondered why nobody had ever told me you needed a key to get into Heaven. That wasn't fair.

God cradled me, and whispered this time, "Rynn, where's the key? Do you still have it?"

I was glad He knew my name. Maybe He knew I was a good person and would let me into Heaven even though I didn't have a key.

"Rynn, how many times did you turn the key? How much longer do we have here?!"

I smiled, and told Him, "I used to have a key. It wasn't for Heaven though. It was for a music box. Or maybe it will work...I don't know..."

"Yes, Rynn," He said. "It will work, do you have it? Where is it?"

I didn't know where it was, though. I hadn't remembered doing anything with it when I arrived in the snowy meadow, before I rose up into Heaven. My eyes cracked open for the first time since I slipped under.

"Oh my God!" I shouted through deep gulps of icy air. "William!"

"Welcome back," he joked, stiffly. "The key?"

"I don't know," I responded honestly. "I usually tuck it under my shirt, but I can't even feel anything in all these layers."

He tossed his gloves aside and I felt his icy hands on my neck, moving my hair and jacket away so he could see.

"I don't see anything, is it on a chain?"

"No, just a ribbon," I answered.

About that time, Pearl stirred behind William, and I became rigid with fear. William noticed the change in me, and turned around to see, with no surprise, she was on her feet.

"Wonder what took her so long," he said under his breath.

She didn't approach, but rather stared at me with chilling eyes, and walked away.

"Hmm," he murmured and then turned to me. "Are you okay?"

I nodded, but the shakes had returned, and it was way beyond my control to stop them. Once assured that Pearl was no longer a threat, William hurriedly went back to looking for the key.

"How many times did you turn the key?" he asked as he searched.

It was forever ago, in my mind, but I replied, "Five."

"And we've been here for what, about an hour? Shit."

"What?" I demanded.

"We have a long time, still, at least an hour, maybe more. You're not going to last if we stay in the water – aha!" He pulled the key out of one of the pockets of my jacket. I must have slipped it in there when I'd arrived, but I had no recollection of it, probably because I did it around the same time I started pissing my pants at the realization of how far up shit creek I'd paddled.

"What do you mean 'I won't last'?" That didn't sound promising.

As he slipped the ribbon around my neck and tucked it safely under my shirt, he answered, "You've already gone into shock, and I brought you back around. It won't be long before you relapse if we stay here in the water." I stared at him, unable to respond. "I'll be honest, though..." he continued. "I wish we didn't have so much time left, because it's going to feel worse up there out of the water."

I sputtered a drunken-scoff, not believing him.

"Trust me," he confirmed. "But you'll have a better chance of surviving if we can get you out."

I was just along for the ride, apparently, because in an instant he was pushing me toward the ice and telling me to hang on. He wasted no time in inspecting the stability of the closest edge, which in fact, did not hold up to his weight. This happened repeatedly, every direction he turned, but each time he checked that I was okay before moving on. As he proceeded through the brittle fringe, he pitched the pieces, big and small across the icy snow and out of his way. Before long, he was significantly farther away from our starting point, which was where I had remained, unable to keep up with him.

"William?" my voice was frail. "William...?"

He turned to look at me, and asked, "Are you okay?"

"Yes, but, I need to ask. What happens if I die out here?"

He didn't answer, but swam back for me instead. I watched him, mesmerized that he was so unaffected by the conditions. He took my hands and wrapped them around his neck, and then returned to the other side and deposited me there. He saw in my eyes the panic that grew while I awaited his answer.

"I don't know, exactly." He went back to testing the ice, but couldn't escape my eyes, and offered, "I think this spot is strong enough for us to climb out...then we can talk."

With a few more testing heaves on the block, he sunk down under the water and propelled himself up with as much force as he could gather. He high-centered it, but had enough weight out of the water and supported by his forearms that he could lift the rest of himself up and out. Not taking chances with the uncertain ice or wasting any time, he lifted me out with ease, and dragged me away from the threatening water.

After a split-second breather, he scooped me up and deposited me in a covering much like the one I'd spent time in prior to my little dip, then started taking off my gloves and unzipping my jacket.

"What are you doing?" I wondered aloud.

"You've got to get the wet gloves off, and I want you to take your arms out of your jacket."

"I really don't know if I can do that," I feigned a laugh. I hated to wuss out, but my muscles failed me a long time ago, and it had only been pure stubborn determination not to lose William from my sight that I'd even been able to stay above water as long as I had while he found a way out.

I was happy to hear him chuckle, as he gently pulled one arm from the soaking wet jacket and folded it across my chest, followed by the other arm. My whole body was in such a ridiculous state, shaking and sore to the point of spasms...I didn't even notice whether it was more or less comfortable out of the water like William had said. I lay there, frozen in every way imaginable, while he unzipped his own jacket and rolled me over to him, where he engulfed as much of my body as he could cover with his own.

I knew he was using the body warmth trick, which made a marginal difference, but more than anything, I was thankful for the chance to finally be close to him. I just wished I could have been in better condition to enjoy it.

"So..." was my attempt at conversation.

He chuckled again, "So..."

My brain kept slipping, as if wanting to drift under the water again, and William must have realized it, because he began speaking rapidly at me. "Rynn, stay with me. Listen, you wanted to know what would happen if you died out here. I don't know. I don't know, because no one else has ever..." he seemed lost for words. "...ever been here...with us. But listen, you've got to stay awake. Tell me something about you. How did you find the music box, and the key?"

I didn't want to talk, I wanted to just lie in his arms listening to his voice forever. I closed my eyes to concentrate on feeling him close to me.

"Rynn!" he shouted, and then he shook me, knocking my head into his shoulder, which brought me around again. I rose up to look at him with confused eyes, and he reacted strongly, "Rynn, you have to talk to me or you'll want to go to sleep, and if you go to sleep YOU WILL DIE. Now tell me how you found the music box and the key."

"But I want to hear about you – I've been *looking* for you!" I sounded like a child, but honestly, I'd been searching and searching and now that I'd found him I was ready for some answers.

"Really? How long have you been looking for me?" he sounded half-irritated and half-amused.

"Uhhh...I guess a few months?"

"Well, I beat you by a long shot, ok? That's not nearly as long as I've spent waiting for..." he trailed off, and for some reason I felt confident enough to chime in.

"For me?"

He was quiet for a minute, but then said, "Maybe. It's complicated, and I promise to fill you in on all the details, but please, for now...just tell me about your story."

With a sigh, I asked, "How much time do you think we have?"

"Long enough for you to start at the beginning," was his response.

"Okay. I guess it started in my Grandma's antique shop..."

I told him of the days spent with Grandma, Tucker, and Nora, and how I inherited the music box and journal, and that I eventually put the pieces of his puzzle together, leading up to finding him. He was right, I did have time to start from the beginning, and every time I tried to ask him a question, he shushed me politely, and promised, "next time."

"William?" I was tired of talking.

"Yes?"

"If I need to warm up, I have a better idea."

He angled his head away from me to see my face. I met his gaze, while my toes traced circles around his. At my waist, his embrace tightened, pressing our bodies closer. Closer. Definitely warmer already. My pulse quickened with the familiar electric current as I withdrew the memory of our humid Miami Beach encounter.

Legitimately torn between losing myself in his eyes or his lips, I froze on the spot. Our breath turned to steam between us and rose to the trees. A smile parted his lips, showing his teeth, white as the snow surrounding us. Heat found my cheeks.

"Come here."

I didn't need to be told twice.

FIFTEEN
ALREADY GONE

When I awoke in the safety of my own house, all I could feel were my aching muscles. I was no longer cold and numb, but for some reason I was still shivering violently. I wondered if that was in fact how badly I had been shaking in William's arms. Oh, those arms. Those lips. Delirious sleep came over me quickly, as usual, and it was mid-afternoon when I woke again.

Finally warmed through and no longer stricken with tremors, I chose to remain on the couch under Grandma's quilt while my mind replayed the events of my most recent and most perilous misadventure. I had covered a lot of ground, so to speak, but I still felt miles away from where I'd hoped to be. While I did manage to find William, it was fruitless in the investigative aspect, due to him insisting that I share my story first.

It was comforting to now know I would thankfully return in good form, no matter the condition I might find myself while traveling. However, it was more than peculiar that I had been so deeply cold that even after the trip was over, the aftermath of shakes had lingered. Why hadn't that part of my physical condition disappeared along with the raw skin and frostbitten hands and feet? I was happy to accept the good news that I wouldn't return injured, but that still hadn't answered the more serious question of life and death. Without a doubt, Pearl was trying to drown me out there, and William admitted to having no sure answer about what would happen if I were to die while "gone."

Easily, I slipped into an over-analytical frame of mind. All things considered, even trying to explore viable explanations for such a phenomenon as this was asinine, but seriously, did I care? Knowing I was entirely unwilling to leave this alone and would continue pressing my luck despite the conceivable dangers, I had to do my best to understand the full potential of my actions.

I figured that shaking was more of a neurological response than physical, so I grabbed my laptop and searched for details, hoping it might be the key to working out the truth about life and death.

What I found about the shivers was pretty simple: when you're cold, your brain sends a signal to your muscles to contract and release rapidly, in hopes of exerting enough energy to warm you up. As straightforward and minimal as this concept was, it was more telling than I had anticipated. This meant that when I returned from the ice bath, I was shaking because my brain had continued working to warm up my body, regardless of the absence of freezing temperatures in my living room. It just took a while for my brain to catch up with reality. So...if death were to occur while passing through a "false" world, I could only presume that my brain would register my body as dead, and would be unlikely to make any further attempts to save me.

I fell back into the couch and closed the laptop. Granted, nothing that I knew about the music box and its curiosities was based on fact, and this conclusion that I had found was pure speculation, but it made sense enough for me to take it seriously. I was eager for the chance to share my new death theory on my next trip, and to hear William's thoughts on it.

While half-frozen, but still far from the worst shape the snowy escapade would leave me in, I had already mulled over the idea that it would be best if I turned the key fewer times so as to avoid dilemmas like I found myself dealing with on that occasion. At that point, it was a knife through my heart to think of having less time to seek out William, but now having peace of mind that we were both aware of each other's existence, that didn't seem nearly as bad. I didn't like it, and I wished I could turn the key a thousand times to spend more time with him, but it wasn't worth going through a situation that could kill me. From now on I would be responsible enough to acknowledge the importance of making it out alive, versus putting all my efforts into finding him.

My head was spinning with the overwhelming highs and lows from what I realized had turned into several months of music box frenzy. It was nearly May, which came as a complete shock once I thought about it. The last time I had dedicated conscious thought to anything other than the current mystery unfolding, had been an embarrassingly long time ago. I heaved myself up and wandered into the kitchen, finding myself gazing out the window and out onto the very spot where I had finally put it all together. With the discovery that I found on that day, one question answered had brought up a thousand more, and the cycle had continued with such a tremendous intensity that I was now looking back on my own life that had moved on without me.

I knew something had to give, but I also knew I had compromised a great deal already by considering limiting the frequency that I would turn the key. It was unreasonable, in my eyes, to think that anything less than once or twice a month would suffice. I would barely have enough opportunities to find and talk to William, and it could take another several months to make any headway in finding out all the details of his life. I was in over my head, but that didn't mean I wasn't willing to be. I just needed to find a better balance between the two realities of my life.

When awareness hit me that I needed to get out of the house, I was both humiliated and defiant. I was having a hard enough time making it one week between key turns, and if I was going to relinquish even more time, I would have to recommit to the life I once led before all of this interference. With high hopes of distraction again, I dialed Nora.

She answered on the first ring, with, "Hey, you're on speaker."

"Hi," I responded. "Are you doing anything tonight?"

"Nah," she answered, "why? You want to do something?" I heard Tucker mumbling in the background, and then the shuffling of the phone.

Closer now, Tucker spoke. "What are you in the mood for, a dinner and a movie date night, or wild and crazy party night?"

It was a toss up, to be honest. I was in the mood for dinner and a movie, but wasn't sure if it would do an adequate job of keeping my mind off William. The crazy party option would definitely do the job, but I wasn't sure I could rally.

I answered with an indifferent, "Uhh...?"

It was still Tucker on the line, and he feigned disappointment in my non-reply. "Dude, you called us, remember? What's it gonna be?"

"How about both? If necessary, I mean..."

Nora returned, confused, "If necessary? What do you mean?"

Defeated and frustrated all over again, but now even more at having to vocalize it, I explained, "I need to take my mind off..." Before saying his name I remembered I hadn't spoke to either of them since learning it was William. I redirected my answer, "Look I have a lot to tell you both, so how about we start with dinner, and see what happens after that?"

"Sure thing, jellybean," came Tucker's voice from beyond the phone.

Nora, closer, agreed. "Where do you want to meet, or do you want us to pick you up?"

"Just pick me up and we'll see. I'm getting in the shower right now."

An hour and a half later, Nora was on my front step, and it wasn't a moment too soon. I met her at the door, eager for the two of them to provide me with the diversion I needed.

"Wow," Nora said as she noticed my enthusiasm for their arrival.

"Everything's okay, right?" It was troubling how many times my little sister had felt the need to give me mothering looks of judgment lately.

Rolling my eyes, but ashamed I'd given her reason to be worried, I assured her with a hug. "I'm fine, but I do have new information. Let's go, and I'll tell you."

Tucker had stayed in the truck, and greeted me with his usual warm smile as I hopped in the back seat. He turned down the Eagles', "Already Gone," long enough to ask, "Where to, ladies?"

"I feel like something shamefully unhealthy," I admitted. I hadn't thought about it, but I barely remembered consuming any meals in the last few months. I know I had eaten, but it had to have been reflexive, rather than planned. Just going through the motions again. Now that I was considering options, I was famished. "How about Joe's? I could really go for some garlic rolls and pizza."

There was a collective Homer Simpson-like groan from the front seat, and I took that as an agreeable vote. Tucker pulled out of my driveway and headed in the direction of the grease and cheese that would hopefully satisfy my stomach and possibly my soul. Too impatient to wait until we could sit down at the restaurant, Nora turned to me expectantly. "Well?" she probed.

"Uh, let's see," I thought aloud. I didn't exactly remember how up-to-date they were in the grand scheme of things. "So last time I talked to you was right after I went on a bender, right? And I told you I'd seen Pearl?"

"Yeah," answered Nora. "You were supposed to wait a week before doing it again, though..."

"I did!" I was automatically defensive. "I waited, and it was torture, but I did it. I turned the key Friday night, and I went to this cute little small town parade – just like the ones Mom and Dad would take us to when we were little. It was adorable, everyone dressed in red, white and blue, waving flags. But I knew Pearl would be there, right? And there was something just..." I didn't want to get ahead of myself, but my latest experience with her had only confirmed the danger she posed. "I knew she wasn't going to be helpful, that's for sure. Even you saw that in her, Tucker."

"So," he asked, "was she there?"

"Yeah."

Nora whipped around to look at me, as if surveying me for injuries. "And?"

"I was on the lookout for her, but she found me first. Snuck up from behind and just started talking to me casually, but she was warning me. I tried to play it cool, but basically her message to me was that if I keep turning the key..." I didn't want to give them reason to tell me not to turn the key anymore, but I couldn't keep anything a secret from them. "...she said 'she gets closer to what she needs, too.' I don't know exactly what she meant."

By then we had covered the three blocks or so from my house to Joe's, and Tucker pulled the truck into a parking spot, put it in park, and turned to me. "So she threatened you?"

"I guess. But — "

"But nothing! Rynn, seriously?" Nora had heard enough.

"Listen! I know what you're thinking, but let's just go inside and sit down and I'll tell you the rest. I haven't told you the really good part! Please?"

Reluctantly, she turned back around and opened the door. We walked into Joe's Pizzeria, and were instantly calmed by the heavenly smells of garlic, dough, and Italian spices in the small room. Joe's was less restaurant and more like a one-room to-go pick up spot with a few red and white checkerboard clothed tables. Linoleum tile floors, two green-curtained windows and a glass door across the front, and the open kitchen behind the red counter that divided the space in half. They did serve beer and wine, though, and apparently we needed it, because the first thing Tucker asked for was a pitcher.

The two of them sat opposite of me in our booth, giving the feeling of an interview. They were just as welcoming as an interrogation panel, too, and I knew I had to do some major convincing. The promising part would be telling them I'd found William. Unfortunately that would be followed by the deal-breaker, when I let them in on the fact that Pearl tried to kill me.

"Okay, so I left Pearl...I just walked away, and she didn't follow. I was really scared," I confessed, "that she was going to follow me and, you know, do something. But she didn't. I just walked around, trying to pass the time until I was pulled out of there. I got nervous, though, and I just plopped down at a picnic table with these cute little old people. I felt bad for interrupting their group, but they were sweet enough to ask if I was okay because I was obviously unnerved about something." I smiled at that moment from my memory. "I tried to be polite and let them know I was fine, but I know they thought I was must have been crazy. And I could feel the person across the table still staring at me, so I looked up to apologize, and..."

I paused to meet their eyes, both of them leaning forward, waiting for me to continue. Our pitcher of beer arrived, interrupting the trance momentarily.

"It was him." I resumed, smiling from ear to ear, making it hard to continue.

The other side of the table erupted in "Who? The writer? How do you know? Did he say anything?" Both Tucker and Nora were talking over each other so fervently that I could hardly make out any of their inquisitions.

"I know it was him, because it was the first person I knew I'd seen before. And, he remembered me, too. It was the man from the wedding that I danced with."

Tucker looked at Nora, as if needing a reminder of the relayed story she had told him. "The random guy you shared cake with?"

"Well," I corrected, "technically he didn't have any cake, but yes, I offered." I had forgotten that I was eating two pieces of cake when I spoke with him. Nice first impression.

Nora interjected, keeping my story moving forward, "The guy she *made out* with." She was engrossed now, which made me feel better about how much I had scared her.

"He said..." My heart fluttered at the memory of his words. "He said, 'I wanted it to be you.'"

Nora literally fell into Tucker's shoulder with a groan. "Wow," I could hear her mumble. They were both silent for a few minutes while they processed such incredible new information.

Tucker rubbed his face with his hands, and through his spread fingers, he finally spoke one word, "Jeez." He filled our glasses, and passed them to Nora and I. "So then what? Did you talk? Who is he?"

"Sadly, no. The trip ended just seconds after that."

NORA WAS DEFINITELY PERTURBED that I had chose to turn the key again immediately following my return from the small-town parade, but it was nothing compared to the fear-induced rant I received when I told them of Pearl's attempts to drown me in the icy abyss. I had expected nothing less, especially after sharing my theory on death during travel. The evening continued with mixed emotions, the two of them stuck between wanting to protect me from Pearl, yet helplessly in awe of the unfathomable idea of William being present and finally aware of me. We discussed all avenues of new possibilities and curiosities this new knowledge posed, but their underlying concern was the danger. If the circumstances alone didn't kill me, eventually, we knew, Pearl would.

I gave them my word that I would take maximum precaution next time I turned the key, but none of us actually knew what that meant. How do you prepare yourself, when you can't bring anything with you to protect yourself, and you have no idea where you'll land? The worst part was a non-negotiable that Nora set in order to limit my opportunities to walk into harm's way: a new once a month rule. It was fucking ludicrous, but if I hadn't agreed to it, Nora threatened to take the key and put herself in charge of all music box dealings. I honestly felt weak in the knees at the thought of the key being in anyone else's hands, even my loving sister.

The next few weeks drug on slower than even I had expected. I made more of an effort in every single thing I did, in hopes of becoming so absorbed that I didn't spend time pondering what possibilities lay on the other side of my own mundane reality. It didn't work. William was in my mind everywhere I went and in every thought. But, it was also a degree easier than anticipated, owing to the simple knowledge that he knew I would be back. In the icy tundra, he didn't seem bothered by me taking fewer turns of the key, and had even insisted on less. I guess when you've lived for centuries, waiting for a moment like this to present itself, another month is a relatively short amount of time to endure.

So, I made plans with Nora often. I visited Tucker at job sites. I even went to see Mom at work at Grandma's old shop, even though I'd avoided it most of my adult life. She knew something was awry by my mere presence, but I wasn't about to go into it and worry someone else. To my surprise, I enjoyed being back at the antique shop, and vowed to come by more often after school. I formed a routine that worked: school, Tucker or the shop, workout at home or a run around my neighborhood, a dinner that required as much effort as possible and included guests if anyone was available, shower, bed, repeat.

The weekends were the hardest. I spent most of my weekend time planning and preparing for my weekdays, meaning every meal was decided, groceries were purchased, and visits were arranged. I became a third wheel, even though Tucker and Nora insisted I had not. They were probably happy to have me around because they knew it was proof that I wasn't going back on my word about waiting between key turns.

When the time finally came to actually sit down with the music box again, I had reluctantly found the rhythm of life again. Nora asked if she could be with me while I went under, although neither of us had any idea how that could be useful. It gave her peace of mind, though, and I was happy to give her that. We made plans that on the agreed upon "third Friday" of May: we would have dinner at my house together and then see what the music box had planned for my evening.

Tucker offered to pick up Chinese take-out for us, as he didn't want to be left out of all the fun and mystery. We all knew things had jumped to the next level, but that unmistakably solidified our interest and devotion to finding more answers. They were in it this with me, and they were willing to make sure I saw this through to the end, and I valued them beyond measure for that.

With our bellies satisfied with Chinese food and dancing with anticipation, we arranged ourselves on the couch and stared at the music box in a way that neither of us had ever done before. Showing their support, each of them placed their hands on my knees while, with shaking hands, I placed the key into the notches. I turned the key modest two turns, and waited for the suffocation to squeeze me through the invisible pipeline that would lead me to William.

Bright light hit my clenched eyelids upon my arrival in new lands. I squinted through the blinding sun in effort to make out my new surroundings, when I heard the most unexpected sound.

"Holy shit," came Tucker's voice from immediately to my right, exactly where he had been seconds before.

SIXTEEN

EVERY BREATH YOU TAKE

Why the hell was I hearing Tucker? With the scenery around me still a blur, I strained, relying on my other senses to tell me what was happening. Two groping hands fumbled around my torso and one finally seized my shoulder, whispering, "Rynn?"

It wasn't Tucker. It was Nora, and the two groping hands belonged to her. "Sweet Jesus, Nora? What are you — how did you?" Articulation escaped me.

Slowly, the view became clear, although on such a bright day it was difficult to see even with perfect vision again. Tucker stood, watching and waiting for Nora and I to stand upright and appear normal again. When we finally came around, he said cheerily, "So I guess we're coming with?"

The last thing I remembered before leaving my own living room was Tucker and Nora's supportive hands on my legs...the only explanation for their presence would be that they were touching me when I turned the key. This was a turn of events I had not anticipated, or even considered. With them now being brought to this unnamed place with me, my instincts kicked in quickly to surmise whether I — or we — might be in any danger.

It was an unusually clear and sunny day, with pure blue skies circling above us. I brought my eyes downward, and was forced to squint through the shattered sunrays broken up by the buildings lining a town square. The three of us wandered into the shade, and we found ourselves among several hundred people bustling about. No clear and present danger that I could see so far.

"This menu looks German," spoke Tucker from a few feet away where he had picked up a sheet of laminated paper off of a bistro table.

Germany. Nora and Tucker hugged each other close as they took in the quaint town, and from out of nowhere came the memory of what in the world I was doing there in the first place.

"I've got to look for William." Obviously he wasn't in view from where I was, so I set off to my right where a large group of people gathered. With my head darting side to side so as not to pass by a single person without scrutinizing them, I weaved in and out of the crowd until running smack into a wooden bench on the far side of the group. With a little luck, and some extra height, I might get a good glimpse of these peoples' faces. I hopped up onto the bench, and saw that in the center of the crowd was a street artist, demonstrating his chalk art skills. Scanning faces, I could see that none of them were William, but thankfully I didn't see Pearl either. As I jumped down and ran quickly to the other side of the crowd, looking for another bench, I realized the unlikelihood that either William or Pearl would spend their time watching a tourist attraction.

"Rynn!" came Nora's voice behind me as I set off at a jog around the town square. I had forgotten about them, and I was going to hear about it in T minus 5, 4, 3, 2... "What the hell? Do you always take off at a sprint every time you show up in a new place, or is it just for our benefit?"

"Sorry — it's just that I know they're here — my mind just went completely tunnel vision on finding William."

"So we'll find him together," she replied, "but I sure as hell don't want to be chasing you around the whole damn time. I know I won't be much help, because I don't know what either of them looks like, but at least Tucker can keep an eye out for Pearl. And I'll...just watch for people that don't seem to be...touristy."

"Agreed," offered Tucker. "Should we all put our hands in and say 'team' on the count of three?"

Nora and I both rolled our eyes, but I was nonetheless thankful as always for the way he was able to ease the tension. With that, we started out on a walk, this time at a much more casual pace. Now, with the sense of urgency somewhat lifted, I was able to appreciate the area in which we had landed. I was taken back by the bright colors surrounding us. The sky was a deep blue like I had never seen in all my life, absolutely pure and clear, and stretching down to reach the tops of buildings that were so filled with variety I didn't know where to look first. Some looked like cathedrals or museums, exuding a royal presence, which would have been intimidating, were it not for the vibrant color of whimsical yellow or radiant orange they had been painted.

A few of the shops and houses lining the market were the more typical European white with wooden "X" cross-beamed exteriors, and others were traditional clay brick, yet still others had ornate patterned brick or palatial turrets and towers.

"What is this place?" I asked, my former idea of Germany being one of less brilliant colors.

"I don't know, but it's great! Let's see if we can find someone like a tourist guide," suggested Tucker.

Just then a couple passed by, and I could just barely pick up on their conversation, which luckily was spoken in English. I jumped at the chance to quiz them, although my rude and unexpected interruption appeared to have alarmed them. As soon as I reached out to them, the man protectively yanked his better half away from my grasp, probably assuming I was mugging them. Behind me, I could hear Tucker whisper, "Smooth," answered with Nora's snickering.

"I'm sorry," I continued with caution, "I'm really sorry, I just — I heard you speaking English, so I just — sorry, I thought maybe you could tell us where we are?"

My question was met with confusion in their eyes. They were still assuming they were being mugged; but apparently by a really, really, bad mugger.

"I know, it sounds funny — but um," I glanced back toward my own better two-thirds, "see, we've been traveling so much that I think it's all just sort-of blending together. We, uh, lost our maps and we ended up here...and, we don't know where 'here' is."

Although unconvinced of my sincerity, but no doubt confident that I could do no harm the couple must have decided they could leave my presence quicker if they just gave me my answers. The man spoke first, responding, "Erfurt. Germany."

When that didn't ring any bells with the three of us, the woman spoke up, "Birthplace of Bach? Where Martin Luther studied at University? The cathedrals — the gardens — the historical houses? Right here — " she raised her hands, as if to present the area around us, "the Fischmarkt?"

"Right," I feigned clarity, "Erfurt. Uh, one more thing, I wonder... um, what is the date?" Proactively, I tried to explain before arising suspicion again, "We haven't seen a newspaper or anything in a while. You know, lost track of time, too..."

The man stared at me a while, then simply stated, "It's May 25." He stared at me briefly, as he considered whether he was finished with us. "2000, he added with narrowed eyes. "In case you don't know the year." And with that, they walked away.

"Well, I have to say," began Tucker. "I think that went just splendid."

"Oh, hush," I snapped, "It's not like we're ever going to see them again."

Nora giggled, and added, "Yeah, they're going to go back to the states and say, 'Our trip was great, except getting accosted by this crazy American idiot-girl.'"

"*Anywho*...Erfurt, Germany. 2000." I looked to the others, who shrugged. "It's cute. You two should honeymoon here. Now let's keep our eyes peeled and move on."

With my mind set with pure determination on William's face, I cut through the crowd. They were all there for the history or the scenery, and I could easily see how this would be a destination worth visiting. We were invading their vacations, though, by dropping in unannounced and chasing through their streets, searching for a hero, yet prepared to meet the villain. I looked back appreciatively at Tucker and Nora. They took the chance to believe against all logic and join me in the crusade to find the man behind the journal, and they stood by me now in the middle of a foreign country with possible danger right around the corner.

Rather than act on the sappy moment that rose up within me, I forced the feelings downward and turned back to the path ahead, where I envisioned William to be.

"Hey Rynn, how many times did you turn the key?"

I stopped so abruptly that they nearly rear-ended me. Turning on the spot, I tried to remember. My hands found the outline of the key where it dangled under my shirt. "Twice," I said confidently. "We should have around an hour, give or take — I've never been able to accurately judge the time on these trips. About how long do you think we've been here already?" Having spent this much time looking for William with no success, I became flustered with the thought of wasting another second standing still.

I had already turned back around and picked up the pace when I heard Tucker's answer to my question, "Maybe 10 or 15 minutes?" It didn't even matter. We had to keep moving and find him.

Before long we had circled the entire area the friendly tourist referred to as "The Fischmarkt." I spun a few times and rested with my hands nervously combing through my hair and staring out at the faces passing by.

Nora stepped up and spoke softly in my ear, "Rynn, maybe they're doing the same thing as we are — and we're just chasing each other in circles. Should we stay put and watch from one spot and maybe eventually they'll pass by?"

"I don't think 'they' will be together. Judging by my last encounter, they aren't exactly a team. But regardless, maybe you're right. I could see Pearl being the type to just watch and wait until we land in her trap, but," before I spoke, I realized how much I hoped my next statement was true, "I think William would be looking for me..." He *would* be looking for me. Was I wrong to think he needed to find me as much as I needed to find him?

As if she knew where I had gone in my head, Nora brought me back, confirming, "Yes — he will. He is. Let's stay put right here and I think we'll have a better chance of seeing him."

To confirm his agreement, Tucker half-sang, half-hummed The Police's "Every Breath You Take."

I didn't know if they were right, and it felt counter-productive to be sitting still instead of out there and looking, but I let them talk me into it anyway.

"What does he look like?" Tucker asked. "Nora and I can at least target our search if we know, like if he's fat and bald or something."

Barely able to crack a smile at his unfailing ability to lighten the mood, I sat myself down next to Tucker and fixed my eyes on the crowds passing in front of us. I recalled the face I unknowingly saw for the first time at the Knicks basketball game. It wasn't even a possibility back then to think the arguing couple was anything more than just that. Like a hypnotic trance, images flew through my mind's eye of all the places I'd been since embarking on this experience. Here and there, William's now-familiar smile, interrupted by Pearl's chilled, self-satisfied grin flashed intermittently. Holding onto the time spent dancing on Miami Beach, and the agonizing near-death nightmare in the icy tundra, where he became my true hero, I thought carefully on how to describe the man I thought I was here to save, but now questioned if it wasn't him sent to save me.

With a deep breath, I spoke slowly and carefully to them. "He's as tall as you, Tucker, maybe a little taller. Dark hair, brownish —

although my hair has been fixed differently according to the various times and places I've traveled to."

I thought of the sweeping bun with tendrils of Miami Beach, and the 90's cut I sported at Madison Square Garden. "But it's 2000, right? A fitting haircut for this year isn't going to be all that different..." I leaned back to take in Tucker's hair for the first time since arriving. It was a pretty clean-cut 'do, a little boxy and understated compared to hipster haircuts of norm these days, but nothing drastic.

Noticing the two of them staring at me again while I sorted through my own thoughts, I quickly continued. "Anyway, it's probably cut short, like Tucker's now? Um, he has dark eyes, like deep blue, with..." I found it embarrassing to describe him like this. I knew he was handsome, but with each detail I recalled, my stomach ached with longing to see his face again, to be close to him, to feel his reassuring presence. With a sigh, I continued, "...with dark eyelashes." I could feel Nora and Tucker exchange a look behind my back, which was absolutely no help at all.

"I doubt he'll be smiling when we see him right now, but, his smile..." I pictured him sitting across from me at the small town barbeque, hiding all the knowledge that I was seeking, smiling at me as if he had just been waiting for me to pop in, yet his eyes still searched for meaning in my existence there in that moment. A contradiction, it would seem, but in my opinion it was his way of showing a conservative interest in the possibility that I could, in fact, be what he had been looking for all those years. I would imagine he had spent far too long being hopeful, though, to be anything less than speculative of these new possibilities. His smile had melted me, though, and perhaps it was the hope I saw in his eyes that made his grin so endearing.

"Where'd you go?" Nora interrupted my thoughts.

"Sorry, uh, never mind about his smile — you'll see for yourself. I hope."

"So he's a 10?" Tucker said, as he grabbed my shoulder and gave it a squeeze.

I hung my head sheepishly, knowing I had given away too much of my feelings. I knew those emotions were there, but I didn't intend to wear them all on my sleeve.

"Okay, just shut up and keep your eyes open for the man of my dreams, alright?"

"Done," he agreed.

For the next several minutes, the two of them would occasionally point out possible men that fit my description, but none were him. I sat, elbows on my knees and chin resting in my hands, with my legs nervously bouncing and bumping my face up and down. I've had the bad habit of fidgeting since I was a kid, and it typically gets worse when I'm tired or nervous. With each passing minute, my fidgeting worsened, until the chime from a nearby bell tower jolted me right out of my seat and sent me pacing.

"Rynn," Nora's voice had the tone of reasoning. "You've had how many trips now, where you didn't see either one of them? It's not a guarantee that you'll find him every time, right? I don't doubt they're here, but...so are all these people. I'm sure he's looking for you, too, but he's probably just looking somewhere else. Do you want to try another area, or maybe go into some of the shops or museums?"

Although there was truth to what she was saying, there was no right answer. I could and probably would cover the entire area in and out, and still be unlikely to find him. I was starting to resent the randomness of the damned places I found myself visiting while on these music box travels. One minute I'm all alone in the frozen wilderness, the next I'm in the middle of a crowd. I had no way of knowing how far apart we could have been when we landed, and it was completely within reason that we each could have been putting more distance between us with each step intended to find each other.

Knowing I was becoming defeated, Tucker made a suggestion. "Look, we're in this great place, and probably only for another 20 minutes or less. You know how they say you find things when you're not looking? Let's go enjoy the sights that we may never see again — like we actually came here with that purpose! Who knows, you may run into him, but if not, then at least we can say we didn't waste the trip sitting around."

Again, there was truth to what he said, and I was more than reluctant to agree that I should move my focus to enjoying the scenery as opposed to finding William, but I threw my hands up and shrugged. What else was I going to do? I didn't want to act like a brat, especially because they were here because of me, and they were only trying to help, but I had a hard time believing I would enjoy any single minute of this unless William was spotted. Being a team player, though, I agreed. "Lead the way," I gave in.

They rose from their seats and took each other's hand with an unsure smile, knowing I was agreeing less than enthusiastically to go with Tucker's plan. I fell in line behind them, watching as they strolled casually down the streets, talking quietly about the sights I was ignoring. We ventured beyond the market area and up roads leading to higher grounds. Unsure of how much time we had left, the idea must have been to just take it easy until we were pulled back to my living room. Eventually the path wound back around to overlook the Fischmarkt. Admittedly, the view was one I wished I could have fully appreciated just as Nora and Tucker were, but with my one eye on the expanse of elaborate and unique buildings below, the other was still scanning faces.

Sadly, in a matter of minutes, the three of us were back in the present day, looking at the Chinese food leftovers and the music box on the living room table. Without speaking, I tucked the key under my shirt, and walked to my bedroom and closed the door. We would all be in helpless slumber in minutes, and I didn't feel the need to chit chat before letting sleep take me away from my disappointment. I heard Tucker and Nora's voices as they moved toward my guest bedroom, and I hoped that they would be gone in the morning before I woke up.

SEVENTEEN

SITTIN' ON THE DOCK OF THE BAY

For the first time in my teaching career, May came to a close with very little anticipation or excitement. Summer brought idle time and little hope of making it through the month's wait until the next turn of the key. Whereas the previous month was bearable due to my dedication to keeping myself involved and busy, I questioned whether I had it in me to do it all again with yet even more time on my hands. Before, I had the spark of having just spent real, honest-to-goodness time with William, rather than the currently fading remnants of the memory to hold me over.

I should have been absolutely euphoric with the feeling of summer. I should have been pouring over books. I should have been spending carefree days shopping. I should have been laying out in my backyard where I could get some sun without anyone actually seeing me in a swimsuit. I should have been, but I wasn't. I was in my pj's indefinitely, most days, with crap on TV around the clock and Lean Cuisine's piled in my freezer for dinner. Nora called often, knowing the mindset I was in. She offered to come over, invited me out with her and Tucker, and enticed me with girls nights out, but I found reasons to decline every time. Dissatisfied with my lack of enthusiasm over the phone, she dropped by unannounced occasionally to urge me out of my funk, however, I was unshakeable.

After two solid weeks of boredom and frustration, Nora showed up on my doorstep and barged right in.

"Where's the journal?" she demanded.

I clutched the key around my neck, fearful she was going to take away everything to do with the music box.

Nora walked around the house, flipping on light switches and turning off the TV, stomping into the kitchen and cleaning up my dishes left in the sink from who knows how long ago.

"Go get the journal, Rynn. I'm not taking it from you, I want you to read it."

Confused, I stood for a while behind her, waiting for her to explain. She took over doing my dishes, which probably wasn't intended to make me feel guilty, but was indirectly the result. All of a sudden, she whipped around, sending soap from the sponge flying toward me. "The journal. Now."

"Why, Nora? I've read it cover to cover so many times already, I —"

"I've read it too, Rynn. Go get it. Please?"

Obediently, I fetched the journal from its most recent spot on my mantle and brought it into the kitchen. Nora dried her hands, started the dishwasher, and turned around to lean on my butcher-block island.

"What's in it, Rynn?" she asked what sounded like a rhetorical question, but I had a feeling she really wanted answers.

If I hadn't been so taken off-guard by her showing up and banging around and barking orders, I might have put up some crossed-arms attitude, but my only response was to blink stupidly at her. She nudged the journal toward me and opened it, shrugging as if she was still waiting for me to say something.

I scanned and reread a few of William's entries, even though most were so familiar I knew them by heart. After seeing the entry detailing our chance meeting back when I was in college, I snapped the journal shut and cut my eyes at Nora. What was she after?

She drew in a full breath, and I braced for the worst. "Day in day out, year after year, Rynn. He was forced to wait, never knowing if the answer was out there or not, but still trusting in it despite the odds. So who the hell are you to go bumming around, depressed because you didn't see him immediately again and now you have to wait *one fucking month*? It's not just about *you,* Rynn. He's been dealing with this for how many years now? You're insulting him by acting like this." She crossed her arms, satisfied that her point was made. "He's looking for you, even if it takes a few tries. You've just got to trust that."

Allowing myself a moment to process, I slumped down on the island. I hated when she was right, but it was a damn good thing she made a habit of it, because otherwise I don't know where I'd end up. Shouldn't the younger sister be the one in need of big-sisterly advice? What a crap job I'd done fulfilling *that* role.

The journal was closed and resting under my arm, and I rose up to take another look at it. The time span was several hundred years — I had known that. He had documented everything that could lead him to answers, not knowing when those answers might come, or even if they would — I had known that, too. This journal was his lifeline, until it was lost, and therefore terminating his only means of continuing his story. He could never have known the journal would have found such a captive audience in me, and my disappointment in the abrupt stop in the entries was countered by the indebted awareness that had it not been for him losing the journal, I never would have put all of it together in order to find him. My life would have moved on, for better or for worse, without the slightest inkling that William had ever even existed.

I brought myself upright again and stared at my loving sister. She was waiting patiently, although with arms crossed and an apprehensive affect.

"Nora, do you think..." I wasn't sure of how to word my question.

I wasn't even sure of the question itself. "Do you think I'm the answer he was looking for?" I hesitated before continuing, "Or am I just the poor schmuck that came along and got all wrapped up in it, thinking I was?"

She leaned back on the counter behind her, gently crossing her arms as she thought. "I don't know." She looked at me for a moment, as if searching my face for hidden confirmation of my question. "I don't know, and I doubt he does either." That wasn't what I was hoping for, but it was what I expected. "But...I guess that's what I'm trying to say. What I'm trying to show you. It all comes down to trust, doesn't it? Think of the trust he's had to rely on, for centuries now. Put yourself in his shoes...what do you think his perspective is on all this now that *you've* entered the picture."

I had jumped blindly, throwing caution to the wind. I doubt, after a lifetime spent waiting, that he was as impulsive to think his prayers had been answered all of a sudden. In fact, I could go as far as assuming he might even be guarded and defensive, given how long it had been since the key had been lost.

I didn't have to speak my thoughts to Nora. She had watched me sort through the possibilities, concluding with a sigh, that she was once again...right.

"Perspective," I whispered, holding up the journal. "Just what I needed. You must get tired to bringing me back to reality, lately, huh?"

Smiling, she answered, "Can't say I blame you. You do happen to be in the middle of a mind-blowing problem." She walked around the island and grabbed me into a hug. As she held me close, she warned, "I know this is big. But that doesn't mean it's all you have. Let this unfold — you might be a willing participant, but you're not in control of it." She stepped back to gauge my response. "So in other words, get your head out of your ass and live your life — the one you have right now, that will pass you by *again* if you're not careful."

I nodded in resignation. "Let's go do something, I need to get out of the house."

AS THE END of June drew near, I tried like hell to keep an even disposition, but the mounting relief that I could once again pursue forward progress was too much to contain. The sky shined brighter, the flowers smelled sweeter, and life was good again. When the time came, I turned the key and eagerly waited to emerge.

It was India. It was a crowded street. It was another frustrating trip spent chasing in vain. I returned in what seemed like no time at all, and collapsed onto the couch, wondering if this was how it was going to be...and for how long.

July passed. I pushed through the fog of the music box and found myself at a golf resort, probably somewhere like Scottsdale, Arizona. No shit, I was completely outfitted in proper golf attire, with clubs waiting in my personal golf cart. I could see other patrons at faraway tee boxes and sand traps, but given the size of typical golf courses, I knew this would be another waste. After half an hour of driving around, I reentered my living room, disgusted.

With August, came the new school year, and thankfully something which to dedicate my time. The new group of students and schedules and paperwork dictated enough of my life that I happily realized one evening that my calendar showed the month's end already having arrived. Once again, I turned the key, hoping for the best, but unfortunately accustomed to set out on a misadventure that might very well lead me in circles yet again.

When my senses returned to function appropriately again, I was immediately hit with a swirling wall of wind. I was surrounded by it, forcing me to shake and wiggle, even feeling the need to clutch at my shirt, lest it pull a Marilyn Monroe and show my goods. I stepped out onto a ledge, taking in the rest of my location. Below were a few walkways, winding up to different industrial-looking buildings. Everything was gray, with cement walled structures and towers, concrete sidewalks lined with faded metal railings protecting the drop toward rocky cliffs below. Beyond the rocks, devastatingly powerful waves crashed. After spinning around and moving toward the other side of the ledge, I could see those waves seemed to surround my new location on all sides.

It was an island. The wind, the water, the gray buildings...I searched past the ocean and found land several miles away, and recognized the distinctive hills and streets of San Francisco. When I squinted, I could make out the Bay Bridge to the left, the Golden Gate Bridge on the right, and the sprawling city skyline right in the middle, which meant I was on Alcatraz Island. We had been there before, on a family vacation when Nora and I were younger. I had fond memories of that trip, and I had long since wanted to return to the city.

At least I could enjoy another visit to San Francisco, even if I didn't find William. I figured that was the best kind of attitude to adopt, anyway. The question was whether I should look for William here on the island, or if he may be on the ferry to the pier...or if he might even be back in the city, for all I knew. I took advantage of my current vantage point while I could, and looked down below at the crowds, scanning the tourists' faces, for the one I hadn't seen in too many months.

Families...couples...tour groups...the usual suspects. I circled around a few times, searching the farthest points my eyes could see, and watching people enter and exit from buildings, referring to their maps for their next stop. None of them were the face I was looking for.

I had to whip back to the rail, though, because suddenly and almost in disbelief, I saw him. He was there, walking toward me, but his eyes were set on the path in front of him.

Without thinking or hesitating, I called out to him. He heard me instantly, but it took him a few seconds to find my flailing arms waving to him. I couldn't believe it, and I dumbly let time pass as if at a standstill, just staring at him. Finally, he laughed under his breath and mimed to me to come down. I nodded, and turned away, heading for the doorway into the building.

I descended spiraling industrial staircases and wandered past offices, the library, cellblocks, and the cafeteria on the way out. It was a shame I couldn't slow down and appreciate all of this again, but it was a small price to pay in order to get to William. With the exit just ahead, I bolted for it, but was stopped short when someone stepped in front of me.

Startled, I blushed knowing I was being rude by running and breaking the National Park rules. "Sorry," I said as I moved out of the way, allowing the person room to pass through. Smug ice-blue eyes glared at me.

"You look like you're in a hurry," Pearl jabbed playfully. "What's your rush, I haven't seen you in so long!"

Sweet fuck-all, seriously? I crossed my arms in attempt to be intimidating while I ran through options in my head of how to get out of this. The more I tried to put off the air of confidence, the wider her smile grew. She knew my game, and she knew she'd busted me. Instincts kicked in, and I did all I could think of: run. Rather than trying to run past her, I turned and retraced my footsteps hoping to circle back through the rooms I'd just been in to find another exit or beat her back to this one. With one quick look back, I could see that she wasn't even chasing after me.

What the hell? It was unnerving enough to be merely in her presence, let alone to see that she doesn't even need to chase me when I run. What was she, omnipresent? Or had superpowers?

No. I wouldn't accept that she was any more special than I was. She simply knew what she was doing...and I, on the other hand, not so much. I confirmed this suspicion when I peeked around a corner with a view of the same door where I'd just met her. She was still there, cautiously eyeing all directions, both inside and out. My only chance would be to find another exit and a path around the back.

She hadn't seen me peek around the corner, so I snuck back out of view and up the stairs again, hoping William hadn't moved an inch. Once again I found myself in the powerful winds at the top of my former lookout, and I fought the force of the gusts to the rail where I had first spotted him.

With a huge sigh of relief, I saw him right were I'd left him. "William!" I shouted. "William! Up here!" I could barely hear myself over the noise of the wind. With everything I could muster, I yelled again, "William!"

He looked up again, raising his hands in the universal gesture of confusion. I pointed down towards the door. "She's there!" I hoped he understood, because it was so damn noisy I knew he wouldn't understand a verbal explanation of what I'd just been through with Pearl. Simultaneously as he glanced toward the doorway I'd indicated, he started moving in the opposite direction. I couldn't see a trail leading around the building, but William was moving stealthily as if he knew where he was going. When he was standing directly under me, he cupped his voice, voicing what I thought was "ferry."

I gave him a thumbs up, repeating, "The ferry?" and gestured in the direction I thought I remembered it being. He nodded and pointed the same direction. He wanted me to meet him at the ferry. I think. He didn't wait, but rather disappeared quickly out of sight and into the building under me. Oh, God. I had to find my way around Pearl and get to the ferry. If I could get down there fast enough, I could follow him.

Not a moment ago I was afraid I'd be in trouble for running, and now I was all out sprinting, with no regard for the poor tourists in my way. Two at a time, I bounded down the stairs and dodged families stopped at information posters. I had to hurry, not able to be sure of how much time I had left. The recreation yard didn't seem likely to have a way out, but I tried it anyway. The good news was, there was an open gate. The bad news, was that it lead right back to Pearl. I went back inside, and decided to play the role of lost tourist needing to make the next ferry. If I was lucky, I could either sneak through a different door, or hide behind the park ranger if we had to pass by Pearl.

Just as I was about to flag down someone, I saw the gift shop.

Surely the gift shop had it's own exit that didn't lead back to the prison cells. Jackpot. I exploded through the door and booked it down the jackknifing trails headed toward the dock. On my way down, I noticed all the exotic plants spilling over the retaining walls, with sweet little old ladies tending to them. I remembered those volunteers on my previous visit, and their warnings not to take any clippings or flowers from the park. Now one little volunteer gardener stared me down as I dripped with sweat tearing down the lane, smiling and shouting the only excuse I could think of: "Practicing for the triathlon!"

I looked back at the little lady I'd just blown by, and to my horror, saw that I was being followed. Pearl was at the top of the hill still a good distance back as I went through a tunnel halfway down, but now I had to find William at the bottom with her on my heels.

"Fucking hell!" came out of my mouth on its own accord. Racing around the Old Model T Alcatraz Firetruck on display, and curving around the crowds listening to a welcome speaker, I scanned the lines waiting for the ferry. It was a forever-winding line, roped off in sections, and I just hoped William was somewhere near the front and could see me coming.

Hating to slow down, I jumped the rope instead of using the entrance into the lines, hearing grumbles from people who had probably waited a good half-hour or longer to be in their current spots. I had bigger concerns than pissing of grumpy tourists, though. Pearl was closing in on me, and I couldn't see William anywhere. Surely I hadn't beaten him down here? I made my way to the front of the line and could feel the angry stares from people roped off to be next in line. Just as I was about to get chewed out, I heard him.

"Rynn!" He was waving me on from the loading ramp with one foot on the boat.

The attendant that stood between me and the other side of the rope looked at me with an apologetic expression. "Look," I said, "I got lost — and I — I'm gonna get left by my tour group — and — and then I'll miss my tour bus, and — "

"Well that's just too bad," spoke up a lady behind me. I ignored her, instead looking back to see that Pearl had reached the bottom of the hill and was weaving her own way through the grumbling people.

"Please," I pleaded. I looked up to William, who could tell I was having a hard time.

"Sir?" he yelled. "I'm sorry — she's with me. Please, could you let her on?"

"Please, please," I begged. He looked at me, and then to the lady, who was grinning with confidence that my ass was about to get ordered to the end of the line.

"Alright," he said as he unhooked the rope and let me through. "Go, go! They're about to board — hurry, or I'll be in trouble!"

I couldn't help but to look back and side-eye the fuming woman now on the other side of the rope. At the top of the ramp, William grabbed me and pulled me through the doorway of the ferry just as a blow horn sounded, interrupting background music of Otis Redding's "Sittin' on the Dock of the Bay," announcing that we were departing. A ferry attendant eyed me, knowing I had slipped on without permission, but he just shrugged, unconcerned. I stuck my head out to see Pearl, who was now alongside the poor line attendant who was now getting an earful from the very unhappy woman in line.

William's laugh behind me was a wonderful startling surprise. I turned to him, feeling a rush of emotions take over me. My hands reached up to hold his face, not sure if I was wanting to hug him or kiss him or cry into his chest with relief.

I didn't get a chance to decide, though, because he gently took my hands in his, giving them a comforting squeeze, and said, "Let's go sit."

I followed him up the stairs to the open air, where he sat and turned to me. He was smiling, but there was something guarded about him. It troubled me, but I tried to look past it. "How many turns?" was all he said.

"The key?" I asked. I couldn't even remember. "I usually turn it two or three times." I felt guilty that I didn't even remember. It had become such a disappointment to go in search of him every time and to have no luck, and I remember wanting to turn it more so I could have more time, but my promise to Nora that I wouldn't go overboard had actually kept me in check. "Yeah, just two or three."

"Let's hope it's three, or we're almost out of time." He was all business. I don't know what I expected, but I thought finding him would have been more...celebratory. I blinked hard. He was all business, and I was all party. Together, we made a mullet. I had to shake my head to get back to our conversation, this time with less...expectation.

"Pearl nearly caught me back there — I thought I'd slipped around her. I don't even know how she saw me. She — "

"Pearl?" he interrupted.

For the first time it occurred to me that 'Pearl' wasn't her real name. "Oh, we started calling her 'Pearl' after my friend Tucker saw her at the Janis Joplin concert. It was just..." Should I be feeling embarrassed?

"Your friend?"

"You know," I said, feeling a little pouty, "you said next time it would be *you* answering questions."

He smiled and nodded in agreement. My stomach hurt with the beauty in that smile. "I know. Sorry, you just seem to keep me on my toes, I'm still trying to figure out what's going on. So, can I ask about your friend? Do you mean it hasn't been you turning the key?"

"Oh, no — it has. Just one time my sister did, and she nearly got eaten by an alligator or crocodile or something, and then my friend Tucker did because he felt kind-of left out and scared because now he's my sister's boyfriend and he was worried about how she almost got eaten by that alligator or crocodile or whatever, and I'm rambling. Sorry."

He was trying not to laugh, which made his damn smile that much more irresistible. "So then, twice, it's been someone other than you?"

"Yeah. Okay, is it your turn now?" He waved his hand as if telling me to proceed with my questions. I had to gather myself for a minute, because all I wanted was time with him. I wanted enough time to appreciate how amazingly handsome he was, which I apparently couldn't do simultaneously as talking to him about his ordeal. I literally had to close my eyes in order to articulate my statement, although I could still see him and his windblown hair tousled around, his dark blue eyes, and obviously muscular build under his windbreaker. Simply put, I asked him, "Start from the beginning. The short version, I guess, since we may not have much time."

"Agreed. But tell me your name — your full name, I mean. I'm ill-equipped without at least knowing that."

"Well, Rynn is short for Corynn. So Rynn McKay. I'm a teacher — kindergarten. I'm from Texas, I don't remember if I told you that last time?"

"Alright, Rynn McKay from Texas. My story." He leaned back as if getting comfortable, putting an arm around the bench behind me and leaning a little closer so he could be heard over the wind. I tried my best to concentrate on his words, and not his appeal. "The short version is that Pearl's real name is Charlotte, and I used to work for her father on his farm on the island of Nantucket. She wanted...a relationship back then." He stopped to look at me, "Back then, meaning late 1700's." Satisfied that I hadn't been freaked out, he continued. "I was a farm hand, and courting the boss's daughter wasn't appropriate, and I didn't want to risk my job. I made that clear to her, which she didn't like. So, she had some voodoo doctor/medicine man curse the music box that you now have. She gave it to me, thinking it would curse me, but what she didn't know was that it cursed her as well."

"So what was the curse? Eternal life? That doesn't seem so bad."

He laughed as he looked deep into my eyes. When he spoke again, it was as though he was looking through me.

"The man you desire has denied you;

You wish him to regret.

Now you give this gift to him.

The effect you seek is set.
Turning the key will lead him astray,
For years he shall wander in vain.
Searching, for the one who'll end
This life that is now his bane.
So if he will not have you,
No one he will have.
Though, be warned, my lady, for you shall find:
a curse always has two halves."

I thought the wind had picked up again, so strong that it bent me over, but I soon knew I had run out of time with William. The last thing I felt from the ferry leaving Alcatraz was his hand reach out and clasp both of mine. With another comforting squeeze, he was gone again.

EIGHTEEN
OPEN ARMS

It was another two months before I was able to find William again.

Unfortunate, but thanks to Nora's previous intervention, I had come to realize it was not the end of the world. September's music box outing took me to a makeshift storm shelter in a Ft. Lauderdale airport in 1947. With a raging hurricane wreaking havoc above and around me, I chose to ride it out and just trust that I would live to turn the key another day. I had worried for William's safety, but our experiences together thus far resonated, reminding me that he had survived centuries of possibly worse conditions seemingly unscathed.

Autumn arrived, still looking and feeling more like summer in Texas as opposed to the nice changing colors of Fall that other states boasted. Even as much as I would have loved to live somewhere that truly experienced differentiation between seasons, for some reason the approach of Fall in Texas still leaves me giddy with seasonal excitement year after year. From October 1st until New Year's Day, my house undergoes its own changing of colors, from orange and black, to orange and brown, to green and red.

In the midst of the elated joy the onset of the holidays brings, I marveled at the way my life had been interrupted to such a degree that I had to physically work at keeping up with what used to be everyday life. I knew I had lost myself, but it was almost because of the fact that I had started to finally find myself again that I was able to recognize the loss in the first place. I acknowledged that I had slipped, and that Nora on more than one occasion had to reach down and pull me back up to reality, but for whatever reason I could feel a change drawing near. Subtle and gradual as the fall foliage turning, but as definitive as differences in each holiday of the holiday season, I anticipated what was to come with a peace in my mind and heart.

Some people have a time in their lives that pinpoints "before and after," and mine had happened as soon as I read the first journal entry. Life divided itself into two parts in that moment, and while I once worried that I would be debilitated by the waiting...the wondering...I was confident now that I would move forward each day, each month, willing to spend years if I had to in order to help William; it was my choice to do so. That choice did not, however, translate to letting myself fade into the background, but rather proceeding with my life and my plan, having been enriched by the possibilities and promises the music box offered to me and only me.

It was difficult to aptly describe the uprising conviction within me, but it was present nonetheless. In fact, it didn't matter if I could articulate to Nora or Tucker, or especially William about this long awaited balance, because that was precisely the point. Although I couldn't say it was all about me, when obviously William had more reason than anyone to that claim, I could say it wasn't *just* about him. I kept coming back to the simple premise that this all fell in my lap, not anyone else's. At that moment when I discovered the peculiarities of the journal, and the key fitting the music box...the moment when my life separated into the "before and after;" it was that moment when I could have tossed it all aside, unwilling to accept the full aspect of consequences that could have come from delving into the mystery, sending myself "Into the Mystic," like the song we danced to in Miami Beach.

Someone else may have — probably *would* have tossed it. I didn't.

I jumped in head first, and no matter how swept up in its' allure, in the end I had only been empowered by it and stood a stronger person today because of it.

So despite a fruitless visit to Ft. Lauderdale in September, I happily enjoyed the Fall season's resplendent buzz in the air just like every other year of my life. My house was whimsically decorated and the oversized candy bowl was ready at the door for neighborhood trick or treaters' visits in a few days. As I prepared mentally to turn the key, it was with less necessity this time around, and with more curiosity. What would this travel bring, if anything?

I gave it three turns and waited patiently for the pressure to lift again so I could go on my merry way. With a wonderful fulfilling breath, I took in my new surroundings; although the first thing I noticed was the dark night sky, noises and flashes of vibrant lights immediately trumped the darkness. I had never been to Times Square, but this was what I imagined it would be like: huge billboards reaching from the street to the sky, taxis and people darting every-where; only my vision of Times Square would have been in English. Here, large Japanese characters covered the street signs, the shop windows, and billboards. I had seen pictures of this place; it was Tokyo.

"The most heavily populated place in the world?" I asked to no one in particular. Passersby glanced briefly in my direction before deciding to ignore me and continue on. With low expectations for this trip, I quickly scanned the crowds. Until noticing that umbrellas obstructed most faces, I hadn't realized the mist present when I arrived had picked up to a fairly decent drizzle. Quickly, I ducked into what I would call a diner in America, to get out of the rain.

"Hey!" I looked up to see a man waving at me. I responded by pointing to myself, as if to ask, "Me?"

"Your friend — back here," he motioned to a doorway. What was he talking about? "American friend?" he asked. I nodded, unsure of what he meant and smiled stupidly as I pushed the door open. The room I now entered was dark, with a red glow of lamps and the smell of years' worth of cigarettes lingering. The man gestured for me to look at the ceiling, where speakers played Journey's "Open Arms." He smiled at me, as if the song choice were picked just for my benefit and he was clearly overjoyed about it.

I nodded appreciatively to him while I looked around. People were sitting in booths, and the man waved me back toward a guest that seemed to be talking his way out of his waitress's inquisitions. The guest waved her off politely and moved toward the edge of his seat in order to stand up, when his eyes locked on mine.

We shared a disbelieving chuckle, and he looked up at the waitress with an apologetic smile before moving back to the spot he was attempting to leave. When I reached the seat opposite him, the waitress seemed genuinely thrilled that not only was William staying, but that he also apparently brought a friend. When I found nothing in my pants pockets, which appeared to be some nice 1980's style slacks, I also had to mime politely to the waitress that I didn't need anything. Unable to suppress a laugh when I noticed William's spiked hair and linen Miami Vice suit, he looked down and replied with a shrug, "I've been through worse."

"I really didn't expect to be able to find you this time." I admit he flustered me, but I had adopted his "all business" approach to our... relationship. At least that's what I kept telling myself.

"Where are we? I've only seen the inside of this room."

"Tokyo, as far as I can tell, but I've never been here before, so it's just a guess."

"Tokyo," he pondered aloud. "Well, I'd buy you a drink, Rynn McKay from Texas, but I don't have anything to pay with." He smiled, somehow not on pins and needles to jump into the continuing story of his life and how I threaded myself into it. How did he do that? "So how much time do we have?"

"Uh, three turns, so a while still, since...since I found you so fast."

"Are you okay?" he asked, lowering his eyes to study my expression.

"Oh, yeah, I'm good. Uh, you know, just so many questions. I don't know where to start."

His eyes fell on the ribbon around my neck, and asked, "Is that where you keep the key?"

Clutching it through my shirt, I nodded.

With narrowing eyes, he pressed, "And it's safe there? I can't tell you how important it is — "

Not meaning to interrupt, but needing to assure him, I interjected, "Yes — yes! I'm a little *too* concerned about keeping it safe. I don't take it off. Ever. Except in the shower." Maybe I shouldn't have admitted that to him.

"Well, I appreciate your concern," he smiled. "I thought losing it once was going to be the end of it...I don't want to even consider..." he shook his head, as if dismissing the thought dismissed the possibility. "And the music box is safe?"

"It's safe. I mean, it's not locked away, or anything — I like seeing it out, since it was given to me by my grandmother...even though I know it's so much more than just a music box, it still represents her... and I've had it hidden away for too long already."

Either satisfied with my precautions or respectfully declining a thorough interrogation of my safety measures, he changed the subject. "Ok, so can I ask some questions this time?" Playfully scoffing at him, I crossed my arms unhappily. He raised his hands, defending, "I know, I know...I just have one, really, and then it's all yours." With a seriousness now, he asked one simple word, "Why?"

"Why? Why what?"

"Why are you here? Why are you putting yourself at risk when you couldn't have imagined what you were getting yourself into? Why did you believe in this?"

I wasn't sure I could verbalize my answers for him, and I took a long time considering where to start. With a sigh, I began, "I have a lot of good things in my life....my family, my job, my students...I couldn't have found a complaint if I'd have tried. I didn't necessarily feel like anything was missing, either — I was completely content.

Truly..." as I said it, I knew it was the truth. "But I was guarded and safe, to a fault, I guess. My perspective finally shifted when my mom brought me these things; my grandmother's things. A silly cardboard box that contained what I inherited when she died when I was a kid. It was something I couldn't face before then, because I was so close to her. It sounds dramatic, but I just chose not to go through that pain again. I had tried before, though. A few times I worked myself up to being strong enough to go ask my mom for that stupid box, but I never went through with it. I'd find an excuse and dive into something I could control, like school. So this time was different. I stayed strong and realized how absurd I'd been all those years." I blinked away the beginnings of tears. "The fact that I had done that, opened up the box, for the first time after so many years and so many times of trying...it was a good moment for me. And then I found the journal.

All of a sudden, rather than be concerned about how I would fare after dealing with old emotions of Grandma's death, I couldn't help but focus on the curious voice in the journal — your voice. Maybe it was something unintentional at the time, taking my mind off coping with reality by letting myself get carried away in your words...your confusion...your story. Either way, I just had to know more. I kept thinking I could help you, and so I read and reread, and then I found one particularly interesting entry. All that time I thought all this had landed coincidentally in my lap, sure to change *my* life. But then I read of a day that you...you met *me*."

Whether it was conscious or not, he had little by little inched toward me while I was talking, until my last words gave him a startle and snapped him upright. I could see him going through no telling how many memories, looking for the one where our paths had crossed before our official introduction. I had never expected him to remember me, it was too long ago and to top that off, he had been away from his journal for an even longer time, which was his only way of staying connected to his travels and the people he met along the way.

He eagerly moved forward once again, waiting for me to

continue. His flawless features, even with his ridiculously rad 80's hair, unexpectedly struck me again. It was hard to shake the stirrings in the pit of my stomach, so I closed my eyes to refocus. The journal entry. College. The South Mall. *Come on, Rynn.*

"I don't remember the date — *your* date, I mean. For me it was March of 2010. I was in college on a break between classes, and I was sitting on the grassy area we called The South Mall. You were there, and you asked to look at my newspaper..." Not sure if that was enough to jog his memory, I let him ponder for a while.

His hand rested over his mouth in a classic thoughtful position. His eyes were far away, deeper than the table they rested upon. The longer he stared, the more convinced I was that he didn't remember.

"I can...I can vaguely remember the setting. The problem is, I opened my eyes to so many strange and different and beautiful places..."

"I know," I assured him. "I haven't been at this nearly as long as you have, and...I can barely remember all the things I've seen. Hey, if it makes you feel any better, I didn't remember you either," I lied.

He smiled his crooked smile again. Damn crooked smile...the same smile that was to blame for the way I actually did remember that first encounter on The South Mall...with butterflies in my stomach from the cute guy that asked for my newspaper.

"Was that all? Were there other instances that we met and I might've forgotten?"

"No, not that I know of...but I guess there were several occasions that we have no way of knowing how close we could've been to meeting." Aww jeez, I was practically talking as if it was fate that brought us together. "You must have been close to my Grandma's house, though, because you left the journal on her property."

"That was your grandmother's property? I lost it in 1922 — my time. But I didn't know what year it was in the time we had traveled to. I wonder if it was it her property when we were there?"

"Who knows, if you don't know what year it was. All I know is, we found the journal there in the river pasture when we were kids."

He seemed to be keenly interested in this, although he didn't share why.

"Does that mean something?" I asked.

He shrugged and shook his head, answering, "Not sure, just brings up more questions, really, but we got sidetracked, I think. Before you mentioned the day I met you, you said you had thought it was all coincidentally happening to you...I had the feeling there was a 'but' coming after that. Did your outlook change?"

We were headed back to the lame fate talk again, but I figured I should be forthcoming with my thought process thus far. With a deep breath, I attempted again to explain my perspective. "You could say so, yes. I don't want you to think I was — or am — an 'it's all about me' kind of person. But before I was seeing the big picture, hell, before I even knew there *was* a big picture, I just thought it was really random. For example, the music box was part of my inheritance. It didn't work, we didn't know its history, it was just another 'treasure' my grandma had in her antique shop. It wasn't even necessarily one of my favorite items, so there wasn't much reason for me to have it. Random, right? And then, the journal. We found the journal on the day my grandma had her stroke, so obviously we completely forgot about anything else. She died not long after that, and we literally never thought about it again. But I must have tossed it in the box with the other inherited things — in fact, I didn't even know what it was when I first found it in there. So, that's also random.

And then, finding the key in the journal, reading your story and wondering why the hell you didn't know where you were...that was just weird. But to discover the key that was concealed in this odd journal that had been lost, or hidden, stuck between a rock and a tree for decades actually fits the music box? I'm sorry, but that's just crazy. Random wasn't even accurate anymore. So yes, I thought it must be more than that — like there was a reason for it, a purpose. Maybe it was selfish, but, for the moment, I assumed it was about me. I knew I wanted to help you, but I also thought there was something I needed to gain from the experience."

He waited to see if I was finished, and when satisfied that I was, he responded with, "But?" I still hadn't adequately answered. He wasn't being rude or abrupt; in fact everything about him was engrossed in what I had to say. He genuinely wanted to know more.

I felt like it had taken me a long time to get back to the point of what he was asking, and now that I was there again, my cheeks flushed at how idiotic I sounded. "But," I continued, "when I saw myself in your journal, and knew the music box had brought you so close to me on at least that occasion, I began to believe I really could help you find what you were looking for, and that had to be why all this had so 'coincidentally' landed in my lap."

"So your official stance on the situation is..." he joked.

"My official position is that it's not about me, it's about you. I know that, now that I've seen the bigger picture, and especially after learning more of your life and story. It's about you. But I believe...or at least I want to believe, that I can help you. That's where I fit into this. That's why all the randomness chaotically aligned and pointed at me."

Silence followed my words. He was pensive again, but I wasn't at all concerned that I had done the wrong thing by letting the free flow release. Only mere seconds passed, before he posed his next question.

"What if it's not all about me?"

I laughed under my breath. "No? Who else then, Pearl — sorry, Charlotte?"

"Searching, for the one who'll end this life that is now his bane."

"Yeah...I'm going to help you find 'the one.'" He looked at me curiously. "What, do you know who it is?" He shook his head. "But you have theories?"

"I've been considering a theory, yes."

"Well, I just poured my heart out expressing an obsession with finding a way to help you, so...now would be a good time to share." Why was he holding back?

I could tell he was feeling the heat from being put on the spot, but I'd spent the last few minutes in that spot and was happy to be free of it. "Do you remember when I first saw you at the picnic? You sat down across from me and — "

"— of course," I interrupted. It was doubtful I would ever forget that moment.

"I saw you and knew you were the one I'd spent the evening with in Miami. Do you remember what I said?" I nodded. "I said, 'I wanted it to be you.' I was absolutely elated not only to have finally found out who had been turning the key, but beyond that, I..." He met my eyes as if gathering strength from them, and said, "I spent every day after that night in Miami wishing I had just abandoned the damned anchor I carry because of this curse.

You lowered my guard. I awoke the next day angry for the first time. Trust me, I've been downright furious with Charlotte, with the curse, with the world...but I deal with it. But I'd never felt like I'd missed an opportunity, and that morning I did. I knew nothing could have changed the fact that even if I'd talked to you for hours about my life and the curse on that night at the wedding, nothing would have changed the fate I succumb to every single time — I would have still been pulled into the black hole that leads me back to my own house and my own life, maybe just a memory to you or maybe wiped away as if I had never been there. But for the first time, I wished I'd just told someone — and maybe, just maybe, if it was you I had told, maybe I could have been lucky for once. Maybe it could have been you that I'd been searching for. You that may have been 'the one' the curse promised was out there."

I couldn't believe what I was hearing. If he would have just said something that night...

"When I saw you again at the picnic, I couldn't believe my fortune. I was jumping out of my skin, knowing I had found the person that now held the key, and it was you. It was you that I had thought of for days after that night in Miami, until I thought I had forced your memory out of my mind for my own sanity's sake. But I saw you, and I knew there was a reason you had been brought into my path. So Rynn, you've convinced yourself that it's all about me, but...I, on the other hand think it's all about you. I think that I spent over a century actively looking for you, and even longer waiting, unable to turn the key after it was lost...waiting and praying for *you* to find me."

More than stunned, I didn't want to speak for fear of fucking up the perfection of what had just transpired. Although I was struggling to make sense of his words, my dumbfounded blinking must have made him uncomfortable. "I'm sorry, was that too forward? I, I only wanted to be honest — "

"No!" I declared a little too excitedly. I reached across the table to take his hands reassuringly. "I'm still processing, that's all."

He flipped his hands to hold mine now. "Why don't we go for a walk? No sense in spending the whole time in here, don't you think?"

"Sure, it was raining, though..."

Grinning, he responded, "Sounds perfect."

The rain hadn't picked up any more than before I had ducked into the diner, but it had kept steady enough to soak the streets. We dodged puddles and our clothes became quickly saturated after only walking a single block.

I considered making a stab at small talk, but how does one move the conversation from curses and destinies to say, the weather?

"What if you're wrong? What if it's not me?" I was already feeling a dizzying responsibility. "Where do we go from here?"

He stopped walking and took my hand. As I turned to face him, looking up into his unconcerned face, I could see that he clearly didn't share my doubts. "It's well within reason that I could be wrong. And I'm going to go home and think long and hard about all that you've told me today...but I want to be right. It's hard to describe, but I've heard the words of the curse over and over in my head for centuries now. I've interpreted them dozens of different ways, but there's one analysis that I keep coming back to."

He took my other hand as he spoke. "Paraphrasing, I believe that Charlotte's plan was to take away what I took from her, which was in her eyes, the chance to be loved. I know she didn't love me. If anything it was lust, and most likely it was just romantic feelings that were heightened by my denial. But the line, 'So if he will not have you, no one he will have,' seems pretty clear to me. If I wouldn't have her, then I wouldn't have anyone.

Also, though, 'Turning the key will lead him astray, for years he shall wander in vain.' I did that. I turned the key, and for years it did lead me astray. Even when it took me to you, I still didn't know it because there was no way of knowing who and where and when I might find 'the one.' It was smoke and mirrors, in a way. Just enough confusion that I came face to face with you and never knew it until you told me tonight. So, though it alludes to there being someone that can end the curse, it never did lead me to them."

Maybe I was dense, but he seemed to be talking in circles. "Don't you see?" he continued, "*I* didn't find you. It didn't lead me to you, just as the curse says. The thing is, that last part, that says, 'Though, be warned, my lady, for you shall find: a curse always has two halves.' This was something Charlotte hadn't anticipated, and this is where I really start to speculate, but I think this line is in a way, a disclaimer. Charlotte was cursed to the same extent that I was. Because of her vindictiveness, she did this to herself. And I don't know for sure, but I have wondered if she didn't have something to do with the music box ending up so close to where we left the key."

"Okay, William, I was pretty lost before, but now that you've started 'speculating,' I'm gonna need you to break it down a little more."

Nearby was a park, and William pulled me by the hand to a bench. It was still raining, but we were so heavily involved in our conversation that it hadn't bothered us a bit. I sat with crisscrossed legs, sideways so my full body and attention could face William. With one arm outstretched over the back of the bench, and resting his hand on my shoulder, he asked me, "Do you know anything about how your grandmother acquired the music box?"

NINETEEN

I MELT WITH YOU

We did know a little bit about how the music box came to be in Grandma's shop, but I hadn't thought about it since the night Tucker had called my mom to inquire about it. The details only returned to me as I prepared to recount what we knew.

"Oh my God, William." I stared wide-eyed at him, disbelieving what I had overlooked. "She and my Grandpa would travel all over, looking for what she called 'treasures.' The diamond in the rough, you know? Another man's trash sort-of idea. They had an eye for it — they would have things shipped home, and it would look like crap! Then they would clean it up or make repairs and sell it for two or three times what they paid." I remembered thinking of the shop as more of a museum than a store, but they did actually do very well because of their keen eye and quick fixes. "So, my mom said they got the music box on a trip to Nantucket! She said my Grandma had struck up a conversation with some woman that was noteworthy because of her striking beauty...they talked about Grandma being from Texas, and the woman said she'd been there. When Grandma told her she owned an antique shop, the lady insisted on going home to get something for her to take back with her. She came back with the music box, and my Grandma fell in love with it..." I had forgotten that my mom said Grandma considered it one of her most favorite pieces. "My Grandma always believed there was a story behind every mirror, within every desk drawer, and the music box was no different." I smiled. "She was right."

William looked off in the distance briefly, then said, "It was 1962."

"What was 1962?"

"When your Grandmother visited Nantucket. It had to have been. After we lost the key, the music box was useless. It just sat there, reminding me that I would be stranded in my own life forever...It sat in my house for 40 years, until one day it was just gone. My first thought was that Charlotte had somehow found the key and was retrieving the music box in order to start up the traveling again, but I waited and waited to be pulled out of my daily life and into another land...but it never happened."

"Hold on," I interrupted. "Why would Charlotte want to turn the key? What would *she* have to gain?"

He stood and paced in front of our bench. "I'm still just guessing here, and please don't think I'm conceited or anything because of it, but...Charlotte had moved away from her parents' farm, which was passed on to me. She would return occasionally, but I think she became a bit of a Nomad. Because we never aged, we couldn't get close to anyone. I would see occasional evidence of her presence for months or even years at the little cottage I once lived in on the farm, but I had moved into her parents' house by then, and I was keen to avoid her. So, the only time we were ever in each other's presence was when I turned the key. From the very beginning she would try to capitalize on our situation of being whisked away as if it were romantic or something. It never changed. Every single time, when she could find me, she took her chances and tried to win me over. Then the music box was gone, and I didn't see her except when I would notice life at the old house. Anyway, when the music box was gone that day, it was when she was back on the farm in the sixties.

Like I said, I thought maybe she had found the key and was planning to use the traveling to her advantage again. But that never happened."

So much to process. "I don't think you're conceited for thinking that — she's mad, obviously — there's no telling what goes on in her mind." He raised his eyebrows as if to say he agreed, and I probably didn't know the half of it. "Why would she give it to my Grandma, though?"

"Well," he started, "you said they had talked about Texas? I'm thinking as soon as your Grandma mentioned that, Charlotte's ears were perked. She's sharp. I promise, she'd probably held onto every detail of the day we lost the key and my journal; she had walked around that whole area, and I remember her mentioning there being a town below the hill. If your Grandma described anything like that area, and then told her she owned an antique shop...Charlotte basically hit the jackpot. In her mind, it was her only chance of joining the journal and the key again."

"Yeah, but why not just ask my Grandma the name of the town, and then hop on a plane and get the journal and key herself?" It seemed like such a long shot to send the music box with a perfect stranger.

"You said you found the journal between a rock and a tree? It must have slipped off the rock when I tried to grab it, which kept it just out of sight for all those years. Who would have imagined it would still be there in that same spot where we left it? Even she would have assumed it to be found by someone, and I'm sure she was betting on that person being either your Grandma or someone in her family. She was right, actually, she was just off by a few decades."

My eyes glossed over as a trance-like revelation came over me. "The shop was called 'Doyle's,' their last name. Still is, actually, but my mom took over. It's right down the hill from the entrance to Grandma's land where you left the journal. The road to Grandma's house had a gate that was never closed, but there was a cute little sign on it. 'The Doyle's.' If Charlotte had seen that, she would have known immediately that my Grandma was that Doyle." I shook my head. "Unbelievable."

He came to sit next to me again, and chuckled, "You get used to it."

We had been talking for close to an hour by then, and still had some time left by my estimate, but I knew I had so many more questions that would go unanswered when we ran out of time.

"So, when you said Charlotte had cursed herself...I think I'm finally catching on. Are you trying to say that all of her efforts to curse you have actually worked to your advantage? She sent the music box with my Grandma, hoping that it would bring the two of you together again through these excursions, but...but really she just delivered it right to me," I hopped up, feeling the excitement of the proclamation I was about to make. "She sealed her fate — " I looked at him, pointing, "actually, she sealed yours. And mine. The music box is mine now...and so I'm...I *am* 'the one,' aren't I?"

I wanted to do an end-zone dance right there, and William's smile indicated that it would be okay if I decided to, but I thought twice about it and returned to the bench instead. Turning serious once again, I asked him, "What does this mean?"

"It means we've covered a lot of ground today and will have much to think about when we return to our homes." He gently pushed a strand of hair out of my face, as he looked to the sky. "It stopped raining."

"Mm-hmm." He probably didn't want to start yet another serious conversation without adequate time.

"You really want to hear another theory?"

"Yes! I don't want to waste a single minute — next time I might not find you so quickly, or at all!"

He sighed, and asked me a question rather than answering mine. "Before all of this, before you found me, and all you had was my journal...what did you think? What were your theories on what I was looking for?"

I thought back to the days I would sit and happily read his journal, pondering these questions for myself. What was he looking for? What was so powerful that it would keep him going all that time?

"Well," I started sheepishly, "I remember thinking it had to be one of two things."

"And?"

"Love. Or answers."

Just then a car stopped at a stoplight in front of us on the street, radio booming. Perturbed with the interruption of such a critical moment in our discussion, I closed my eyes until the light turned green and allowed the car to move on and out of earshot. While I waited, I searched within my own musical memory stores for a words to replace the noise that I feared might get stuck in my head. "I'll stop the world and melt with you" surfaced for some reason, although appropriate for the current circumstance. I hummed along as the car's music faded into the distance.

"Are you singing?" noticed William.

"Sorry," I blushed.

"What are you singing?"

"No," I swatted his question as if it were an annoying fly. "Bad habit. Anyway, I answered your question. Now it's your turn."

"Okay, fair enough. Love and answers. Those are roughly the same possibilities I come up with as well." He leaned closer to me, pretending to examine my face for something I may have been hiding. "And I guess we'll have to wait and see which you possess."

I was suddenly parched, and he could tell I had been struck speechless. Poking fun, he added, "Hey, you wanted to know! Now, I really think we're running out of time. Do me a favor?" I shrugged, wondering what favor he could possibly need at that particular moment. "What were you singing?"

I cut my eyes at him. "I don't sing."

"Ah, but you *were* singing. I heard you."

"No, that was an accident. I was just trying to get the radio noise out of my head. And it was humming, which is *not* singing."

Not taking no for an answer, he stood up and held out his hand, saying, "I'm in the mood for another dance. But," he twirled around, bringing my attention to the area around us, "we don't seem to have any music."

"You can't be serious." I stared at his hand, feeling the heat rise to the surface of my skin all over my body.

He reached down and grabbed my hands, pulling me up to meet him. "Come on...please? At least tell me what it was, maybe I know it."

I buried my face in his chest. That was a mistake, because if I was already feeling nauseous because of what he was asking of me, I then became weak in the knees at the musculature I could feel against my forehead. Good grief, not only was he too handsome to look at for prolonged periods of time, but he was built, too. I squeezed my eyes tight and concentrated on not vomiting.

"Hey," he prodded. "Okay, don't sing — just tell me what song is in your head."

I looked up at him as he released my hands and wrapped his arms around my waist. "I always have a song in my head," I told him. "It's just the way my mind works."

"I like that. So what's the song in your head now?"

"Modern English," I sighed. "'I Melt With You.' And I swear if you ask me to sing again, I'll junk punch you."

He knew I was serious, as he looked down at me, shaking from his poor attempt at controlling his laughter. "I know the song. Calm down. How about this? You can have the song in your head, and I can have it in my head. No singing necessary, we can just dance to our own drum, so to speak?"

My sigh indicated my consent.

"I think I only know the chorus, I hope that doesn't throw off our steps," he teased.

"Ha ha," I mocked. "Let's just sway like a middle school dance. I don't think you can really mess up those moves."

He barked a laugh, turning his head as if covering up a cough. "I never had the luxury of that awkward experience." His smile faded and he became serious once again. "You know, I think I *would* stop the world and melt with you, if I could. It's almost true, those words: the world as we know it stops when we turn the key, and we melt together, wherever we are."

I froze. He swept down to meet me, our lips close enough to feel the breath between us. His hand left my waist and moved to support my head, as he pulled me toward him. It wasn't electric, like the last times. It was waves crashing upon rocks. It was skydiving. It was the anti-gravity ride at the fair. It was an intensity I'd ever experienced, and the only thought in my head became the plea that the music box didn't take me at that moment.

Tokyo faded, but thank God not because time ran out. The smell of wet pavement, the wetness in the air, the blinking lights and honking horns disappeared and there was only us. And because it was only us, I pushed him backward to the bench, pinning him down as I sat atop his lap. He startled, pulling his head back a bit to see if I had really just done that.

His surprise melted into desire. One hand reached around my waist and the other tugged at my neck, compressing the space between us. A breathy groan came from him, and I wanted to seize it from the air around his mouth. The scruff of his chin found a path to my neck, pushing my head back for more purchase. My hands tangled in his hair.

He gently pulled at the collar of my shirt, exposing the hollow of my collarbone. His lips ran the length of it, to my shoulder as he inched my shirt farther, farther. My flesh was white hot.

In my ear, he confessed, "You were worth waiting for."

DON'T CRY because it is over, smile because it happened. In a way, that became my new mantra. I returned to my happy home with the anticipation of Halloween in a few days, and uplifted spirits from the scintillating memory of Tokyo. Without a doubt, I was more than ready for the next opportunity to turn they key, but when I felt myself slip into an overly anxious mood, I reminded myself to smile because it happened.

Nora and Tucker had always spent Halloween night at my house helping pass out candy, and I was in high spirits knowing this year would be no different. The three of us enjoyed cooking an early dinner together, both of them listening avidly to my delivery of information I received from William in Tokyo. Tucker took every opportunity to roll his eyes at the mushy parts I divulged, which weren't nearly as many as I kept to myself.

"Holy shit, you told him you were going to junk punch him?" Tucker spouted. "I thought you liked the guy." He looked squarely at Nora and asked, "You wouldn't junk punch *me*, would you?"

She threw her hands in the air and complained, "How about we *not* discuss anyone's junk, alright?"

I had to agree, and held up my glass as confirmation. It was nice to have this normalcy of everyday life to spend with them, even if normal for us did mean unveiling a centuries-old curse, fulfilling its prophecy, and concluding that it was me who might end said curse for a nearly 250 year old man I had a major thing for.

As we sat down to the table with a spread of steak, potatoes and salad, Nora spoke aloud, repeating words from near the end of my story, "Love and answers. So that's where we're at right now?"

Savoring a bite before answering, I then replied, "That's my guess based on what I had already assumed from the very beginning of my involvement. He said that was his guess as well, but his theory is probably stemming from hearing the curse ring in his ears for hundreds of years."

Tucker spoke up to ask, "And what exactly does the curse say?"

I had to paraphrase, not able to recall every word. "Basically that if William wouldn't have Charlotte, then he wouldn't have anyone. And, the music box would lead him astray — for years he would wander in vain...something about looking for the one to end his bane.

Then the last part was about Charlotte: a warning that a curse always has two halves.

So William is probably thinking that if Charlotte's purpose was to curse him in love — to ensure that he never would have what he had denied her, then that must be exactly what 'the one' might offer. Or at least that's the most likely option, since I obviously don't have any other answers."

"Rynn," came Nora's mothering voice. I knew what was coming. "You just seem so casual about all this. I know you're...a little head over heals for this guy, and for the excitement and the adventure. But I don't want you to accept all of it without giving it long and hard consideration."

"Nora, I know you're trying to protect me, but — "

"Damn right, I'm trying to protect you! Have you forgotten that Pearl — or Charlotte, whoever she is, tried to drown you? That's just ONE aspect of this. And what about the fact that she, and William both are apparently...immortal? They've been alive for centuries, Rynn! How exactly does that work out, if the two of you really hit if off? Growing old together usually applies to both people." She knew she'd lost her cool, and tried to recover before irreparable damage. "I'm just saying, what now, Rynn? Really, what now? You need to do more talking and less slow dancing, so you can maybe work on the answers part. Before it's too late, I mean."

I processed her accusations for a few minutes, all of which were valid and had received hours on end of my own review in the past days. The truth was, I left off where William and I had: Love and answers...we'll have to see which one I possess. In my opinion, it could be one or it could be the other, but I hoped it could be both.

"I've thought a lot about all of it, Nora, I really have. But I don't have answers, and I probably won't until I spend more time talking to William. Of course I'm already in over my head, which is what you fear for me. So: love and answers. Right now I don't know which one, if either, that I can offer him...but I do believe eventually, I could. You know what they say about the greater the risk, right?"

The rest of our dinner conversation took on a lighter tone, with more about the two of them and less about William or the music box. We drank some wine, filled many a bag of candy, and retired to watch *The Wizard of Oz* half asleep after the last of the trick-or-treaters rang at the door. All in all, it was another successful Halloween, and I had already planned to take down my orange and black the following day after school, in preparation for the orange and brown of Thanksgiving.

My alarm woke me as usual, and I fumbled into the bathroom to start the shower. The day after Halloween is hard for a Kindergarten teacher, with cranky students who got all hopped up on sugar, then went to bed late, and probably to stayed up half the night with stomachaches. And then most of them would have handfuls of their loot in their lunchboxes, which created another month of candy-raged afternoons. I undressed and decided to spend an extra few minutes in the shower to ensure maximum wakefulness.

Once I was thoroughly conscious, I stepped out of the shower to the aroma of my pre-set coffee, brewed and ready for me. But in the mirror — a mirror I loved so much, from Grandma's shop, was a picture drawn with one finger in the condensation. It was a key. My key.

"No," came from within me somewhere. I searched above and below the pedestal sink. I shook my clothes, looked under and over and behind the shower curtain, all the while knowing it wouldn't be there. And if the key was missing...

Sprinting naked through my house, slipping on wet feet, I thundered on the hardwood floors into the living room to the mantel. I could see that the music box wasn't there as soon as I entered the room, and tears were already dripping off my chin. There was something there, though, in the place where my music box formerly sat, and I inched closer to see what it was. A few steps before reaching the mantel, my tender bare feet stepped on something.

It was difficult to focus with tears welling in my eyes, but I could see that whatever I had stepped on wasn't the only one. Several small white balls where scattered on the floor. I reached for one and rose to see it better. Blinking through the water in my eyes, I saw past the item between my fingers to the empty space where the music box should have been.

And then I could see. And I understood. A broken necklace was looped over a candlestick that used to stand behind the music box on my mantel, with its torn strings falling over the edge, spilling tiny white pearls all over my floor.

TWENTY

PLEASE COME HOME FOR CHRISTMAS

She was in my house. Just minutes ago — or was she still there? I stood naked and shivering, with only Grandma's quilt to offer cover. I'd never felt so vulnerable, and I knew it wasn't fear for my safety; it was that she'd taken what had become my most valuable possession.

That didn't mean I wasn't still afraid for my safety, though. Like a child, scared of the boogeyman, I slid to the corner, placing my back against the wall. At least she couldn't attack me from behind. I slumped to the floor and wiped my tears. *I will fight her fucking naked, but she will not see me cry.*

Seconds ticked on the nearby wall clock, echoing throughout the empty room. Minutes. Silence. Stillness. Silence. Was she gone? Was she watching from somewhere in the house? Ten minutes passed before a honking horn outside startled me to consciousness. The room became relevant again with the smell of coffee and the bathroom fan still running down the hall. And the pearls. Those goddamn pearls scattered all over the floor.

I had to get out. In ten minutes I had called a sub, dressed, and was on the road weaving through morning traffic toward Nora's apartment, watching my rearview mirror for lights following me.

"Did William know we called her Pearl?" After the shock of me showing up at her door, Nora had questions and I only had guesses for answers.

All logic pointed to the likelihood that Charlotte had been eavesdropping on William and I in the Tokyo restaurant. For a clever person like Charlotte, all she would need to do was get on the internet and search my name. With social media, it would have taken only seconds to find me, and even set up a believable account to send a friend/follow-request. I accepted the fact that she likely found me easily as a blessing, though, since she could have gone and poked around at Doyle's if she didn't find me on the internet quickly. The thought of her chatting it up with my mom, or worse, using God knows what sort of persuasive tactics on her for information, was chilling.

As for how she knew exactly where I lived, I couldn't be sure...I had pictures of my school, my house, and my local hangouts all over my social media pages. Advertisements, practically, to anyone paying even the slightest attention. It wasn't worth the anguish to explore all the ways she could have gotten to me. It was done. The only question now was what to do about it.

My hope was that if Charlotte was capable of finding me, then maybe William could as well. The worst part was that even if Charlotte turned the key, William could spend ages looking for me and not know that I wasn't there. We had already endured countless visits unaware of each other's presence...how long would it take for him to realize?

Without question, I would be starting my own search for William, but somehow I had been talked into being the one giving up all the information, leaving me severely deficient and in no position to begin a manhunt.

"So what now?" asked Nora eventually.

"Good old-fashioned stalking, I guess," I answered. "I'll start by looking up whatever I can on Nantucket. That's all I have to go on..."

Panic caught in my throat, knowing it was true, and it wasn't going to be enough. "Um, can I stay here for a while?"

Nora couldn't stay home, but promised that she would stop by my house to gather an overnight bag for me on the way home. I couldn't stay any longer than that, and I would have to go back to school the next morning — a sub for one day is hard enough on kindergarteners — but I really hoped she or Tucker wouldn't object to staying with me if I had to return to my Pearl-violated house.

How in the world was I going to manage tracking him down? I didn't even know his last name, and I was only assuming he still lived on the island of Nantucket. Making matters worse, between regular school obligations, and the extra holiday keepsake projects I would be cramming in for the kids, I was approaching the absolute craziest 6 weeks of the school year, which didn't leave me much optimism for fitting the investigation in during my "down time."

A downward spiral should have enveloped me by that point, given the zombie-like depressions I'd experienced for lesser complications, but a voice of common sense threatened to beat my pathetic ass if I wasted a single minute feeling sorry for myself. I'd already shed my tears; it wouldn't do any good to wallow in sadness when I could be actively working towards finding him.

I was "the one." Reminding me of this, which I accepted as truth, helped put things in perspective. Everything Charlotte had done to thwart William, and now me, had only worked against her, and I intended for this setback to have the same outcome. In a way, it was empowering, knowing Charlotte had felt so threatened by me that she resorted to stealing the only lifeline between William and I. I was a force to be reckoned with, and she knew it — maybe even before I did.

Dividing my day into separate sections, almost dividing myself into two different people, was my plan of attack. With effort I managed to pull off my day job: the schoolteacher superhero, busy with the whirlwind of day-to-day planning and teaching coupled with

Thanksgiving projects, eventually becoming the on-holiday teacher, jumping into the fun and festive meal preparations with my family. By night I was Rynn McKay, P.I. Scouring the internet for Nantucket information, I left no stone unturned: public records, newspaper articles, Chamber of Commerce listings, you name it. The problem was, I only had one thing to go on, which was one name — and a name like William, (surprise, surprise) comes up often to say the least.

Thanksgiving had come and gone, and I still didn't even have a lead. I looked up Nantucket farms, of which there are a few, but none listed William as having anything to do with them. I know he told me Charlotte's parents had passed the farm along to him, which was my main rationale for believing he was still on the island, even though he had never said as much.

My goal was to have either something concrete, or at least something promising enough by Christmas vacation so I could fly up there when I was out of school. I had decided to call the local Nantucket librarian or county clerk to see if they had any archives or genealogical registries to check out, but I was at school until five and six o'clock every day preparing the endless extra Christmas keepsakes, ornaments, and special kindergarten holiday memories. With Nantucket's time zone an hour ahead of Texas, it was too late to catch anyone by phone.

In the back of my mind, I held onto two possibilities: one was that he would somehow know of what had happened, and find me first; and two, that I would soon have a break from school, which meant two solid weeks to spend on the phone or on the island digging for something to lead me to William. I was counting on him finding me, since my investigative skills had proved lacking, but I was determined not to be discouraged. I was 'the one' and I would prevail. Just as I had stuck with this from the beginning, trusted myself, and proved to William of my dedication once already, I would continue and now show Charlotte that I could overcome whatever adversity she threw at me.

I kept my head down and finished the holiday season at school, but I was never so happy to close my classroom door and leave for two weeks with visions of my hard work paying off with a long-awaited reunion.

Monday morning I was on the phone with first, the librarian, who didn't have access to actual families or their records, but was more than willing to show me how to look up my own family history if I wanted to "pop in." Next I tried the county clerk, who was helpful in assisting me in my request for information, however I didn't have a last name, making it a little difficult to direct her in how to search her records. Again, it was suggested that I come in so that we could look more thoroughly. I committed to a date after Christmas, and she thoughtfully offered to look through birth certificates for any "William" dating back to mid 1700.

It was Saturday, and here I was, already at a standstill. Christmas would be the following Monday, and all my plans of spending the week building on new information, making headway and feeling good about where I stood in my investigation had now gone cold. A month and a half had passed since my last turn of the key, meaning we were now 2 weeks overdue for another travel. Would Charlotte have known the pattern I had adopted and follow it so as not to raise William's suspicion? Perhaps she had planned to send the two of them on excursions immediately and often, creating more opportunities to tempt him like she had done in the beginning.

If she were acting smart, she would follow my pattern, but being smart and being sensible were two different things. My need for William to know it was Charlotte in control of the music box now depended on her hopefully reckless character surfacing again and outing her for what she had done. I had the week ahead of me to ponder this, while piddling through the internet countless times and making half-hearted attempts at contacting anyone who could tell me anything about the farms on Nantucket.

I tried decorating. I tried baking. I even tried shopping. I turned on holiday music, banking on its habit of nausea-inducing cheerfulness to elevate me to my typical self, but it only made things worse.

By Friday, I had abandoned the Christmas spirit and concentrated solely on the search. I barely noticed that I hadn't gotten out of my PJ's since Wednesday, I hadn't left my laptop for even a minute, and I had accidentally redialed several people that I had already spoken to on previous occasions with no luck.

When my doorbell rang sometime that evening, I was dozing on the couch with the laptop teetering on my chest and awoke with a delirious hope that it could be William at my door. Barely sturdy enough to stand upright and answer my visitor, I opened the door to see Tucker with a pizza box.

"Hey, I'm your entertainment for the evening. Hope you like anchovies." He walked passed me into the house.

"I...what are you doing here?" Had I missed something? "Where's Nora — anchovies?"

"At your mom's getting ready for Christmas Eve. Hey, uh," his eyes fell on me with a judgmental face I didn't ordinarily see from him, "when's the last time you showered? I love you, girlfriend, but you look like shit."

I looked down at my appearance, and grumbled. "I promise, it wasn't another one of my slips into a funk this time! It was more like a dive into an obsessive bounty hunting...in search of a...you know, a man born mid 18th century on Nantucket Island..." I wasn't sure that was a better excuse.

"You don't know that he was born on Nantucket," was Tucker's response.

"Yeah, he said he worked there all his life, and they left it to him when he died."

"Maybe, I'm just saying, you said 'born' on Nantucket, and technically, you don't know that. So," he shrugged, "it's just worth mentioning, that's all. The devil's in the details, right? Listen, I'll set up here and you go take a shower. Nora may come over later if she and your mom finish whatever they've got started back home."

A little disoriented by the point Tucker had made, and wondering to what extent that little assumption might have made a difference in my legwork thus far, I obeyed and took a refreshing shower. My plane tickets and reservation at a Nantucket cottage were set for Tuesday through Saturday. If William wasn't actually born there, I would have to apologize upon arrival to the sweet county clerk for her fruitless search. That would be okay, I reasoned; it was all information I needed to consider in order to lead me to William...no harm done, I hoped.

Tempted to pull on some new PJ's, I decided against it and chose some jeans and a sweater instead. Tucker wasn't exactly an invited guest, but I could manage at least a little effort for his thoughtfulness in bringing me dinner. He had found makings for a salad in the fridge and, as promised, had set up dinner for me on the island, and had gone as far as turning on some Christmas music in the background. I usually loved this time of year, and would have loved this moment if not for recent events.

We made small talk; he told me about a big job ongoing at work, and I filled him in on my investigation. Moments like this made me so thankful for his friendship. He had been supportive from the beginning, and never tired of my constant chatter about William at any point. I was a lucky girl, and my heart swelled, knowing that if he was that true to me, then he would be exponentially more wonderful to my sister.

I was smiling again, and it felt good. I turned toward the living room as one of my favorite Christmas songs began: the Eagles, "Please Come Home for Christmas."

Tucker was beside me in a heartbeat, pulling me to him in a tight bear hug and swaying to the tune. I giggled, knowing what was coming next. Soon he was singing dramatically, pulling and pushing me, in and out and under his arms and back again to sway together for the next few beats, and then he would repeat.

I was laughing and twirling him by the end of the song, and just like always; it was exactly what I needed. I felt restored, and although my mind was still far away, with William and the island of Nantucket, I had been grounded again enough to look forward to continuing my search...*after* spending the holidays with my family.

I pulled Tucker close for a hug when our dance had ended, and I looked up at him to express my gratitude. "I don't know what I'd do without you guys, Tucker. You've been my best friends my whole life...I'm a lucky girl."

He leaned forward to kiss the top of my head. "You're gonna find him. If we all have to go around the world to track him down, we're gonna make sure you do this." He squeezed me tight again, and we spent the rest of the night watching cheesy Christmas specials with the room lit by my Christmas lights and the crackling fire.

WILLIAM HAD CONVINCED Rynn to wait between the turns of the key, and although she put up a fight, she conceded to his request. To the day. To the hour. To the minute. And she was late. Two weeks late, to be exact.

There was any number of reasons she may be late, William knew, and he tried for two weeks to remember that without worrying. Family gathering. Girls' night out. Death in the family. His knees bounced as he considered all the hopeful possibilities of what could have come up to delay her. Since her miracle appearance in his life, his world had been turned on its end, and the extra lift in his step was undoubtedly her doing.

Besides the fact that he found himself believing for the first time in his life that there could be an end to the curse...there was more now. There was her. Something in her smile. Her kiss. He couldn't wait to see her, to hear more of her life and how she came to know his secrets. But today she was late.

After another hour, his nail beds bordered on bleeding. A path had been worn in the rug around his dining room table. His fingers had run through his hair so many times it hadn't bothered laying down again. She wouldn't be late like this.

Something was wrong.

Loss of interest, maybe. Fear — that would be within reason with Charlotte lurking around and trying to kill her. How had he just expected Rynn to accept this without objections? A knot formed in his stomach. If she was no longer willing to risk her life for William, he could understand wholeheartedly. But hadn't there been something there, something between them?

He shook his head, but entertained the possibility of Rynn sharing a spark with someone else. Maybe that's what had really happened. Who could judge her? A normal guy with a normal life and normal baggage would rank higher than William, carrying his curse and bringing a crazed Charlotte on their "music box dates."

Gripping the back of a dining room chair with white knuckles, he made an affirmation. That couldn't have been it, and even if it was, Rynn wanted to help. She wouldn't have given up, not without telling him first. So maybe there was something else going on. Charlotte?

He had expected her to be on the attack during every music box trip, but perhaps she saw more value in staying behind in the shadows, watching, and learning. Charlotte could have been gathering information and waiting to make her move this whole time. Even a move in real life, perhaps.

William kicked himself for missing this. He'd gotten so caught up in Rynn, what if he let his guard down against Charlotte, and now... now what? He considered finding Rynn after the last trip to Tokyo, but feared bringing himself into her daily life until they had more chances to discuss...well, to discuss what the hell to do. If Charlotte had only half the information William knew about Rynn, she could have found her and taken the music box and key. Or hurt her. His breath caught in his throat. Jesus, or worse.

He had to know.

Maybe she had only moved on, which now seemed to be the most hopeful possibility. But if Charlotte had made her presence known in real life in any way, Rynn would be looking for him, and that would prove infinitely more difficult than she could imagine. He had to go to her.

With enough to start a simple internet search, William searched all the spellings of "Rynn" he could think of, paired with her last name, "McKay." Thankfully, although not wisely on her part, Rynn had a social media presence and had even created a very thorough teacher webpage with personal touches, including a mention and a picture of her first house purchased on her own. He started a search of the area near her school, cross-referenced with what social media showed to be her favorite restaurants and coffee shops. Confident this was the general area that she must be living, he used Google Maps street-view to find the house in her "sold" picture from her webpage. Within two hours from sitting down at his laptop, William found the house and purchased his plan ticket for Texas.

Within an hour of landing, William had arrived by taxi on her street.

Before even reaching her steps, he could hear Christmas music inside playing, which was fitting for the girl who said she always had a song in her head. Relief spread through his chest. She was okay.

Rynn suddenly walked into view from the window, catching his eye unexpectedly. He found himself awestruck, overjoyed that he had reached this moment after waiting so long. She was listening to the Eagles, "Please Come Home for Christmas," with her perfect smile stretched across her face. A man walked into view just then, behind her...and they shared an embrace that forced William to look away, confused. He stepped back off the steps, feeling guilty for spying on her. *She's safe*, William reminded himself. It wasn't Charlotte's interference that stopped Rynn from turning the key, which meant Rynn was safe, and that was all that mattered.

He glanced back, knowing he would only confirm his findings. They were dancing. Happy and playfully, just as he remembered dancing with her in Miami. She twirled and rocked and swayed, until eventually they came together, holding each other close. She looked up to him lovingly, speaking to him with honesty in her eyes, to which the man responded with a kiss on her forehead. He didn't realize he was holding his breath until the kiss took the air from his lungs.

William stumbled as he turned from them, falling to a seated position on her front steps. She was happy, and that was what was important, he told himself. It was within reason for her to decide to move on. It didn't matter, there was no use in feeling sorry for himself. She was happy.

He remained on her steps long enough to gather himself, and without looking back, he called another taxi to take him to the airport.

TWENTY-ONE

THERE ONCE WAS A MAN FROM NANTUCKET

Getting to Nantucket was quite a process, starting with air travel to Boston, ground travel to Hyannis, and finally, sea travel to the island. The entire day was spent en route, which would have been frustrating, given my timeline, but the beauty of the scenery along the way and beaches from which I had departed gave me promise of hope to come. My ferry arrived during a sunset like I've never seen before: gray clouds set against an almost neon pink sky. I was so struck with awe that I nearly forgot the reason I had come to the island in the first place.

Bitter wind whipped up around me like a tornado cutting through the already icy temperatures. I had left home wearing my heavy peacoat in an attempt to save space in my carry-on, though it had served no necessary purpose in Texas other than cause me to sweat profusely. Now, I clutched the peacoat, paired with a thick crocheted scarf, and pulled down my sock hat in an effort to shield the abrasive gusts from my spoiled-by-Texas-winters skin.

My final taxi ride would have been a quick one, but seeing that the whole town was still lit up like a storybook Christmas, I asked the driver to take a joyride around the main attractions. He chatted with me lightly about the past week's events, including carolers, costume contests, and visits from Mr. and Mrs. Claus. It was beyond charming. Normally, I would have rolled my eyes. Now, on the other hand, harboring such unexpected romantic longings since my introduction to William, I tried to avoid the lightheadedness that accompanied novel fantasies created by such an overwhelmingly amorous setting. How could one *not* want to fall in love here?

I thanked the taxi driver with a generous tip and well wishes for the New Year, and got settled in to my cottage. It was adorable, directly on the water in the Nantucket Boat Basin, and featuring all the appeal you'd expect from a northern island getaway. It was so irresistibly warm and cozy, in fact, that despite knowing it was time I should be finding dinner somewhere, I chose rather to get comfy and curl up in the soft bed. There was no fighting the exhaustion brought on by an entire day of trekking halfway across the country, and in minutes I was dreaming.

Waking up in the cottage-style room with an appetite for not only food, but also for insight into William's life here on the island had me up and ready to go before 7:00 the next morning. My excitement was physical, felt in everything I did. I chose to walk in the cold instead of taking a taxi, so as to embrace the mere fact that I was finally no longer in Texas, sitting on my ass and scouring the internet. My search was concrete now; I was here, among the people that knew him, and I was going to find him.

With a hot coffee and lemon-poppy seed muffin in hand from a near-by coffee shop, I was in heaven already, and I hadn't even made it to the county clerk's office yet. It was as if I had finally reached the place that had been waiting for me my whole life. Everywhere I looked was sublime, from the water to the passing boats, the friendly locals and the excited tourists, the lighthouses and the moors. I planned to experience all that the island had to offer, as soon as I had William by my side.

A brisk walk with my coffee refilled led me down the street to the office of the very sweet Laurel Adams, who was delighted to meet me in person after my curious phone requests. "My goodness, you're here! All the way from Texas, it is so nice to meet you! Come in here and let me show you what I've found. So why exactly are you looking for this William?"

Well, that was tricky. "Love interest" might be cause for alarm, just as "really cute cursed guy" would. I smiled, and lied, "Old friend of my great, great..." shit, how many greats would that go back to? "... grandfather. We, uh, found journals that continually mentioned a William, it was clear that he was a close friend, so I was just hoping to learn more about him."

"How interesting!" Her eyes were wide with blank wonder. "So your grandfather was from Nantucket?" She blinked stupidly, as if I had just made her day.

I gave a simple and poignant, "Mmm hmm," then asked to see what she had found.

"Oh, yes! Okay, I made this list here for you, and if you want to just make yourself at home, you can browse through the records in here for more information." As she spoke, she escorted me down the hall, offering a small room with a table in the middle, surrounded by filing cabinets.

"Oh, Laurel," I remembered, "I'm sorry, but my friend brought it to my attention that I had only *assumed* William was born on the island...is there a way we can open up our search to include new residents?"

"Oh, sure, although I'm not promising as much success as those birth certificates. But I'll go see what I can find. Oh, and you can use that computer right over there," she pointed to the corner of the room, "if you want to try to look up anything on these names."

Laurel brought me the records for all boys with the name of William born on the island between 1730 and 1780, which amounted to a pretty thick file. As I buried myself in the disappointingly random names, she worked on finding any Williams that had moved to the island during that same time frame. I worked diligently between the paper mess of files and the computer to search for a picture attached to any of the names. Of course, there were little, if any, but it was a good start. By lunchtime I thanked Laurel for her help, paid her for my copies, and headed for the library with a stop at a sandwich shop along the way.

I spoke briefly to Teresa, the librarian, reminding her of our previous week's phone conversation and asked her to show me to the collection of the island's historic newspapers and access to the microfilm. Once set up at a table near the microfiche, I laid out my paperwork from the clerk's office. My plan was to continue checking out the birth records and then move on to the new residents, but I decided to take a break and just browse through the historic newspapers since I was already seeing double from the fine print of handwritten records.

The collection was impressive, dating back to the times of the thriving whaling industry, documenting a world so far removed from my own. I could have spent days in there, and perhaps I might need to. I started at the earliest date, just leafing through the delicate pages, marveling at the manner in which the people of the island lived and flourished, until the Great Fire of 1846 destroyed a third of the town and ultimately led to the end of Nantucket's spot as a leader in the whaling community. The story of Nantucket's darkest time unfolded in the pages of the newspapers before me. My heart sank for the people of the island as I read through its history, and before my efforts of being optimistic changed to dreary, I urged myself to get back to work.

I alternated my time between the desk covered in papers, to the microfilm for searching newspaper articles, to the stacks of originals for a break, taking into account the rationale that you find what you're looking for when you're not actually looking. I had found a rhythm in my process, and was sitting back down at the table when the librarian came in to let me know the library would be closing at 5:00.

"Oh," I jumped, surprised by her presence. "Sorry, what time is it?" My watch showed 4:45. "Thank you, I'll probably be back tomorrow, then."

She nodded and said that would be fine, and bid me a good evening. I gathered up my papers and spent the last few minutes scanning more of the old newspapers. Tomorrow would have to be more productive, I thought to myself. Maybe I would make a list of current farm owners in the morning, and spend my afternoon visiting with them in person.

So day one may not have been hugely successful, but I still felt like I was on the right track. I would press on in the morning, and see what the rest of the day would bring. The afternoon sun was a welcome sight, after having been behind the library walls most of the day. I considered a walk around town to kill time before dinner, especially since the weather would be nice, at least until the sun went down.

With all my paperwork tucked into my handbag, I strolled along the main tourist thoroughfares. Not looking for souvenirs, I didn't go into any of the shops. Instead, I enjoyed the Christmas spirit that still lingered on the streets and among the crowds spending their vacations on this enchanting island. For the moment, I might as well have been a tourist. I hadn't set my expectation to find William on day one so that I wouldn't be let down if it didn't pan out, and now was exactly that moment. I could have planned to be dining with William this evening, but, if I had, I would be essentially stood up by my own failure to find him already. Instead, I would be dining alone, and I was okay with that. Dinner for one. The question was, where?

Didn't tourist towns always have racks and racks of flyers and brochures everywhere you look? I looked behind me, through the window of a shop, which was actually a high-end art studio. Mmmm, maybe not there. Walking along the row, I peeked in as I passed windows, until finally I saw exactly what I was looking for: the wooden racks with small openings for the many local businesses to advertise by schlepping their flyer into the slot. I entered the shop and, rather than stare at them all and stand in the way, I collected as many as I could hold and then headed back to my cottage.

I fell into the bed for a quick rest, while pondering my wardrobe. While considering my options, I rolled over and flipped through the restaurant flyers, thinking my attire would probably be determined by the restaurant. "Sharp casual" at Brant Point Grill sounded like a winner, so I traded my jeans for tights and my sweater for a belted dress. I washed my face and reapplied my make-up, followed by a brush and fluff of my hair. Knee-high boots completed the outfit, and I gathered the assortment of brochures along with my manila file folder of records to peruse at dinner. On my way out the door, I noticed an informational binder and a few additional pamphlets on the entry table, so I grabbed those as well.

My stomach rumbled as I walked with extra pep in my step toward my rare-occasion fancy dinner. I sat down, marveling at the atmosphere, thoroughly pleased with my choice. Although I wished I had hurried up enough to enjoy the view in the daylight, the lights of the harbor were still magnificent. I ordered enough food for two: an appetizer of clam chowder, an entrée of steak and lobster with aspara-gus, and a dessert of chocolate cake, which I couldn't even look at, and had boxed up to take home as soon as it was served.

A teacher's budget couldn't afford luxuries like this often, and I was using up a sizable percentage of my savings on this trip; it was so absolutely divine, though, like nothing I'd ever treated myself to before. I vowed to do again at least every now and then. The waiter offered to refill my glass of wine, and I decided to take him up on it, extending my time in the elegant ambiance while I looked at the flyers in my folder.

Hot air ballooning, hike and bike trails, chartered boats...the usual suspects. There were also beautiful beaches, obviously, muse-ums, and the library I'd just spent half my day in; art shows, plays, helicopter rides, guided fishing, etc. Most of these were seasonal, anyway, and weren't even offered during the winter, not that I'd been looking for ways to occupy my time. There would be no shortage of things to do, though, if I were ever able to return on a true vacation.

With all the flyers browsed, I took a look through the binder from my room. In the welcome letter was a list of personally suggested attractions from the rental owners. I recognized all the same venues as I'd seen on the flyers, until one new one stood out. Bennett Park was the name. Wondering why this hadn't come up in any of my internet searches, or in my stack of flyers, I got my waiter's attention to inquire.

"Oh, Bennett Park is lovely, but unfortunately it won't be open until the spring," he answered when I asked him about the surprise listing.

"Do you know anything about the owner or the history of the park?"

He was caught off guard by the question, "Well, I don't know, ma'am, I haven't lived on the island for very long. Would you...like me to ask someone else?"

I ignored his question, and was already pulling out the manila folder of my photocopied records. I flipped and flipped until I found a document that had previously meant nothing to me, just like every other faceless name in the folder. Joseph Bennett, and son, William, documented arrival on the island in 1768. It could be nothing, but...it was the first link to a possible farm of any sort. Against the odds, I dialed the number listed in the binder, as I got out my wallet to signal the waiter that I was ready to pay.

The number went to a polite recording about the hours of operation and seasonal dates and events. I looked up the website on my phone for anything that I could go by. The very basic site offered sparse information, but I could see that the park itself wasn't open. A sister site, however linked to more thorough off-season offerings, as they shipped all sorts of herbs, seeds, bulbs, and even products like soaps and organic fragrances year round. Someone was obviously working the off-season, even if not right at the moment because it was evening. There was no William Bennett listed on the contact information, and in fact there was no one by the name of Bennett at all. Margaret Tinley was the operating manager, with a phone number and an email address provided. I dialed and it, too, went to the messaging system.

"Happy Holidays," came my waiter's voice, returning my check and interrupting my thoughts. "Thank you for joining us tonight."

It's the holidays, I now remembered. Surely the owners and employees took time off, and might not even be back until I'd be gone. Surely William would be there, though? He had no family to spend the holidays with. I ran off so quickly I forgot my chocolate cake on the table, which I really was hoping to eat for a late night snack. It wouldn't have traveled well, though, since I had made up my mind to take a cab to the park immediately.

When the cabbie heard my request, he looked back at me like I was most definitely a little off. "Uh, well, miss...The place isn't open until Spring, and anyway, it's 8:45 in the evening. No one would be there this late at night."

"I know," I told him, "but they do still run the shipping business in the off-season, and I —"

" — Miss, if I take you to Bennett Park at this hour, I'd be leaving you at a locked gate, and I'm sorry, I won't be doing that."

With a sigh, I resigned. "Okay. Hey, do you know the owner?"

"Of Bennett Park? Not that I know of, I just know they get a nice load of visitors. Now, I hate to be like this, but if you stay any longer in the cab, I'm going to have to start the meter."

Defeated, I exited the cab, and decided it was worth a try to see if they may have salvaged my chocolate cake in the restaurant, since I wouldn't be making any surprise appearances on anyone's doorsteps tonight. When I reentered, my waiter acknowledged me with his pointer finger in the air.

"I thought you might be back," he said a minute later, with a wink. "I set it aside. I know you'll enjoy it."

I was still too full to eat it that night, but when I woke up the next morning, I fist pumped through my blankets, remembering it for my breakfast. What better way to start a day of stalking than with a piece of chocolate cake so large it required a meal-sized to-go container? An hour later on the street, I shook from the nerves, the cold, and the sugar as I called for a taxi, fighting spasms of excitement: the moment had finally arrived for my search to be over.

Thankful I wasn't getting into the same guy's car as last night, I asked the new driver to take me to Bennett Park. As he drove, he asked if I was aware that they were closed for the season. "Yes! Jeez, I know," I blew up at him; must have been all the sugar and coffee. "I know, thank you, I'm going to see the owner."

The driver ignored me for the rest of the drive, letting me sit in silence with just my guilty conscience for company. When we reached the park, I could see that last night's driver knew what he was talking about, because there, as he had said, was a locked gate. There was a keypad, but that didn't help me at all. I told the driver to hang on, and I got out to inspect my options. Relieved, I saw an intercom and pressed it immediately.

"Yes?" came a crackling voice within seconds.

"Hello?" was my stupid response.

"I'm sorry, we're closed for the holidays — we'll, uh, be open again on the 3rd." The voice was ambiguous through the static, but I had to know.

"Wait, please! William?" I asked excitedly.

"Who is this?"

"It's Ryan...I'm looking for...for William."

There was silence on the other end. The mike was still open, providing pops and static while I waited to see if I had found *my* William or another dead end. I looked back at the driver, who was probably more than happy sitting back, watching his charges tick higher.

Had I taken some insignificant detail and made it into more than it was? There was still no response on the other end of the intercom, leading me to think detective work was just not for me. I gave it a few minutes, but eventually had to accept that all I'd really done was bug a poor business owner on his holiday vacation. I turned back to the cab and opened the door to get in.

"S'that your boy?" asked the driver as I was just about to tell him to take me to the library.

"Huh?" Looking back, I could see a dark SUV tearing down the road toward us, kicking up dust behind it. The automatic gate opened, and I got out to see who was driving the vehicle, expecting an angry landowner ready to yell me off his property. It pulled to a swift stop right on the other side of the gate, and the door flung open. When the dust settled, William appeared. He approached cautiously, for some reason, but I was running to him, beside myself and spilling tears of joy.

I jumped up and wrapped my arms around his neck. "It's you, it's really you — William, I *found* you!"

"How did you...why are you here?" he asked.

His question caught me off guard. "It was Charlotte — she's a *lunatic* — it was Halloween night. She broke into my house and stole the key and the music box. And just to make sure I knew it was her, she left a broken pearl necklace on the mantel where the music box had been. She must have been close enough in Tokyo to hear me call her 'Pearl.' She's — she's — oh God, William, she scared the shit out of me, and I was devastated that I'd never see you again, but I looked and looked...and I found you."

He moved gently backward out of my embrace and pushed his hands into his pockets. "I was afraid something like that might have happened." Seeing the taxi, he walked quietly away from me and paid my fair.

When he returned, I couldn't help but to unleash weeks of frustration. "What do you mean? You knew?" Fire spread through my veins. "I've been looking for you for*ever*, but you knew and you didn't come find me? It would have been ridiculously easy, if you would have bothered — "

"It was," he said plainly, nodding.

"What — what are you talking about?"

"You were always so prompt turning the key, right down to the minute. So when it was time and nothing happened, I suspected something." His speech was strained, as if recalling difficult memories. "I gave it some time, not wanting to jump to conclusions, but eventually I knew something must have happened." He paused, looking down and nudging a rock with his shoe. "Between social media and your school website, I found you easily, even your house. I was on a plane the next day. I was afraid Charlotte had found you, I thought she had..." He stopped, waving his arms to release the rest of his argument into the air. "I wanted to know that you were safe, but when I got to your house I saw you. I saw that you were with someone, and I understand, Rynn, I do. So, I just don't know why you're here now, instead of at home...with him."

He wasn't pouting, but he was hurting. I didn't know what the hell he was talking about, but I was careful not to throw out a tone that was full of accusation.

"When? When did you come to my house?"

"Friday," he answered. "Rynn, I'm not mad, you had no obligation to me or my situation. I'm glad you've found someone. I'm happy for you. Really."

"William, I don't know what you saw, or what you think you saw, but..." The only man I'd even seen other than my own family recently was Tucker. "Oh my God, William. Did he have blonde hair? Curly, kind-of messy?"

He was looking at me like I was prolonging the torture, and turned to stare off into the distance as he leaned back on the SUV.

"It was Tucker, William! My best friend — my sister's *boyfriend!* He came over because I'd gotten so involved in my search for *you* that I lost track of the world...again. That seems to happen a lot lately. He — he — he did exactly what he always does as my best friend — he cheers me up — he forces me out of it."

William cut his eyes at me, waiting for my continued explanation. "You were dancing...he kissed you."

I shook my head, remembering the moment. "No, he kissed my

forehead. And that's just Tucker, he sings like an idiot, we dance, and you can't help but be in a better mood. I told him I was lucky to have him...that's when he kissed my forehead and told me he would help *me* find *you* even if he and Nora had to search the whole world with me...he promised me that we'd find you."

He didn't respond, instead walking in a slow circle to the gate and back. I watched him, thinking surely he believed me, but his reaction was disheartening.

When standing directly in front of me again, he said, "I'm sorry. Rynn, I — it's not even — " He spun, raising his hands to rest on the top of his head and waiting, apparently for the right words to come.

With one swift movement, he turned and gathered me up in a hug that lifted me face to face with him. His eyes were closed as he spoke, "I tried not to be hurt, Rynn...but —"

Words went silent. Pressure consumed us. Bennett Park disappeared.

TWENTY-TWO

MICHELLE, MA BELLE

The force tore us apart and we resurfaced separately. I knew Charlotte had to have turned the key, but why wouldn't we come up for air together like Nora and Tucker had when I brought them with me? I was touching him, just like they had been touching me, but this time I was suffocatingly alone when my eyes opened.

Fresh air swirled as a wind kicked up through the meadow around me. It smelled good, like home. My eyes did a sweep of the area, hoping to see William, yet prepared for Charlotte. Chattering voices suddenly called out ahead of me, just beyond the brush that concealed me. I stopped short, but it was clear soon that it was kids talking as they marched through the meadow. In my stillness, I noticed the sound of slowly trickling water nearby.

In the clearing ahead, I caught sight of gleaming blonde hair, just like Nora's when she was young. The blondie trailed behind two others, a girl and a boy who were obviously a few years older and leading the procession. She alternated between a fast walk and then a few strides at a jog, struggling to keep up.

"Wait for me! Tucker, Rynn, *wait!*"

My stomach dropped. Like a movie scene that feels like it's

zooming in at the same time as it's zooming out. The three kids came into focus just as the surroundings began to stand out as well. The hill behind them: my old house, and my grandma's. The clearing around them: what we called the river pasture, and where we spent most of our free time. The tree in the distance: that's where we found the journal.

I watched the three of us and couldn't help but smile. We were so happy and carefree — before I let the walls come up around me. My breath stalled, caught in my throat. The last time I came down to the river with Nora and Tucker was the day my Grandma had her stroke. That meant she was still alive.

That day played in my head again like a slideshow, right down to our clothes. Nora was in a hand-me-down purple sweatshirt and jeans. Tucker wore one of his dad's old baseball caps and a red windbreaker. I was in green leggings with an oversized sweater that nearly touched my knees because I was so short.

I watched us march on, crossing the field. Red jacket, big sweater, and a purple sweatshirt a few strides behind. My heart lost its steady rhythm and picked up an erratic thumping, tapping, thundering so loud I was sure the kids' parade would halt at the sound. I crouched down, hiding my face.

It was the day. The day we found the journal, they day I really lost my grandma. By the looks of us kids, we had just arrived to play and it would be a while before getting distracted by the tree and rock. Maybe I still had time.

As soon as the three of us were out of earshot, busy playing and lost in imagery no doubt provided by Grandma's stories, I made a beeline for the hill. The three musketeers became just a memory again.

I pushed passed the point of burning muscles, until my arms pumped and my legs shredded through the tall grass on autopilot. I'd run through that field enough times before the age of nine to navigate it with my eyes closed. The realization that William and Charlotte were somewhere nearby fluttered and bounced in my consciousness, but this time, I wasn't worried about finding either one of them.

Grandma's house came into view through the trees, and I pressed onward while it grew larger and larger. A stranger shouldn't run through your front door unannounced and out of breathe, but that didn't seem to register at the time. I charged through the door, and in seconds heard the voice that shaped my childhood. "Holy hell, kids, you're gonna bust down my door one of these days!"

She came out of the kitchen with a wooden spoon in one hand and the other hand palm-up under it, ready to catch drippings. Rather than looking alarmed, she moved her free hand to her hip and gave me a well-you-better-have-an-explanation-for-this-or-I'll-use-this-spoon expression.

Instinctively, my hands raised in a non-threatening gesture. She was alive. I'd made it in time. The last thing I wanted to do was give her a heart attack.

"Grandma, it's me." She searched my face. "It's me, Rynn, and I'm sorry that this is so weird, but I have to tell you something."

I gave her time to look me over, surely seeing me as the all-grown-up Rynn. But she didn't speak just yet.

"You cheat at cards every damn time we play. Your favorite Beatles song is "Michelle." You're colorblind but won't tell anybody. You suck at cooking, but you bake like a pro, so I hope that wooden spoon is stirring up snickerdoodles." She fought a grin, but kept listening. "You've never missed my school plays or dance recitals." My temperature rose and tears formed. "You hate your name, Eleanor, so you insisted that Nora not be named after you unless she could have a nickname."

I would have continued, but she came at me, spoon and all, and enveloped me in the embrace I never would have felt again if not for the music box. If I could have stayed there until time ran out, I would have, but there was so much I needed to tell her.

"Grandma, I don't know how much time we have." I led her to sit on the sofa. "Listen, I'm here because the music box — the one in your shop." Her brows turned up, confused, and I realized that if I told her that I inherit the music box, I'd have to tell her of her death.

A sob escaped, despite my best effort to be strong. "Listen, this is super important, then I'll fill you in. Do you have a notepad or something somewhere?"

"Yeah," she said as she reached over to the table by her easy chair. "I use this when the Miss America contests are on, I like to keep track of their scores." The snort that came out of me helped keep the sobbing away.

"This is going to sound weird," I broached, "but do you have anything planned...like a will or anything?"

"Jesus, Rynn, what'd you do, grow up and become a damn lawyer?"

God I loved her. "No, no — I'm a teacher! But we need to write some things down if you don't have plans for your inheritance. Nothing big," I reassured her. She got a look on her face like I was going to tell her someone was going to swindle her. "Just small things. Mainly that music box. Grandma, it's a matter of life and death." Or really, eternal life and the end of a curse.

"So I'm gonna kick the bucket? I planned on living forever, damnit."

I smiled through more tears. "Eventually, I guess we all will, right?" I couldn't do it. What good would it do to ruin our reunion?

She got her mechanical pencil ready. "When I, Eleanor Doyle, kick the bucket..." I rolled my eyes and she snickered. "I want my granddaughter, Corynn McKay to have from my antique shop: the music box... what else?"

I guess she wanted to make a list. "Uh, okay, well, that's the big one. And your quilt. The one that was great-grandma's." She wrote it down. "And just some little things from the shop, like ceramic figures and stuff."

"Sounds like a bunch of crap you'll really cherish, huh?"

It sounded like a jab, but there was sarcasm behind it. "I will. I will when I receive it, I promise. You know you were my favorite treasure in the shop, anyway, don't you?"

She smiled and leaned over to kiss my cheek right below my eye. I held her face close to mine, never wanting to let go. *No tears*, I reminded myself, *no time.*

I told her to give the vanity to Nora and to figure out the rest on her own, leaving out the part that it would all be lost shortly anyway.

"Ok, so, wanna know how the hell I'm here?"

I'D PREPARED myself for tears. Expected it to be the hardest conversation I'd ever had, given that I'd shaped my entire adult life around...not being like her. Because it hurt too much. Who wants to face their Grandma twenty years after her death and explain that they purposefully became her total opposite?

But we laughed until we cried. Only she could listen to the tragedy I called my grief, and shoot profanities at me about how ridiculous I was. She was fascinated in an I-told-you-so way about the story of the music box, unable to help herself, pointing out that sometimes stories could be more than pure fiction. My sides ached and I found myself gasping for air by the time a beeping in the kitchen rang out.

"Oh, I guess that's my cookies. And they're peanut butter, sorry, smartass."

She pulled out one batch and started spooning peanut butter batter onto another cookie sheet. I prayed that I had enough time with her to taste them when they cooled, one last time. "Oh, I forgot my tea, too. Want some?"

I waved her off, and she grabbed a teacup from the microwave, door still ajar from when I barged in. She tested the temperature with a careful sip. I just wanted to watch her move. Watch her live. She caught me eyeing her and I realized that I'd been hoping for more time with her before the music box pulled me away, but I was fighting something else for my time with her. Today was the day she had her stroke.

Too much emotion came over me with the thought, and the air felt too thick again, just as it had on the day I sat down to open the twenty-year-old cardboard box with my name on it. "Hey, I'll be right back," I told her, not able to stomach the reality that I was about to lose her again.

She placed the cookie sheet in the oven as she called out, "You have to pee even when you're time traveling?" If only I could have laughed.

In the bathroom, I gripped the counter and stared at my reflection. My eyes had recovered from the initial tears upon my arrival, but now threatened to break like a dam under duress. Years' worth of tears would flood the tiny bathroom if I couldn't hold it together. I ran the water and splashed my face with it, breathing in through my nose, and out my mouth, to steady myself.

As I fumbled blindly around the counter for a towel, I bumped into jars of lotions and make-up containers, until finding the soft fabric beside the rattle of a medicine bottle. With clear eyes once again, I found the bottle to make sure I hadn't overturned it, and saw it upright and opened.

Out of habit, I looked for the lid, but something else caught my attention: scattered around it were a few empty capsule shells, and in loops of neatly arranged circles around the bottle, was Grandma's pearl necklace.

Ice formed in my feet, pushing its way up my legs, rooting me to the linoleum floor. It spread to my stomach, lungs, and out my arms.

"No," I coughed. "No!"

The ice turned to boiling rage. This couldn't be happening. I turned to leave the bathroom, but the sound of glass breaking in the kitchen shattered any last hope that I was wrong. Grandma was holding onto the counter with one hand when I came out of the hallway, but she was on her way down. Her other hand lay limp at her side.

"Oh, God, hang on, I'm coming!" She slumped again, now to a sitting position on the floor. Her face was confused, like I'd let this happen to her. I knew it wasn't meant to be, but it felt like an accusation. "Lay down, Grandma."

She attempted words, but they bounced around in her mouth, broken apart by lips that had been erased of their muscles.

"Shhh, it's okay, I'm going to call Mom. It's going to be okay, Grandma," I lied. Somebody had to come find her, she couldn't sit there like that, helpless. But I couldn't talk to my mom, either. I decided a phone call with no answer on the other end would attract enough attention to at least get someone to come check on her. The rest, I supposed, would be history. A history, I now realized like a punch in the stomach, that was my creation.

I dialed my mom's extension at the nursing home where she worked at the time, muscle memory on the rotary phone thankfully kicking in. When I heard her voice pick up, a gasp escaped me without warning. With my hand clamped over my mouth, I stretched the cord across the kitchen near Grandma. Maybe it would at least look like she collapsed while on the phone.

"I'm not leaving you," I whispered, tucking her neatly permed hair behind her ear. "I want to look around and make sure there's no sign of me being here — in case I don't have much time before... before I have to leave."

I ran to the bathroom, knowing the only evidence I needed to conceal was the pill capsules Charlotte had spilled. Back in the living room, I placed the notepad in view as if Grandma had just sat down to ponder her granddaughters' inheritance. Dear God, nothing suspicious about that.

Grandma remained motionless, with terrified wide eyes searching for meaning, while I tore through her house looking for anything else to stage or hide. What was she thinking of me?

"You're the most amazing woman I've ever known...you know that, right?" I returned, staring deep into her eyes and grabbing her hand. My tears dropped straight onto her blouse as I hovered over her. She couldn't answer, but her wandering gaze found me and locked. Her hand squirmed within mine. The soft skin of her fingers interlaced with my own, and she squeezed gently.

I fell into her shoulder, needing more time, needing her to understand. The pressure should have come then, to take me away, to save me from living through this all over again. But there was nothing. Only the fabric of her shirt, now wet and rough, rubbing my cheeks raw as my cries rocked me. I just wanted to bury myself, fearing meeting her eyes again.

A car door outside brought me back to attention. I moved to get up, but Grandma still had ahold of my hand. She gripped tighter, preventing my escape. "Grandma," I choked, "I have to go or someone will see me. I love you. I love you," I sobbed. It was goodbye all over again. Worse this time.

She held me steady. I moved closer to see straight into her eyes; maybe they could tell me something. With strained movements and forced air through her motionless lips, she formed two words: "Help. Him."

I nodded, wiping my nose on my arm sleeve. "I will, Grandma. I promise, I will." Noises on the front steps. "I have to go." She released me.

My only thought was getting out. I still had time. The doorknob jiggled, and my dad's voice boomed from the other side. "Eleanor??"

Get out, get out. I knew I could slip out the back door, but something was nagging at me. The front door creaked open, and the voice became louder. "Eleanor, you home?" Seconds, that's all I would have. Dad's footsteps paced through the entrance, just as I darted into the bathroom. "Eleanor, Eleanor! Oh Jesus, Eleanor, Eleanor! Eleanor, are you with me?"

The front door was still open, and with Dad occupied in the kitchen I walked down the front steps like I'd done a thousand times in my youth. My sobs had subsided. My breathing controlled. My resolve set. And Grandma's pearl necklace around my neck.

CHARLOTTE MUST HAVE TURNED the key eight or nine times, because I stalked around for what seemed like hours with still no sign of return to William's arms in Nantucket. All thoughts of finding either one of them were nonexistent when I was in Grandma's house, but with idle time to think since then, a frenzy stirred within me.

It was my fault. The greatest loss of my life, and it was my fault.

No, I told myself. I wouldn't take all the responsibility. This started long before me, and I didn't have to own that. There was no one to blame but Charlotte. The frenzy roiled into a fever, hot and effervescent.

She would pay.

I had an idea where she was. From our land on the hill, I could see the town where I grew up. Main street. The grocery store. Gas stations. And right on the edge, closest to me, was Doyle's. It was a Sunday, so it would be closed, just as it had been when the "break in" occurred on the same day as her stroke. I was beginning to understand.

The shop was a small place, because she and my grandpa couldn't afford anything bigger, and when they bought it, it was in disrepair. When they got all the major repairs finished, they put in new windows, doors, and lighting. They never touched the floors, though, because that's one of those things they said "adds character." Grandma always said the shop was the first antique they ever bought.

The back door was left ajar, inviting me in. My skin blazed, completely incensed that Charlotte would tread on such sacred ground after what she did.

This had been my sanctuary. A magical place. The rich color of the wood, the intricate details of the jewelry...I would look into every mirror and wonder about the reflections they had held in another time.

And Grandma's stories — from young forbidden romances to battles over land or freedom. I knew they weren't true, most of them, but that's what I loved. The delicate weave of fantasy intertwined with the possibility of reality. Charlotte couldn't possibly fathom what she'd taken from me. Or maybe she could.

The lights were off, but the sunlight from the outer windows reflected in shards off the polished wood furniture. Unnerved by the stillness, I raised my arms to a defensive stance, ready for what may already be coming for me. No creaking wood floors. No breath hanging in the air. No movement, not even outside.

Just then a shadow passed, breaking the sheen of an armoire. I jumped in the direction of the movement, but it was her voice that cut right through me, as she stepped out into the open.

"Adorable place, I never thought I'd see it again." Her eyes were caustic, boring holes in me. She smiled. "Nice pearls."

That was it. I hurled myself forward with no plan other than to take her down. She was swift, making one move to the left like a bull-fighter, sending me stumbling passed her. The spindled legs of an elegant desk scraped the hardwood floors as I sent it careening into a mirror. Glass erupted, glittering the desk and dancing to the floor.

"You," I breathed. "You —"

Something small with crystalline fragments flew at me, shooting rainbows across my vision. Whatever it was, it was too solid to shatter upon contact, which meant the impact was absorbed completely by my forehead. I didn't want to lose sight of her, but the damn thing hit with such force my eyes watered despite every effort to stop it. I staggered backward, coming to rest on the desk I had sent flying.

Charlotte moved silently away from me like an ocean current rippling away from the shore. *Like hell she will.* No matter what I did to harm her, I knew it would be futile, but that wasn't going to stop me from trying.

Under me, the desk crackled with the crunch of the shattered mirror. I felt around for a long, slender piece and heaved myself toward the window, slicing part of the curtain off to wrap around the end as a handle. Charlotte was practically skipping away, laughing.

I had nothing left to do but charge. She turned, hearing my footsteps, and lowered her shoulder to me. Something in me expected this, and I rolled back to back with her, bringing down the shard of glass as I came full turn. It scored a bloody tear across the left side of her arm. She jumped, alarmed at the blood, but recovered with a quick foot to my stomach, lunging into me with all her weight. One step forward, two steps back.

I remembered the icy pond, where my best offense was to bring her under with me. Fending her off would only wear me out, and she was too powerful anyway. I had to keep coming at her.

Her thrust had sent me into a tufted high-back chair. When I gained footing again I took the chair with me, spinning like a discus thrower, and launching it in her direction. She ducked, but couldn't dodge completely. The legs caught her right in the neck, sending her to the floor as the chair collided with the center counter where Grandma usually perched.

While she was still getting to her feet, I took a running leap and tackled like a linebacker. We slid a good ten feet, but she was attacking before we even came to a rest. She punched, but I was too close for her to gain enough leverage. I had to stay close. In one hand I somehow still had the glass, and in the other I grabbed her mess of black curls.

Her legs thrashed, performing acrobatic kicks that would be impressive for the Cirque du Soleil, but I held steady. I thought I had her finally slowing down when a growl tore through her as she sunk her teeth into the flesh of my neck. White hot flashes marred my vision matching the physical jolts of pain throughout my body.

Grandma's necklace tore, spilling pearls all over Charlotte, lodging in her hair. Exhausted and shaking, I feebly attempted all I could manage with my weapon. I raised the shard and sunk it into Charlotte's side, just as the tugging sensation pulled me away and back to William.

TWENTY-THREE

AIN'T THAT A KICK IN THE HEAD

"Rynn, stop, *stop!*" My right arm connected repeatedly with William. Awareness sunk in that I was no longer in the wreckage of the shop back in Texas. He hugged me tighter, the only way to avoid my attack. "It's ok, Rynn. Rynn! It's over."

I beat at his back until my arms burned, and he let me. Every fiber of my muscles screamed in protest until I could no longer manipulate their movement. My body sagged. Limp in his arms, William held the rag doll I'd become. He eased me down to the ground, leaning me back in his lap.

"It was her," I breathed into his chest.

"Charlotte?"

I nodded against him. "Do you know where we were, just then?" I removed my face from his sweater to watch him answer.

He half-shrugged, "Not exactly. I was at the edge of a town, so I just roamed around looking for you up and down the street. When I didn't find you there I went back and explored the woods beyond my starting point. What was it?"

Bile snuck into the back of my throat. Verbalizing this was going to make me live through it all over again. "That was my hometown. I surfaced in the woods behind my family's land." I heaved, but clenched my eyes and swallowed hard. "I saw myself. And Nora and Tucker — from a distance, I mean. It was the day we found your journal, which was the day my Grandma had her stroke." The day she was poisoned. "I hauled ass to her house thinking I could catch her before...before it happened." Before Charlotte killed her. "And I did." I let my head fall backward into the crook of his arm. I needed more air on my clammy face.

"I got to see her. One last time. We talked and I told her everything, especially how important it was that she pass the music box on to me." A ripple of ice moved through me. "Charlotte was there."

William had been sincerely listening, but his attention shifted and his muscles petrified when I mentioned her. Near my head he flexed his hand in and out.

"Her stroke. It wasn't just a stroke." I rose to a sitting position, burying my face in the heels of my hands. "Charlotte was there." I couldn't sit still all of a sudden. I wanted the shattered glass in my hand again. When did I get up and start pacing? "It was her."

He shifted his weight to his hand and pushed himself to stand. Brushing off, he asked, "Her? What was 'her?'"

"She must have been in the back of the house. I went to the bathroom because I realized I was probably about to run out of time with her — I just needed to compose myself, in case...in case it happened right in front of me. I needed to prepare."

"Charlotte *wanted* me to know," I spat through gritted teeth. "She emptied capsules of Grandma's blood pressure medication into her tea, which caused her to stroke. Then she laced my Grandma's pearl necklace around the pill bottle."

His face turned a sickly white. "So are you saying she," he ran his hands through his hair, "she poisoned your Grandmother?"

And it was my fault.

I had been so proud of myself, "the one." But at what cost?

"Rynn?"

I ran behind the SUV and let the whole thing wretch through

me. William followed, patting my back hesitantly. Images flickered. My Grandma's terrified eyes. The panic when my dad found her. Charlotte's vicious smile. Her bloody face. I heaved again, losing the rest of that goddamn chocolate cake.

William ran to open the door of the vehicle, and returned with a bottle of water. "Here," he offered. I took it and motioned him away, needing a moment alone. I rinsed my mouth, but the taste of guilt wouldn't wash away. Nose running, eyes watering, and coughing down bile, I sunk into a hollow shell of myself. How would I live with this?

Feet paced behind me. They moved faster and faster until connecting with the SUV, echoing with the sound of buckling metal. The jolt rocked me off the bumper where I leaned, nearly sending me into my own puke.

"Get in the car," he demanded. I followed, unfit to ask questions. He searched me over when I closed the door behind me. "Are you ok?"

"Huh?"

"I'm sorry — look, I know you have a lot to think about right now —"

A sound escaped me. It felt like a laugh, but sounded like a high-pitched cry. "Are you *joking*? A lot to think about? I made Charlotte hate me by proving to be 'the one.' I made her know I would be a threat to her and her fucking curse! But she got me worse than I could ever have dreamed. And now I know it's all my fault. I led her right to my Grandma, and I had to lose her all over again. I've got blood on *my* hands. And I don't even mean that figuratively — I found Charlotte in the antique shop and we tore the whole place up trying to get at each other. I fucking *shanked* her with a piece of glass."

He grabbed my head and pulled it forward to rest on his shoulder. Several times, I heard him attempt words, but stop short. "Ok, first: Charlotte is a...foul, conniving...there are no true words for her. You want to blame someone for what's happened? All of it, from day one right up to today — you blame Charlotte." I lifted and gave my head a convulsive shake, but he continued. "I know you feel responsible. I get that, Rynn." Tears filled my eyes and I willed myself to blink and hold his gaze. His eyes were the only things on earth tethering me to the hope that I could live through this pain.

"You just can't. You can't take this and call it yours. If I could find a way to change what happened, I would, but you have to remember that none of this would have happened if she hadn't set this curse in motion."

I choked on a sob, and he leaned forward, kissing the corner of my eyes to stop my tears. "You didn't do this. You are the person who took something unfathomable, and committed to it...to me, before you even had any idea what you were up against. You have given yourself to danger, to the unknown, to the possibility of losing yourself and that *kills* me. But that is who you are — and I know it's not just who you are to me, Rynn. You are the person who gives yourself, your every fiber, to everything you do."

"How can you assume that about me?"

"How can I not?" He pulled my chin closer. "I will help you get through this, I promise."

I closed my eyes, praying it was true. "What do we do now?"

"I don't know, I'll be honest. I never thought we would reach a point quite like this. I always thought it would be...obvious if I ever found the one...*you*. Since your presence, I just assumed I would know what to do. But, I don't know yet. If you don't mind, though, tell me what happened in the antique shop with Charlotte." I felt another gurgle rise in my stomach. He sensed it. "I know you probably don't want to go into it, but I'm not just curious. I need to know. I have a tiny sliver of an idea, so knowing what happened could mean finding the answers we're looking for."

I recounted the events of the shop for him as best I could, but the details weren't as important as the fact that we fought like wild beasts, which was evidenced by my animalistic attack on her.

"We've never encountered a danger that posed a threat like this. Well, what I mean is," he corrected, "that of all the situations we've been in, nothing has actually affected us. We somehow skate around it. But you actually got through to her, so to speak." He winced at the bad pun. "I'm sorry, poor choice of words, but do you see what I'm saying? Just the fact that she *bled* is indicative of something major."

"Why? Why was it different this time?" I looked down where her blood had previously stained my hands, still unbelieving that I'd had to take such measures.

William could read my guilt, and quickly came to my rescue. "Rynn, she poisoned your Grandma. She's essentially a murderer, if that offers any perspective. My point is: you are causing an affect on her even she couldn't have imagined." I couldn't think straight. I dropped my head between my legs, because that's what people tell you to do when you feel like you're going to faint.

From my lap I tried to speak. "What's your idea, William? I can't handle much more of this talking."

"I don't know if I can put it into words, what I'm thinking."

"Then give me a minute. I need to process, and more thinking might send me over the edge."

"Of course. I'll take you back to the house and you can freshen up. Do you have bags somewhere? I can call for them."

"Call for them? What, like you have a butler or something?"

"I have employees. They aren't here right now, but I can get someone to take care of it."

I sighed in resignation. "My bags are at the Nantucket Boat Basin." At that point I didn't care how the bags got to me. I found him. I lost my grandmother all over again. I attacked Charlotte like a monster. It was all too much.

"HOW LONG HAVE YOU BEEN HERE?" he asked as we drove through the large expanse of Bennett Park. I hardly registered William speaking, as the beauty of his land and the usual music box sleep lulled me into a welcome daze after my hysterics. Vine covered pergolas and archways led to ponds, orchards, and wide-open spaces that must be bursting with color in the spring. I don't know what I expected William's "day job" to be, but this blew me away.

"What? Oh, I got here Tuesday evening," I answered. Normal conversation breathed fresh air into my lungs as if I had been dragged under water by the weight of our previous topics. I pushed my doubt-filled thoughts aside and filled him in on my search process that was ultimately defined by luck.

"I'm shocked," he yawned, shaking off the drowsiness as well. "I never would have believed I could be found."

"I can see how you'd think that — why exactly *are* you so hidden?"

"Because I'm two and a half centuries old," he said dryly as he cut his cobalt eyes in my direction. "The more I keep to myself, the easier it is to blend into the background. I don't even keep staff employed here longer than two years. The less people get to know me, the better...that's just how it's always been." He pulled up in front of a beautiful old house far away from the commercial area of the farm.

"Is this your house?" I asked, stunned. It looked like the little cottage I had rented, but on steroids. Sitting on a slight hill stood two stories of flawless Nantucket design: shingles, original windows, balconies, and a lighthouse in the distance...I was awestruck.

"Not originally, but it is now. I moved into it around the same time I started laying the groundwork to change the old farm into what it is now. It was Charlotte's parents' house. She used to come stay here, like I said back in Tokyo. But eventually I decided if the farm was mine, the house would be, too. Over the years, it took shape like the rest of the land." He shrugged as he spoke, as if it were no big deal.

We stepped inside and from somewhere in the distance I could hear Dean Martin crooning, "Ain't That a Kick in the Head?" The work he'd done on the interior of the house was remarkable. At some point a true remodel must have been in order, but what he had done was more of a restoration that salvaged as much of the house as possible. The walls and ceilings showcased beautiful beams, and the wood floors were intact, though polished to perfection. The walls were new, painted with a subtle hint of green so pale it would have appeared white if not for the contrast of ivory trim around the doors and windows.

He hadn't decorated, so much as displayed unique items. Some shelves were adorned with old tools and kerosene lamps, whereas others utilized driftwood and common flotsam to bookend an impressive library. There were no pictures, but instead he had sketches of his travels, and also of contraptions that looked like items he might have created for use on the farm. I could almost see the story his life on this land told within his house.

"Did you do all of this?"

He looked around, nodding modestly. "It's nice to finally share it with someone."

It wasn't that he didn't seem proud of his work, but he definitely wasn't gushing to show it off. More than anything, he watched as my eyes swept across the house, as if I were the only person to ever see these walls.

"Can I take a look around?" I asked.

"Of course," he replied. "I'll give you the tour."

We were still standing in the foyer, but the entire area spread out in front of me to combine the kitchen, dining area, and living room. He had knocked down walls to open up the spaces, replacing the original supports with amazing weather worn wooden pillars, and the kitchen looked like it had been completely gutted, except for one thing.

My fingers traced unique grooves scarring the well-worn pieces of wooden countertop. "These were original," I commented.

He nodded. "This section here," he ran his hands along a stretch of the mahogany-stained counters about six or eight feet long, "was along the opposite wall, there, which was the entire kitchen space at the time. I made the rest," he spun, pointing to the surfaces covering two additional walls of the kitchen, "to match it."

"You made it?"

He seemed confused by the question, answering, "I made everything."

"Everything?"

"Don't underestimate the amount of time I had to work on my craftsmanship. Plus, I didn't really have anything else to do."

I chuckled. It felt good. "But, you did all this work...by yourself?"

"For the most part, yes. I told you, I keep to myself," he responded shyly.

"So when you said you're glad to finally share it with someone, you really did mean for the first time?"

"Yes," he said with a pained expression, as if vacillating between defending himself or not. Opting against it, he then showed me the rest of the house, which had several rooms that were furnished neatly and ready for guests, although they had never entertained any. He had prepared this house with the same trust that he had turned the key in the music box: continually, every day, waiting for a chance opportunity that he couldn't even be certain would occur. I shivered, thinking this perhaps might be that day, finally coming to fruition.

"I have coffee made," he offered as we arrived downstairs again. "If you want, we can make a cup and then I'll show you the best part. And some caffeine will help us fight the sleep."

"No coffee, thanks," I smiled apologetically, my stomach still knotted after losing my breakfast. "I'll power through."

He led me toward the back of the house and opened a set of French doors. We stepped out onto a large stone patio floor outlined with native grasses swaying in the wind, with outdoor chairs and couches arranged to admire the most beautiful feature of the space: a majestic lighthouse, and the promise of the ocean beyond it. Even though I couldn't see the water for the rise in the land, I could hear it. So alive. I had to close my eyes, unable to fathom any place in the world that could top this.

"Are you okay?" he interrupted.

"I — I," words once again failed me. "I'm overwhelmed." Overwhelmed by beauty. Overwhelmed by grief. Overwhelmed by fear. I wanted to trek to the lighthouse, climb up to the top, and jump. Let the wind take me out to sea.

"Have a seat — I'll go get some blankets," he told me.

"Actually," I hesitated. "Do you have some mouthwash or something? I did just puke."

He smirked and led me to his bathroom. When we both returned, we shared a comfortable silence only interrupted by steamy breaths hanging in the cold air. At least he knew I wasn't up for talking just yet. His scent, on the blanket, on his clothes, on his neck, was intoxicating. I burrowed closer and closer, wishing I could drown in him, never coming up for air.

His arms cradled me, engulfing my frame. The warmth of his breath under the blanket clung to my skin and baited my self-control. A kiss, placed at the bottom of his jawline, set his whole body in motion. He shuttered as he leaned into me, meeting my lips with century's worth of anticipation released.

I leaned back to rest on the arm of the sofa, and he followed eagerly. Wild hands traced my outline, moving clothing slightly to expose skin, which he in turn caressed and kissed. A shiver rocked me, both from the exposure of skin to the wind as the blanket had long fell away, and also from his lips on my ribcage.

William stopped at my sudden uncontrolled movement. "This won't do," he said.

I stared at him, dumfounded that he wanted to stop. "No?"

"Of course not," he continued with a devious grin, "it's too cold out here to be removing clothes."

"YOUR IDEA. Is it that it has to be me? There's something I need to do to end this?"

He traced spirals on my bare back, looping around and around as he chose his answer. "Yes, I think it's you. But what that means, I don't know."

"You don't think I have to...kill her, do you?"

His lips pressed together, along with his brow. "No, I don't think so, and I'm not even sure you could. But then again everything is changing now. No, I think it's actually something more...symbolic. I think you need to win, and she needs to lose. But how, I don't know."

I quietly pondered what that could mean.

"I need some water." I needed to stick my head in an ice bath and scream.

Wrapped in a sheet, I walked past the kitchen, deciding on fresh air over water. The chilling temperatures had no effect on my already raw nerves. Charlotte was evil. Charlotte killed Grandma. Charlotte had to be defeated. These were the facts. But how?

Pressure again. Darkness. And this time I wasn't even touching William. With no time to process, the world came into focus with sharp contrast. Humid air stuck to me. My breath hung heavy around my lips, barely moving past my mouth. It was pitch black, but something rustled so close to me that it tickled my arms. I moved a fraction and met more of the same sound at every angle.

I looked up to see that the moon offered a faint outline of what surrounded me: corn stalks. *Perfect. Now I'm in* Children of the *fucking* Corn.

Panic sang in my ears. Every direction would be the same, and I could wander in here forever and never know if I was getting closer to the edge. So I decided it didn't matter anyway and sat down to think. The best that could happen would be to wait it out and return to William's farm. The worst would be for Charlotte to stumble upon me and I'd have to fight.

It was quiet. Unnervingly quiet. There was no sound beyond the wind moving through the stalks, crackling the leaves. I waited ten minutes. Twenty. Thirty. Who knows how long. Surely, soon I would be pulled out of the darkness. Then came the most horrific sound I never knew I would fear. An engine. A rhythmic turning of blades. And it was getting closer.

I sprang to my feet without thinking. The owner of the land wouldn't be plowing in the middle of the night. It was Charlotte. There's no way she could have known I was in the corn, but she wouldn't pass even the outside chance to plow me down.

I hopped in circles, looking for headlights, but found only darkness, penetrated by the engine noise thundering louder. Fine, no lights. If I tried to run away, I'd probably end up like those goddamned idiots on horror films and fall just in time to be enveloped by the blades. I decided instead, to walk slowly toward the noise and when I was sure of where it was, I'd break perpendicular to it and out of the way.

My heart throbbed, surging blood through my veins. The air was so thick I feared I'd pass out if I tried to exert much energy. The sound was to my right. I turned to face it and took my first steps toward it. Within thirty seconds and a few steps to adjust my direction, it was close enough to vibrate the ground under me.

I lowered my stance to a slight crouch, ready to move like an athlete either direction. Stalks snapped and crunched. The ground shook. It was approaching faster than I'd anticipated. The sea of corn suddenly parted in front of me and I sprinted left with just enough time to dive out of the way and watch the slow-moving machinery growl as it passed. My first instinct had been to run in the other direction for safety, but I remembered William's theory.

Heavy equipment was not my area of expertise, so I chased alongside from a distance, trying to see if there was a spot to jump and grab onto without sending myself into the blades if I missed. As to be expected, it was pretty much a death trap any way I looked at it. Handlebars stuck out from the sides of the cab, but I couldn't tell if there was much of a foothold because the cornstalks were so dense toward the ground. If I was going to do this, I had to go in blind.

Whipping the corn away as I ran, I sprang like a rattlesnake and managed to wrap both hands around the bar. My feet thrashed around under me, struggling to gain foothold on a step while the flailing corn-stalks whipped at my arms. The engine made a strange sound, and suddenly it quit moving forward. I swung from the handlebar as the machine came to a stop. She heard me. She was coming to kill me now.

Do I get down? Do I try to open the door? I couldn't breathe. The blades slowed in their dizzying spinning. With one hand on the handlebar, I moved the other to the door handle and brought my feet up to a crouch against the frame. I gave the handle one swift jerk, and the door cranked open, just as I launched my feet into the cab and caught an alert but startled Charlotte right in the chest.

She hit the other door with a crack. On the offensive immedi-ately, she returned and bounded on top of me, sending my head hanging out the open door. With the dim light of the moon, I could see a thin scar on her arm where I'd cut her. A scar. A *scar*. I was winning.

"What happened to your arm, *Pearl?*" I laughed, nothing like myself.

Her eyes flashed. I saw stars before even realizing she'd punched me. With no vision, I aimed my fists, elbows, and head-butts anywhere they could connect. Repeated thuds marked direct hits, but they weren't all mine. It was a mess of furious wrestling, and despite what I'd always heard about catfights, I knew if I could grab her hair and lift her face, I'd get in a better shot.

Her thick curls provided the perfect grip, and as I pulled her back I cocked my arm straight for her jaw. Blood sprayed my face. Maybe I got her nose. She recoiled just a nanosecond, but I was ready. Both arms heaved her higher off me, giving my legs the room to reach her chest and send her again, into the door.

"Rynn!"

Charlotte's eyes flickered toward the direction of William's voice. She sneered, "Is he coming to save you?"

"You and I both know I don't need any help."

"How's your Grandma? Oh, that's right..."

I was in mid-air suddenly, flinging myself at her when the pressure consumed me, bringing us back to Nantucket. The cold air bit at my once-again naked skin. Rage still curdled my blood. I flexed my hands in and out, shaking off the memories of the beating they'd given. William was at the door wrapped in a comforter quicker than I could even bring myself to full consciousness.

"You're okay," he breathed into my neck as he held me close.

"I'm going to kill her."

He met my eyes and pressed his forehead against mine. "I was afraid you'd say that." He wrapped the comforter around me. "Did you do some damage again?" He was grinning. I think he liked this feisty side of me.

"You're enjoying this, aren't you?"

"Not exactly, I just...I feel like for centuries now I've been at a standstill, and now all of a sudden things are moving forward faster than I can keep up with. But it worries me when I can't get to you, though. I feel helpless in a whole different way now."

The usual fatigue began to creep up on me again, but my mind was still actively reliving the fight. "I don't think you need to worry about me. I was winning," I told him. "She was trying to play mind games with me, because she knew it. I'm getting to her."

"Well don't get too cocky, she's not going to lie down easy. Let's go inside and talk about this before we freeze."

"No. If we go inside we'll fall asleep — for hours." There was too much I needed to talk about. All of a sudden, I felt like I was close to something but I couldn't reach it. I nudged my head towards the outdoor sofa and we tucked the comforter around us. "Why do you think she turned the key again — so fast after returning from what I did to her?"

"You scared her. Maybe she wanted to retaliate and show you she would fight back."

It could be true, but something in me felt like there was more. My eyes grew heavy. "Ugh, I don't want to sleep right now."

"You can't fight it," William laughed. "We should go get comfy or we'll wake up frozen."

"Has it been like this forever? You sleep like that after every single time?"

William thought for a moment. "Yes. I had to fight through it once in the beginning when Charlotte turned the key in the middle of the day unexpectedly and I had to return to work with her father after the episode was over. But ever since then, I've been in control of the key and I would only turn it at night so I could sleep it off."

"Me, too. Is it the same for Charlotte?"

"You mean, does she sleep, too?"

"Yeah. Tucker and Nora fell asleep afterwards, also. So I'm just assuming she does?"

"Actually," he seemed surprised, "when I woke up from that very first time, Charlotte was still in my house, and I remember she looked crazed and wild. She said she had watched it in the fire all night, and it never burned." He turned to me. "She said she watched it all night. I couldn't have stayed awake if I was just sitting by myself watching a fire, I promise you that. Maybe she doesn't feel the same effects as we do."

"But she knows you do? That *we* do?"

"I've never thought about it, Rynn, do you think that means something?"

"Look, she's smart and calculating with everything she does. Don't you think she remembers things like that? We know she's spied on me and broke into my house, there's no telling how much she knows about me. She probably spies on you, too."

He conceded with a nod. "You may be right, but what would it matter?"

I wasn't sure, but I couldn't stop myself from rambling. "She knows. And maybe she thinks she can use it against us? You know, wear us down. But what point is there to that?"

We thought silently for a minute. "Okay, so going with this train of thought," he reasoned, "you wear down your opponent when you're in a fight. So you can get an edge."

"And if she's wearing us down, then she must be feeling threatened. William, do you think she knows I'm here with you?"

"I wish I knew, but I haven't seen her except for when we're transported by the music box."

"Why else would she feel so threatened? I'm sure she didn't expect me to travel with you after she took the key, so when I turned up that probably scared her. But if I were in Texas — so far away from you — I still wouldn't be posing an immediate threat. William! She knows I'm here, and unless she's got fucking cameras on your house, that means she's here, too!"

He looked like he wanted to talk me out of it, but he was already grabbing the comforter tighter around him and moving toward the door. "No time to sleep. Get dressed."

"Why?"

"I know where she is."

TWENTY-FOUR
HEROES

The black SUV tore through the landscape William spent centuries chiseling with his bare hands. "Where are we going?"

"The cabin where I used to live. The place we first turned the key. If she's really here, that's where she'll be."

A sickly shiver spread cold over me. She could be that close? Close enough to be watching me, watching us?

The sun had set over the moor, leaving a dusting of gray on the land. A break in the trees opened up to an unassuming wooden cabin. It was small, but in good shape, as if William still used it.

"It's now used as a gift shop in the Spring, but she'll know it's empty during the off season." He shrugged at my unspoken question. "She used to stay here, but I decided at some point I didn't have to be so hospitable. Ready?"

"Sure?"

He nodded. I didn't know if I should be cautious or go kick the door down. Was she armed with more than an ornamental key?

William went with the kick the door in plan. We rushed the cabin with a ruckus announcement of our presence, to find a bloody-nosed Charlotte huddled in the corner. She jerked her hand, and I hurled myself through the air just as she made the connection with the key and music box, giving it a turn.

We surfaced in an isolated desert. I couldn't see anyone for miles, and while I knew they were there with me, I decided to save my energy for the return. She didn't even turn the key a full turn, so I knew we'd be back in the cabin in no time.

Sand blew with the sticky wind. Waves of heat wiggled over the horizon. Beautiful pools of sparkling water danced in the distance. If I spent any more time there, I might actually chase the mirage.

In mere minutes I went from dusting sand off my lips, to landing from my airborne assault on Charlotte, sliding into her. She fired off another turn of the key. Just like I suspected, she was wearing us — or me, down. If she continued like this, I wouldn't have any fight left in me after the accumulation of so many trips through the music box continuum. If I could just get the key from her before she turned it again...

Pressure. Darkness. Skyscrapers towered over me, but I couldn't see much more than that. Torrential rain soaked the streets and brought out smells of a city that absorbs every footstep tread across it, and there were many. Again, she barely turned the key, so I backed up to the wall behind me and kept my eyes peeled.

Minutes ticked quickly by with no sign of her. Was she waiting, too? Biding her time until we returned? David Bowie's voice from inside a passing car sang "Heroes," just as a scuffle to my right interrupted my thoughts.

"Get *off* me!" A woman shrugged away from a hooded figure, but it was clearly Charlotte's voice. Until I could be sure what was going on, I remained hidden from her view. The figure made a grab at her, and she threw her arm out away from him, the object in her hand catching the glow of a streetlight. The key.

I let my head fall back against the brick of the building. I'd been so preoccupied with fighting her off, both in reality and in our new surroundings, I hadn't considered that I could simply take the key from her and return with it. A sideways look in her direction revealed

William, cautiously stepping closer to her as she walked backwards. There were enough people on the streets to pay attention, even at what seemed to be the dark hours of morning, so he was smart to avoid onlookers who could raise concern for her "safety."

Her every move glittered the key with light, beckoning me to release it from her grip. I thought it best not to even alert William of my presence, lest his eye contact on mine give me away.

They were moving toward me. I stepped over to a newsstand, bending over to feign interest in the Wall Street Journal.

"What are you going to do, Charlotte? You can't keep turning the key and wearing us down, it won't work."

A shaky laugh escaped her as she jerked oddly with every step. Power surged through me. They were two, maybe three strides away. I could overtake her, get the key, beat her ass, and tell her the fuck off all in one stride.

Almost there...

"She's no match for me, you — you should know that." There was a void in her usual demeanor, like the fatigue that set in for William and I in reality was hitting her here, in the time of the music box. She appeared weak, disjointed. "She — she's nothing compared to me, William. Nothing."

They had moved directly to my right. He stopped walking. "Actually," I turned my head toward him. His eyes met mine. "She's everything."

Her body went rigid as a disbelieving laugh snuck out in short breaths. It was too easy. The key slipped right from her fingers into my left hand. As soon as she turned to see what had happened, I rounded on her with what I think they call a right hook.

As she stumbled backward William wrapped his arms through hers from behind like a professional hit man, shuffling back into the ally. She kicked at the air in a vain attempt at resistance. Her once chilling eyes had lost their sharp edge. They had become dull and cloudy; less severe. I breathed in the satisfaction of her impairment as if I could somehow absorb her power.

Charlotte writhed, futile against William's hold. I wanted to hurt her. In fact, in this condition I could have easily beat her senseless within an edge of her life. Blood coursed through my veins, becoming thick, heavy in my arms and legs. It throbbed in my head. It blurred my vision. Was I wet from rain? Or sweat?

But is that how I was to defeat her? Something within me knew that wasn't the answer.

The rain disappeared, along with the street noise and twinkling city lights. We resurfaced in the cabin, weighed down from too many travels and in need of sleep. I had the key, though, and I couldn't afford to lose my grip.

Charlotte made an immediate grab at the key, which prompted both William and I into action. A scuffle tore through the cabin, knocking over displays of seeds and oil de perfumes. William pushed me away as he pinned her against the checkout counter. "Go, Rynn! I'll handle her, you take the music box and key. Get in the car!"

This wasn't how it was supposed to be. I couldn't run. She would just come back for us, and we would never be free of her. I followed his orders and picked up the music box, but I didn't run. I wouldn't leave him to fight it out with her alone.

Without a plan, save for the notion that William and I had more power while on the music box's time rather than our own present, I placed the key inside the music box. Familiar power and confidence vibrated the key. I would give us time — plenty of time, to do what we had to do.

Once, twice, three times. I turned again and again. Six, seven, eight. I didn't know how long I planned for us to be gone, but at that moment I didn't care. Charlotte and William stopped struggling and stared at me. I continued turning the key. Twelve? Thirteen? I'd lost count and my arm muscles protested. For some reason I didn't want to stop. Something wouldn't let me.

The floor under us buckled. Charlotte slid to the ground as William lost his hold on her. Rather than come after me, she appeared tethered to the space around her. I continued turning the key. William watched me with outstretched hands steadying himself. The room no longer seemed stable around us, buckling and churning. But with every turn I knew I had to keep going.

"What the hell are you doing?" Charlotte shrieked. She reached at me with weighted limbs that barely left her side.

"Keep turning, Rynn," urged William. "I don't know what's happening, but just keep turning!"

The sound of snapping wood penetrated my thoughts, as if the cabin were crumbling to the ground. Instead, though, the contents of the cabin began swirling around us. A blur of windowpanes, wood beams, and rocks from the fireplace created a tornado, and in its eye stood the three of us. The smell of old wood and unearthed soil filled the revolving room. Wind picked up as the cabin raged in circles, but I kept turning the key.

"William?" I shouted.

"Just keep turning!"

Charlotte panted on the floor, still fighting to reach for the music box. Fire burned in my arm as I continued turning the key but I refused to stop. The swirling room moved with such speed that I was unable to discern individual pieces anymore, everything becoming a brown blur.

Wind rocketed upward around me, knocking me off balance and throwing the music box out of my hands, sending it to the ground between the three of us. I panicked, but as I reached for it, the lid flew open with such force that it threw me back to the floor.

Bits and pieces of the room fluttered off the sale racks and shelves, joining in the tornado. Somehow in their circular movement, a repeated alignment of the debris created an image over and over: the rain-soaked street we had just left. Just as soon as I could see the projected picture, it broke up into pieces again, which were pulled into the music box. A new image appeared in the same way: wood, glass, soaps and bath salts from the cabin-turned-gift shop aligned again in the tornado to now show the corn stalks and terrorizing farm equipment.

"William?" I could hardly breathe the words, all the air sucked out of me and incorporated into the images on the moving wall.

"Just hold steady, Rynn, are you okay?"

"I'm okay."

Charlotte's eyes darted around at the images as they shone above our heads and dropped one at a time into the music box. The meadow back home. Tokyo. San Francisco. The projections picked up speed, making it harder to pick out the locations. Miami. Madison Square Garden. I knew I missed some as they flickered above us and were sucked into the music box, but I understood that all of the travels I'd ever taken had somehow now been returned to where they had come.

New images now, not of my own travels, but of before I came to play a part in the curse, shined and disappeared. Hundreds of years flashed, showing me everywhere that William had searched for me. Across the room, he watched me. He steadied himself into a standing position, which was far more than Charlotte could to do. She had sunk farther the ground, with her head resting against what used to be the base of the counter. An expression marked her face, frozen between terror and pain.

William stepped over her, but not easily. The room's motion uprooted his balance, knocking him to the floor.

"William, no! What are you doing?"

"Just stay there!" He crawled on the ground around the music box and in my direction.

"No, *you* stay there! You don't know what the hell is happening, what if the floor opens up?" It seemed unlikely, but so did the tornado of images displayed around us.

He worked against the wind, fighting his way to me. Huddled together, we diverted our attention back to the room.

"What's happening?" I whispered in his ear.

"I think you found a way to end this." He pulled me closer to him, engulfing me with his body.

"I didn't know what I was doing, I just couldn't stop turning the key," I admitted.

"Doesn't matter," he shook his head.

A whimper from across the room brought our attention back to Charlotte. Her eyes wide with fear stared up at another image. "I had a feeling we'd see him," William responded. The other images had been still, as if photographs. However above us moved a heavy-set man with dark, painted skin. He spoke aloud the words William shared with me on the ferry from Alcatraz.

"The man you desire has denied you;
You wish him to regret.
Now you give this gift to him.
The effect you seek is set.
Turning the key will lead him astray,
For years he shall wander in vain.
Searching, for the one who'll end
This life that is now his bane.
So if he will not have you,
No one he will have.
Though, be warned, my lady, for you shall find:
a curse always has two halves."

The music box in the image flamed and smoked as the man lit something on fire inside it. From within the real music box on the cabin floor, the same flames and smoke rose, permeating the room with the smell of burning leaves and spices.

"William?" He squeezed me tighter. "William, if this is the end — what does that mean? We don't know what's going to happen!"

He looked at me, holding my face in his hands. "Rynn, listen to me. I don't know what's going to happen. I wanted an end to the curse for so long I didn't care how it came, I just wanted it to be done. But then you came along. You became something worth living for. All I want is to be with you. But if this is the end — "

" — no, it can't be like that!"

"Rynn, please. Just know that no matter what happens..." He swallowed a breath and closed his eyes. "I love you."

I choked back tears. "I love you, William! You can't leave me!"

He kissed me, hard and urgent. I held him there, pressed against my lips, praying that he never leave.

The smoke from the music box lifted and swirled around us now along with the image of the dark man. Charlotte screamed. I broke from William and looked over to see Charlotte moving, perhaps regaining control. Rather than sitting or standing, though, she continued moving upward. She rose by some outside power, until she floated in mid-air.

I gripped William tighter, fearful that he would be joining Charlotte.

The man from the image repeated his last words, "Though, be warned, my lady, for you shall find: a curse always has two halves."

"It's okay," William assured me as I held him tight.

Charlotte's face revealed a contorted rage as she attempted to fight the invisible force lifting her into the air. Strange, strangled cries escaped her paralyzed mouth as her limbs twisted and disjointed unnaturally. I hid my eyes, not sure I wanted to see what would become of her.

The room's violent storm reached a new level of turmoil. The debris circling around Charlotte picked up speed, pulling her into the tornado one cell at a time. She became a stretched image, and so, too, did the man speaking the curse. Charlotte's color faded, as she blended into the background made up of the cabin's contents. And just as all the other images, she and the dark man slowly drifted, piece-by-piece, into the music box.

An explosion came from within the moving walls of the cabin. William shielded me with his body just as the remaining particles traveling in circles were obliterated into ashes that rained down over us.

Everything was gone. The walls, the floor under us, the rock fireplace, all gone, as if it had never been erected at all. The moon in the clear night's sky gave off just enough light to see the absence of every-thing around us.

And Charlotte. Gone. Erased from time, sucked back into the music box that had created a cursed lifetime for herself and for William. A new wind blew over us, taking even the dust with it, leaving us without a single trace of what had just happened.

"You did it," William said, brushing my hair from my face.

I looked around, taking it all in. "It's all gone." I looked down at my hand and raised the only remnant of William's curse. He took the key from me and twirled it around his finger.

"I feel like...like I've had the shit kicked out of me." He laughed carefully. "For the first time since before the curse — I actually *hurt*." He smiled, acknowledging one small facet of proof that his curse was finally over. "It hurts!"

"So that's good, right? That means you're...normal now?"

He winced at the welcome sensation. "Yes, I think it does."

"Then I guess I'll have to be extra careful with you." I leaned down, brushing my lips against his jawline. He sat up carefully to meet me, but stopped when he caught sight of something behind me.

"Uh, Rynn?"

I turned to see what he was looking at. "What? I don't see anything."

"Exactly. We drove here, remember?"

THANKFULLY WILLIAM WAS ONLY BRUISED and could walk once I helped him stand. We speculated on the possibilities of just how far the effects of the music box could have reached, given the fact that William's vehicle had disappeared along with Charlotte and the music box.

"But why your vehicle? It didn't have anything to do with the curse."

"Just think of all the things that would be different if the curse had never existed. We couldn't possibly imagine all the things that may be changed from what we used to know."

"But the farm? Everything you've done to the land, all of it — "

" — I know, Rynn. I'm trying to figure it out, too." He stopped just as his house came into view. With a deep breath, he turned to me. "Whatever I am now, whatever the curse has decided for me...I don't care what it is, though, as long as you're here with me."

"You can come live with me in Texas and I'll support you on my teacher's salary. I'll take good care of you," I joked, but inside, I worried for him.

He smiled and kissed my forehead. "Let's go see what's in the house."

After a long, cold trek across what we could see still resembled Bennett Farms, we came to the house. The lights were on, inside and out, as Christmas music played and laughter filled the expansive living room and kitchen. Voices carried from within, sinking into the pit of my stomach. People lived there.

"Should we ring the doorbell? We're going to freeze if we're out here any longer."

"Sure," he half-answered, half-shrugged.

"I'm sorry William, I know how much you put into this land." For lack of anything else to do, I hugged him.

From inside, a voice rose above the rest. "Nora, how long ago did they leave? Shouldn't they be back by now?"

Our heads jerked to the window. Then to each other. Then back. Coincidence? There were tons of people in the world named Nora. And why would my Nora be here at William's house, anyway?

The answer came from farther inside the house, somewhere near the living area. "Yeah, it's been almost an hour, they should be back any minute, I guess."

"That's Nora," I barked as I grabbed William and began jumping. "William, that's *my* Nora."

He studied my face, needing to be certain before getting his hopes up. "Are you sure? Who are the rest?"

"I can't tell," I answered honestly. The voices danced together, interrupting the others with such consistency it was too hard to decipher one from the other. "But we have to go see."

William nodded, nervously stepping up to his own door. His hand shook as he raised a finger to ring the doorbell.

The door opened before he could reach the button. Inside the house, my dad startled at our presence on the doorstep and half-yelled at us, "Jeez, you two, why the hell are you ringing your own doorbell? And what took you so long, I was about to go looking for you." We froze on the front step, unsure of how to react to the crowd of my whole family, none of whom William had ever even met, having a party in his house. "Where's the wine? That *is* what you went to get, isn't it?" My father eyed us closely, now, dragging us into the house.

William straightened his clothes and hair, and I did the same. I looked around the room at everyone staring at us, waiting for a logical response. Mom, Dad, Tucker, Nora...and a baby's cry in another room.

William sputtered, "Uh, sorry, they were out of wine."

At the same time I rambled, "The store was closed."

We looked at each other, guilty, but not sure why.

"Aw, leave them alone," came a new voice from same direction as the crying baby. "We've invaded their first holiday together, give them a break." A familiar woman, but somehow still a stranger, walked out cradling a toddler dressed in Christmas pajamas. She handed the baby to Nora, then came over to me.

"Grandma?" The word caught in my throat, alongside a knot that prevented me from uttering another word.

"Nice to have you back," she winked.

William squeezed my hand and met my eyes. "It's good to be back," he whispered, only to me.

PLAYLIST

Saturday Night's Alright for Fighting - Elton John

Golden Years - David Bowie

Here Comes the Hotstepper - Ini Kimoze

Cotton Eyed Joe - Rednex

Kung Fu Fighting - Carl Douglas

Peace Train - Cat Stevens

Loves Me Like a Rock - Paul Simon

Come on Eileen - Dexy's Midnight Runners

Mustang Sally - Wilson Pickett

Maggie May - Rod Stewart

Oh, What a Night (AKA December, 1963) - The Four Seasons

Sweet Caroline - Neil Diamond

Into the Mystic - Van Morrison

You May Be Right - Billy Joel

A Little Less Conversation - Elvis Presley

One Night in Bangkok - Murray Head

You Are My Sunshine - Written by Jimmie Davis and Charles Mitchell

The Sound of Silence - Simon and Garfunkel

Already Gone - Eagles

Every Breath You Take - The Police

(Sittin' on) the Dock of the Bay - Otis Redding

Open Arms - Journey

I Melt With You - Modern English

Please Come Home for Christmas - Eagles

Michelle - The Beatles

Ain't That a Kick in the Head? - Dean Martin

Heroes - David Bowie

ABOUT THE AUTHOR

Kathryn Callahan lives in Texas with her two badass girls and one amazing rescue dog. She is a habitual movie-quoter and coffee addict. She misses David Bowie. She still misses Heath Ledger, for that matter. She daydreams a little too much, but that's when She divines her next big idea. She weathered the perfect storm, and is now dancing in the rain.

www.katcalwrites.com